HARDBOILED

ALLEN & UNWIN
FICTION

STUART COUPE and JULIE OGDEN are the publishers of *Mean Streets*, Australia's crime, mystery and detective fiction magazine. *Mean Streets* was first published in October 1990 and has established a wide readership not only in Australia but in America, England, Europe, Japan, Hong Kong and New Zealand. When not putting together issues of the magazine, or looking after daughters Jay and Sara, both try and keep up with the piles of crime and mystery novels that pour through the door of their Blackheath home. *Hardboiled* is the first book they have edited together—but forthcoming in 1993 is their second (also with Allen & Unwin) in which Australian crime fiction writers have their characters 'solve' famous Australian murders and mysteries.

HARDBOILED

TOUGH, EXPLICIT AND UNCOMPROMISING
CRIME FICTION

Edited by Stuart Coupe and Julie Ogden

ALLEN & UNWIN

First published in 1992
Allen & Unwin Pty Ltd
9 Atchison Street, St Leonards, NSW 2065 Australia

National Library of Australia
Cataloguing-in-Publication entry:
Hardboiled
ISBN 1 86373 221 7
1. Detective and mystery stories. I. Coupe, Stuart, 1956– . II. Ogden Julie.
813.087208

Set in 10½/12 pt Goudy Old Style by DOCUPRO, Sydney
Printed by Australian Print Group, Maryborough, Victoria.

10 9 8 7 6 5 4 3 2 1

FOR JAY OGDEN-COUPE

'Teach the children
The ways of men and animals
Teach them about cities, the history of the mysteries
Their vices and their virtues
About branches that blow in the wind
Or the wages of their sins
Teach them about forgiveness, teach them about mercy
Teach them about music
and the cool and cleansing water.'

(a slight adaptation of Teach The Gifted Children by Lou Reed)

Contents

ACKNOWLEDGEMENTS

I'd like to acknowledge the contributions of a number of people without whom . . . you know the story. Patrick Gallagher was brave enough to be talked into publishing *Hardboiled*. Fiona Inglis spent many hours poring over the manuscript and in the process received a crash course in Americanisms. Later Bernadette Foley took over the arduous, painstaking work of getting *Hardboiled* into its final shape and managed to still remain on speaking terms with two editors who wanted everything just right. Andrew Vachss introduced me to the work of some very fine writers. The writers themselves responded enthusiastically to the idea of an anthology—and remained enthusiastic even after being told what they'd be paid!

Special thanks goes to my wife and co-editor of this book Julie Ogden who, after we'd both spent many hours in front of our computer screens, offered encouragement when I'd throw my hands in the air and say 'Why are we doing this?'

Photographic credits

Stuart Coupe and Julie Ogden photographed by Linda Marlin; Lawrence Block by Patrick Trese; Charles de Lint by Beth Gwinn; Julie Smith by Peggy Skorpinski; Joe R. Lansdale by Karen Lansdale; Andrew Vachss by Peter Papadopolous; Neal Barrett, Jr by Danny Biggs; Wayne D. Dundee by Olan Mills; Rose Dawn Bradford by Sandy Huffaker, Jr; James Colbert by Ron Mobley.

INTRODUCTION

'I'm sorry if I appear hardboiled or cold blooded, but . . . them that live by the gun should die by the gun,' says Race Williams, the creation of Carroll John Daly, in *The Snarl of the Beast* (1927).

This was arguably the first use of the expression 'hardboiled' in crime fiction. It is in fact believed to have evolved from American Army slang. Later Dashiell Hammett's Sam Spade described a detective as being 'as tough as a 20 minute egg'.

Over the years the expression 'softboiled' has been introduced as a description for a somewhat tamer sub-genre of crime and detective fiction. But make no mistake, what you hold in your hands, for the most part, is a collection of fiction the equivalent of an egg that's been boiling for a few hours. Some of these stories are so hard that only the most adventurous readers will be prepared to tackle them.

This anthology, however, is not a collection of stories featuring weatherbeaten, bourbon-soaked, gun-toting private eyes staggering down the urban mean streets. Since Race Williams uttered those famous lines the words 'hardboiled' and 'detective' have seemed almost inseparable, and many maintain that the two are inescapably linked. Hopefully this collection by contemporary American (and one Canadian) crime writers will go some way towards supporting the idea that crime and detective fiction can be hardboiled equally with or without the presence of a detective or private investigator as the central character.

Certainly there are some private investigators in this collection, but they are absent from the majority of stories. The private eyes represented, such as Lawrence Block's Matt Scudder and Wayne Dundee's Joe Hannibal, are in the finest hardboiled mould—they're tough, realistic and contemporary.

Again, in contrast to the traditional perceptions of hardboiled fiction, a number of these stories do not take place in the urban mean streets. Suburban houses, small towns and isolated countryside are shown to be equally powerful settings for hardboiled fiction as the pavements and back alleys of New York, Chicago, Los Angeles and Sydney. It's hard to imagine more relentlessly disturbing writing than, for example, Joe Lansdale's *Night They Missed the Horror Show* which is set in a small Texan town, or Chet Williamson's *First Kill* which takes place in the countryside during hunting season.

Nevertheless all these stories are firmly routed in the hardboiled tradition. To varying degrees all are mean, slangy, witty and tough. Many portray situations of extreme violence—some in a physical sense, others psychological. They are not written by, or for, people who choose to hide away and ignore the reality of contemporary life. They are written for people who accept that the horrors do exist and won't go away if simply ignored—and that confrontation and understanding of these horrors frequently leads to awareness and change.

Violence is a part of everyday life. It frequently occurs at random, whilst at other times it is premeditated. More often than not it is a savage assault on an unsuspecting individual. Some of the stories in *Hardboiled* contain a high level of violence—but it is never gratuitous, never there simply to titillate, to shock, or as a celebration. Certainly readers unaccustomed to realistic writing of this nature may find some stories and scenes in *Hardboiled* confrontational and disturbing. For this I offer a warning but no apologies.

The same applies to some of the language used. These writers have a masterful ability to capture the vernacular of their characters. One of the characteristics of hardboiled diction is the occasional use of incorrect grammar, slang and expressions peculiar to the regions and locations the characters inhabit. It is very much the language of the streets and contains words and descriptions that many may recoil from. But it is integral to the genre—without it the characters would not live, their voices would not have the same resounding impact on our psyche.

Many of the stories in *Hardboiled* extend the preconceived notion of what a crime story should be. This is not a collection of stories where the principle dilemma is whether the butler or the second cousin twice removed is responsible for poisoning Aunty Mae in the dining room of the family's ancestral estate. Nor is it full of trench-coated private eyes trying to save the blonde in distress whilst slugging down enough bourbon to make the difference between the blonde and the Empire State Building rather blurred.

Avid readers of crime fiction may be familiar with some of the contributors to *Hardboiled*—but the overriding purpose is to introduce an array of fine writers who are, for the most part, little known in this country. It is my hope that having read their stories in *Hardboiled* people will be motivated to seek out their novels.

The contributors in this anthology come from a host of different backgrounds. Some are established writers with many, many books to their credit; some are well known in other genres such as horror, science fiction, fantasy and mystery; and some combine genres. A number of stories have won major awards in America and are recognised as classics. In contrast one writer has his first piece of fiction published in this collection.

Enjoy, if that's the right word, *Hardboiled* but don't read it at night if you're planning to get to sleep before dawn. This book is not for the fainthearted!

Stuart Coupe
Blackheath, *1992*

CHET WILLIAMSON's latest novel is *Reign*, which *Publisher's Weekly* called a 'thoroughly enjoyable novel . . . elegant, inventive . . . sure to satisfy.' His other novels include *Dreamthorp*, *Ash Wednesday*, *Lowland Rider*, *Soulstorm*, and *McKain's Dilemma*.

Over sixty of his short stories have appeared in such magazines as *The New Yorker*, *Playboy*, *Esquire*, *Magazine of Fantasy and Science Fiction*, *Twilight Zone*, and many other magazines and anthologies. He has been a final nominee for the World Fantasy Award and the Mystery Writers of America Edgar Allan Poe Award, and he has received six Bram Stoker Award nominations from the Horror Writers of America. He lives in Elizabethtown, Pennsylvania with his wife Laurie and son Colin.

Chet Williamson

First Kill

For days now, the hunter had thought about widows and orphaned children, and decided that he would try and see if the man wore a wedding ring. With his 4x Weaver scope, he thought he should be able to catch a glint of gold on the left hand.

However, the Monday after Thanksgiving was often cold in the woods of northern Pennsylvania. Odds were that blaze-orange mittens would cover most hands, to be slipped warily off only at the sound of hooves rustling dead leaves. Even then, most men fired rifles with their right hands. A wedding ring would still be covered. Still, he would try to avoid a father, making an effort to show the mercy the earth he loved did not have.

But if he could not see the hand, he would accept whatever target was offered.

Peter Keats awoke an hour before dawn, pushed in the button of the wind-up alarm clock, and shivered with excitement and the cold. The fire he and his two cabin mates had set the night before in the wood stove was dead, and he was glad he had worn his insulated long underwear in his sleeping bag. He didn't think he could have stood the chilly air against his bare trunk and legs. He woke his friends, slid out of his bunk, and put on two pairs of socks, one cotton, the other heavy wool. He stepped into his thick trousers, then slipped his feet into ankle-high L. L. Bean hunting boots.

Keats was out the front door before the others had disentangled themselves from their sleeping bags. He breathed in the air, reveling in the sharp crispness that stung his throat. He walked up the hill from the cabin to the outhouse, defecated quickly and efficiently, and walked back again, broke the ice in the basin that sat on the railing of the tiny porch, and splashed frigid water on his face. It made him even more wakeful than before.

Back inside, the men joked, ate donuts, and drank the coffee they had made the night before. Then they finished dressing, ending with the heavy coats of safety orange, put wads of toilet paper under their scope covers so the lenses wouldn't fog in the colder outside air, and stepped outside to hunt, and to be hunted.

It took Peter Keats a half-hour of walking in the near darkness to reach the spot he had chosen the day before, when they had helped each other erect their stands, the elevated platforms in which they would perch and wait for a deer to wander by. One of his friends was a half-mile to the northwest, the other a mile south. Keats could easily hear their shots, and if he did he would hold still for five, ten minutes, waiting even more silently in case of a miss or a wounding, in case the deer should run, limp, or drag itself past his stand.

By the time Peter Keats had climbed onto his perch, he could just make out streaks of rose through the ragged treetops to the east. He settled himself, his Remington pump .760 resting across his legs. His feet dangled over the edge of the stand, fifteen feet above the ground. For comfort's sake, Keats had placed a small, flat pillow under the spot where his knees rested against the sharp edge of the stand.

Keats thought that it seemed colder than it had in years before. He rubbed his fingers against each other inside the heavy mittens, and wished that the orange of his jacket was as warm to the touch as it was to the eye. The deer must really be colorblind if that hue didn't startle them. He had heard other hunters say that it appeared white to the deer's eyes. Well, if it did it did. It didn't much matter, and besides, it was the law.

In his fifty years of deer hunting, Peter Keats had always obeyed the law. His father had taught him that when he had given him his first deer rifle at the age of fourteen. One deer a year, no more. No shooting one for your friend, and no shooting a doe in buck season. Keats had done none of those things, simply because he had never been tempted to. And he had never been tempted, because in his half-century of what he called hunting, he had never shot, nor had he ever wanted to shoot, a deer.

The pattern was set the first year he went hunting with his father. Keats was positioned next to an oak tree, crouching among the acorns on which the deer loved to feed. His father was a half-mile away, and Keats, his heart beating rapidly, waited, waited, feeling youthful erections of excitement come and go. An hour passed, during which Keats stood up several times, stretching his legs. He was standing when he heard the deer approach. He froze, felt the wind on his face from the direction of the sound of breaking leaves, snapping twigs, and saw a buck and two doe push through the brush less than fifty yards away.

He raised his rifle with what felt like the slowness of a watch's second hand, and by the time the buck had cleared the brush, Keats was looking at it through the notch of the open sight. Its smooth coat made it look carved of wood, its brown eyes stared into his like some spirit of the forest, and he felt, holding the deer's life in his fingertip, as though he was defying God, like a vandal in a cathedral. If he pulled the trigger he knew he would violate a far more solemn contract than the one forged between him and his father.

He lowered the gun, and never raised it to a deer again.

Still, he went hunting every year, and patiently bore his fellow hunters' good-natured teasing. He suspected that the old friends he was with now knew the truth, for he no longer even fired a shot or two to make them think he had tried but failed. He had had plenty of chances over the years, and his heart still pounded when he saw a buck approach, pass by him, pause, look up, startled, and run. But he did not lift his loaded rifle to his shoulder.

And it was loaded, always. Every year he went through the ritual of sighting in the rifle at the sportsman's club to which he belonged, cleaning it, taking out the same bullets from the cabinet, bullets that had turned green where lead met brass, and shooting at the targets on the range, until his offhand scores equaled those of men years his junior.

Keats loved the ritual, the preparations, the chance to be with his friends and by himself. His two companions with whom he had come to Potter County shared his love of the outdoors, but he seldom saw them outside of deer season, so that when they did get together there was much to catch up on.

But the solitude was the best part, the sense that there was no one but him in the world to see the sky grow brighter, feel the air become less bitterly cold, behold the dread miracle of winter. He sat and waited, and while he was alert to the sounds of the woods, he also escaped into himself, his past, his thoughts and memories of seasons before.

He thought of his wife, of when they had both been young, though no happier than they were now, of the job at the steel mill he had held for over thirty years before he had retired four years ago, of his church where he served on the budget committee, of his three grandchildren, of the oldest boy who wanted to go hunting with him next year when he was old enough.

Peter Keats thought of many things as the morning brightened, until the sun slashed bright streaks through the latticework of branches, bathing his orange garb with fire, making him a perfect target.

The hunter saw the man in the tree stand just before 7.30. Ever since dawn he had been moving stealthily, stalking. It was estimated that fifty thousand people would be roaming through the quarter million acres of Potter County's state forests today. Since that averaged out to one hunter per five acres, it was only natural that they would come across each other now and again.

That was what calmed and excited and worried the hunter. It calmed him because no one would take a second look at another man dressed in orange; it excited him because the statistic made it certain that he would find game; and it worried him that the game might be *too* plentiful, tripping over one another in the haste for their own prey. A herd would do the hunter no good. He had to find a single animal, cut off from the rest.

That was when he saw the man in the tree. Thank God, he thought, for the orange. Its warm brightness protected him on the cold ground, marked his targets in the chilly air.

He stepped behind a thick-boled pine tree, and peered out at the man in the tree-stand seventy yards away. The man gave no indication that he had seen the hunter.

The hunter slipped the glove from his right hand, put it into his coat pocket, and wadded small bits of wax into his ears. Then he lifted his rifle, a Ruger Model 77, 7 mm magnum, and leaned against the tree. He placed his right cheek against the smooth walnut stock, and looked through the Weaver scope with his right eye.

The man in the stand did not fill the field of vision, but the hunter could make out certain details. The man was older, in his sixties, and had probably killed deer for many years. The hunter found a poetic justice in that fact. His hands were mittened, so the hunter could not tell if he wore a ring. Probably married, the hunter thought. He looked like a married man, happy to be alone in the woods. The man had a little gray moustache, and wore glasses with black frames. His booted feet dangled over the edge of the stand, and he swung them back and forth like a child, a movement that any deer would notice immediately. The man did not appear likely to bag a buck this year.

Still, he was hunting deer, so it was the hunter's obligation to hunt him. Maybe he was only a harmless old man who enjoyed sitting in a tree house holding a loaded rifle, but surely he had taken his toll over the years. Now it was pay-back time.

The hunter flicked off the safety, breathed in icy air, leaned against the tree so that his forehead rubbed roughly against the bark, moved his Ruger in a series of infinitesimal motions until the plain of blaze orange was settled directly under the scope's cross hair. Only then did he place his bare finger on the cold metal of the trigger, let out half his breath in a white puff, hold the rest, and begin, very gently, to squeeze. When he had exerted enough pressure, the firing pin descended, the powder ignited, the bullet left the barrel and flew across the seventy yards in the merest fraction of a second, meeting the man in the tree, expanding the instant it struck the orange jacket, widening as it tore through flesh and muscle and bone. The man flew backwards into a red cloud of himself, and fell from the tree, landing on the dry leaves below like a sack of lime.

The hunter held his pose for a moment, the sound of the explosion reverberating like a great gong. Then he operated the bolt and lowered the rifle so that he still looked through the scope at the man on the ground, ready to fire a second shot at the hint of motion.

There was none. It had been a clean, quick kill.

From the corner of his eye, he had seen the spent shell fly from the ejector, and it took him only a moment to find the gleaming brass amid the floor of dead pine needles. He dropped it into his pocket and walked to the tree-stand, pulling the wax wads from his ears. Although he listened intently, he heard no other sounds, neither voices nor footsteps in dead leaves. No, no one would come. No one would leave their stands and jeopardize their own chances of making a kill. It would be safe to do the field dressing.

It was extraordinary, he thought, the damage a single, small projectile could do to a human body. The man had not moved since he had fallen, and the glassy stare told the hunter he was dead. Heart and lungs had been ripped through, and the blood must have ceased its pumping to the brain instantly. He hoped the man had felt little pain, only one, short, sharp, and savage, before he lost consciousness and his life.

The hunter stood for a long time, looking down at the first man he had ever killed, indeed ever even harmed. He thought he had readied himself for it, but no philosophy, no cause firmly and chokingly believed in, had prepared him for this moment. It had prepared him for the stalking, the sighting, even the pulling of the trigger, but not this. He struggled to stop shaking, told himself it was only the cold, that he could not be shaking from emotion because he had none. He was a machine that had functioned as it was supposed to, and would continue to do so.

Again he repeated his manifesto to himself, like a mantra of destruction, all the proper words about the purity of life, the reverence for nature, the abomination of hunting in a country where no one need do so to eat, the thousands of animals wounded and not found, dying slowly and painfully. He thought about the protests he had made with the others, the signs and speeches that had done nothing to slow the annual slaughter, thought about his decision to do more, administer true justice, turn the tables on the hunters, show them all too clearly just what they were doing to another species, going over it again and again in his mind, establishing his alibi, changing his appearance, going far, far from where he lived, to a place where no one knew him, a place rich with human game, where he could make his kill, and show that any species could be preyed upon.

And now he had killed, and now he must continue, be strong, finish the lesson, plant the seeds of legend and terror.

There. He was all right now, ready to do what had to be done.

He propped his Ruger against the tree and held the stand, put on both gloves, and knelt by the side of the dead man. He unsnapped the man's jacket, grasped his neck, hauled him to a sitting position, and removed the sodden mass of cotton shell and goose down. The hole in the man's back was greater than the hunter had imagined.

He let the body flop back onto the bloody leaves, and saw that some blood on the man's small moustache had frozen. It looked, thought the hunter, as though he had cut his lip shaving.

The hunter took a horn-handled knife with a five-inch blade from its sheath, and tried to forget that what lay before him was a human being, tried to think of it only as a slaughtered animal, as the other hunters would think of the deer they had shot.

He cut open the dead man's sweater, shirt, and thermal undershirt, exposing the pallid flesh and the entrance wound to the freezing air. He yanked the upper clothing off the body, then removed the boots and socks, and sliced through the waistband of the trousers, tugging them off, along with the long underwear, until the corpse lay naked on the frozen bed of leaves. The hunter had read over and over about field dressing, and now he would recreate the procedure. It wouldn't be perfect, for the anatomies of deer and men were different. But they would see, and realize, and tell the tale, so that everyone would know there was an avenger in the forest.

A true field dressing would have begun with cutting the penis and scrotum free, then scoring around the anus, but the hunter wanted no hints of sexual psychosis to dilute the true purpose of his act. He left the genitals intact, and instead slipped the razor sharp knife beneath the skin of the lower abdomen. Blade up, he slid the knife through the flesh until it struck the breastbone, exposing a layer of yellow fat and muscle.

He had not reckoned on the fat. It looked greasy and slimy, and although he thought the presence of blood on his gloves would arouse no curiosity, the same could not be said for the remnants of fat. So he took off the gloves and lay them next to the butt of his rifle. When he was finished, he would wipe his hands as best he could with the dead leaves.

The incision had drawn back the skin, and the warm, moist organs steamed in the cold air, like clouds rising from a valley. The hunter rolled up his right sleeve, made a few quick, short cuts, and lifted away the fat and the sheet of muscle beneath it. His cold hands nearly burned when he touched the hot, wet innards, and for a moment the steam rose from his hands and forearms. He then cut the diaphragm away from the rib cage, and reached up inside the chest until he found the esophagus and windpipe, both of which he severed, accidentally nicking the palm of his left hand in the confined space. He pulled both tubes back and out, and the lungs, now deflated sacks, followed. It was nearly as easy as the books had said.

A little more cutting of the membranes removed the diaphragm, and in another moment he was able to work the heart free and remove it. Then he reached in with both hands, as though he was embracing the carcass, and lifted most of the viscera out, except for the lower intestine, which was still attached to the anus. He dropped the innards on the leaves, where the smoking, multi-hued mound settled itself like a nest of lazy snakes in sunshine. Then he picked up the knife again, intending to sever the recalcitrant lower bowel, when he heard a crunch of leaves behind him, and a voice. The hunter turned his head and saw, twenty feet away, a man with a gray beard, dressed in blaze orange, holding a rifle pointed at the ground.

When Peter Keats had heard the single shot from the south, he had listened for more, for the signals that he and his friend there had established. If Keats heard one, he could assume it was a single killing shot. If two, a downing shot and a finishing shot. But if three, a miss. His friend's hands were arthritic, especially in the cold, and he could not begin to field dress a deer. Keats had offered to do the gutting if necessary, and the single shot had told him it was.

It had taken Keats nearly fifteen minutes to walk the mile between the two stands, and when he had seen the figure bent over something red and white he had thought that his friend must have already begun. But he saw quickly that the kneeling man was smaller and narrower through the shoulders than his friend, and Keats walked more quietly, stepping on exposed rocks and patches of pine needles that offered no crisp, betraying resistance.

When he saw his friend, he could not believe it, and said, 'God,' and stepped on dry leaves. The kneeling man turned then, and looked at him over his right shoulder, and Keats could see his red and glistening hands and forearms.

'What . . . ' Keats began to say, and the man twisted the other way, to his left, toward the tree against which his rifle leaned, stretched, his left hand sliding on the ground as he tried to grasp the rifle's grip with his wet, slippery right hand. He came around toward Keats, one knee on the ground, left leg extended, the barrel bobbing in his efforts to grasp the gun securely.

But before its dark eye could look at Keats, he had raised his Remington, flicked off the safety, and fired before his rifle stopped its motion. The sound of the shot hammered his unprotected ears, and he pressed his eyes shut, waiting to feel the man's bullet tear into him.

The answering shot assaulted his deafened ears, but he felt no pain, and when he opened his eyes he saw the man lying on the ground, still gripping his rifle, blood streaming from a hole in his torn neck like a parasitic serpent escaping its host.

Slowly he lowered his rifle and looked at the two dead men. Then, very softly, he began to cry. He cried for a long time, the hot tears quickly cooling on his stubbly cheeks in the winter air.

Peter Keats had made his first kill.

LAWRENCE BLOCK was born in 1938 and when not travelling lives in New York. He is the author of more than 50 novels featuring a variety of series characters. His private investigator, Mathew Scudder, made his first appearance in the novel *In the Midst of Death* (1976) and has become one of the best known figures in contemporary American crime fiction. The other Scudder novels are *Sins of the Fathers* (1976), *Time to Murder and Create* (1977), *A Stab in the Dark* (1981), *Eight Million Ways to Die* (1982), *When the Sacred Ginmill Closes* (1986), *Out on the Cutting Edge* (1989), *A Ticket to the Boneyard* (1990), and *A Dance at the Slaughterhouse* (1991). Block has won numerous awards for his writing, including the Edgar Award for Best Short Story in 1984 for *By the Dawn's Early Light.*

Lawrence Block

By The Dawn's Early Light

All this happened a long time ago.

Abe Beame was living in Gracie Mansion, although even he seemed to have trouble believing he was really the Mayor of the City of New York. Ali was in his prime, and the Knicks still had a year or so left in Bradley and DeBusschere. I was still drinking in those days, of course, and at the time it seemed to be doing more for me than it was doing to me.

I had already left my wife and kids, my home in Syosset, and the NYPD. I was living in the hotel on West Fifty-Seventh Street where I still live, and I was doing most of my drinking around the corner in Jimmy Armstrong's saloon. Billie was the nighttime bartender, his own best customer for the twelve-year-old Jameson. A Filipino youth named Dennis was behind the stick most days.

And Tommy Tillary was one of the regulars.

He was big, probably six-two, full in the chest, big in the belly, too. He rarely showed up in a suit but always wore a jacket and tie, usually a navy or burgundy blazer with gray flannel slacks, or white duck pants in warmer weather. He had a loud voice that boomed from his barrel chest, and a big cleanshaven face that was innocent around the pouting mouth and knowing around the eyes. He was somewhere in his late forties, and he drank a lot of top-shelf Scotch. Chivas, as I remember it, but it could have been Johnny Black. Whatever it was, his face was beginning to show it, with patches of permanent flush at the cheekbones and a tracery of broken capillaries across the bridge of the nose.

We were saloon friends. We didn't speak every time we ran into each other, but at the least we always acknowledged one another with a nod or a wave. He told a lot of dialect jokes and told them reasonably well, and I laughed at my share of them. Sometimes I was in a mood to reminisce about my days on the force, and when my stories were funny his laugh was as loud as anyone's.

Sometimes he showed up alone, sometimes with male friends. About a third of the time he was in the company of a short and curvy blonde named Carolyn. 'Caro-lyn from the Caro-line', was the way he occasionally introduced her, and she did have a faint southern accent that became more pronounced as the drink got to her. Generally they came in together, but sometimes he got there first and she joined him later.

Then one morning I picked up the *Daily News* and read that burglars had broken into a house on Colonial Road, in the Bay Ridge section of Brookyln. They had stabbed to death the only occupant present, one Margaret Tillary. Her husband, Thomas J. Tillary, a salesman, was not at home at the time.

It's an uncommon name. There's a Tillary Street in Brooklyn, not far from the entrance to the Brooklyn Bridge, but I've no idea what war hero or ward heeler they named it after, or if he's a relative of Tommy's. I hadn't known Tommy was a salesman, or that he'd had a wife. He did wear a wide yellow gold band on the appropriate finger, and it was clear that he wasn't married to Carolyn from Caroline, and it now looked as though he was a widower. I felt vaguely sorry for him, vaguely sorry for the wife I'd never known of, but that was the extent of it. I drank enough back then to avoid feeling any emotion very strongly.

And then, two or three nights later, I walked into Armstrong's and there was Carolyn. She didn't look to be waiting for him or anyone else, nor did she look as though she'd just breezed in a few minutes ago. She had a stool by herself at the bar and she was drinking something dark from a lowball glass.

I took a seat a few stools down from her. I ordered two double shots of bourbon, drank one, and poured the other into the cup of black coffee Billie brought me. I was sipping the coffee when a voice with a Piedmont softness to it said, 'I forget your name.'

I looked up.

'I believe we were introduced,' she said, 'but I don't recall your name.'

'It's Matt,' I said, 'and you're right, Tommy introduced us. You're Carolyn.'

'Carolyn Cheatham. Have you seen him?'

'Tommy? Not since it happened.'

'Neither have I. Were you-all at the funeral?'

'No. When was it?'

'This afternoon. Neither was I. There. Matt. Whyn't you buy me a drink? Or I'll buy you one, but come sit next to me so's I don't have to shout. Please?'

She was drinking Amaretto, sweet almond liqueur that she took on the rocks. It tastes like dessert but it's as strong as whiskey.

'He told me not to come,' she said. 'To the funeral. It was someplace in Brooklyn, that's a whole foreign nation to me, Brooklyn, but a lot of people went from the office. I could have had a ride, I could have been part of the office crowd, come to pay our respects. But he said not to, he said it wouldn't look right.'

'Because—'

'He said it was a matter of respect for the dead.' She picked up her glass and started into it. I've never known what people hope to see there, although it's a gesture I've performed often enough myself.

'Respect,' she said. 'What's he care about respect? I would have just been part of the office crowd, we both work at Tannahill, far as anyone there knows we're just friends. And all we ever were is friends, you know.'

'Whatever you say.'

'Oh, *shit*,' she said. 'Ah don't mean Ah wasn't fucking him, for the Lord's sake. Ah mean it was just laughs and good times. He was married and he went home to Mama every night and that was jes fine, because who in her right mind'd want Tommy Tillary around by the dawn's early light? Christ in the foothills, did Ah spill this or drink it?'

We agreed that she was drinking them a little too fast. Sweet drinks, we told each other, had a way of sneaking up on a person. It was this fancy New York Amaretto shit, she maintained, not like the bourbon she'd grown up on. You knew where you stood with bourbon.

I told her I was a bourbon drinker myself, and it pleased her to learn this. Alliances have been forged on thinner bonds than that, and ours served to propel us out of Armstrong's, with a stop down the block for a fifth of Maker's Mark—her choice—and a four-block walk to her apartment. There were exposed brick walls, I remember, and candles stuck in straw-wrapped bottles, and several travel posters from Sabena, the Belgian airline.

We did what grownups do when they find themselves alone together. We drank our fair share of the Maker's Mark and went to bed. She made a lot of enthusiastic noises and more than a few skillful moves, and afterwards she cried some.

A little later she dropped off to sleep. I was tired myself, but I put on my clothes and sent myself home. Because who in her right mind'd want Matt Scudder around by the dawn's early light?

Over the next couple of days, I wondered every time I entered Armstrong's if I'd run into her, and each time I was more relieved than disappointed when I didn't. I didn't encounter Tommy either, and that too was a relief, and in no sense disappointing.

Then one morning I picked up the *News* and read that they'd arrested a pair of young Hispanics from Sunset Park for the Tillary burglary and homicide. The paper ran the usual photo—two skinny kids, their hair unruly, one of them trying to hide his face from the camera, the other smirking defiantly, and each of them handcuffed to a broadshouldered, grimfaced Irishman in a suit. You didn't need the careful caption to tell the good guys from the bad guys.

Sometime in the middle of the afternoon I went over to Armstrong's for a hamburger and drank a beer with it, then got the day going with a round or two of laced coffee. The phone behind the bar rang and Dennis put down the glass he was wiping and answered it. 'He was here a minute ago,' he said. 'I'll see if he stepped out.' He covered the mouthpiece with his hand and looked quizzically at me. 'Are you still here?' he asked. 'Or did you slip away while my attention was somehow diverted?'

'Who wants to know?'

'Tommy Tillary.'

You never know what a woman will decide to tell a man, or how a man will react to it. I didn't want to find out, but I was better off learning over the phone than face to face. I nodded and took the phone from Dennis.

I said, 'Matt Scudder, Tommy. I was sorry to hear about your wife.'

'Thanks, Matt. Jesus, it feels like it happened a year ago. It was what, a week?'

'At least they got the bastards.'

There was a pause. Then he said, 'Jesus. You haven't seen a paper, huh?'

'That's where I read about it. Two Spanish kids.'

'You read the *News* this morning.'

'I generally do. Why?'

'You didn't happen to see this afternoon's *Post*.'

'No. Why, what happened? They turn out to be clean?'

Another pause. Then he said, 'I figured you'd know. The cops were over early this morning, even before I saw the story in the *News*. It'd be easier if you already knew.'

'I'm not following you, Tommy.'

'The two Spics. Clean? Shit, they're about as clean as the men's room in the Times Square subway station. The cops hit their place and found stuff from my house everywhere they looked. Jewelry they had descriptions of, a stereo that I gave them the serial number, everything. Monogrammed shit. I mean that's how clean they were, for Christ's sake.'

'So?'

'They admitted the burglary but not the murder.'

'That's common, Tommy.'

'Lemme finish, huh? They admitted the burglary, but according to them it was a put-up job. According to them I hired them to hit my place. They could keep whatever they got and I'd have everything out and arranged for them, and in return I got to clean up on the insurance by over-reporting the loss.'

'What did the loss amount to?'

'Shit *I* don't know. There were twice as many things turned up in their apartment as I ever listed when I made out a report. There's things I missed a few days after I filed the report and others I didn't know were gone until the cops found them. You don't notice everything right away, at least I don't, and on top of it how could I think straight with Peg dead? You know?'

'It hardly sounds like an insurance set-up.'

'No, of course it wasn't. How the hell could it be? All I had was a standard homeowner's policy. It covered maybe a third of what I lost. According to them, the place was empty when they hit it. Peg was out.'

'And?'

'And I set them up. They hit the place, they carted everything away, and I came home with Peg and stabbed her six, eight times, whatever it was, and left her there so it'd look like it happened in a burglary.'

'How could the burglars testify that you stabbed your wife?'

'They couldn't. All they said was they didn't and she wasn't home when they were there, and that I hired them to do the burglary. The cops pieced the rest of it together.'

'What did they do, arrest you?'

'No. They came over to the house, it was early, I don't know what time. It was the first I knew that the Spics were arrested, let alone that they were tryng to do a job on me. They just wanted to talk, the cops, and at first I talked to them, and then I started to get the drift of what they were trying to put onto me. So I said I wasn't saying anything more without my lawyer present, and I called him, and he left half his breakfast on the table and came over in a hurry, and he wouldn't let me say a word.'

'And the cops didn't take you in or book you?'

'No.'

'Did they buy your story?'

'No way. I didn't really tell 'em a story because Kaplan wouldn't let me say anything. They didn't drag me in because they don't have a case yet, but Kaplan says they're gonna be building one if they can. They told me not to leave town. You believe it? My wife's dead, the *Post* headline *Quiz Husband in Burglary Murder*, and what the hell do they think I'm gonna do? Am I going fishing for fucking trout in Montana? "Don't leave town." You see this shit on television, you think nobody in real life talks this way. Maybe television's where they get it from.'

I waited for him to tell me what he wanted from me. I didn't have long to wait.

'Why I called,' he said, 'is Kaplan wants to hire a detective. He figured maybe these guys talked around the neighborhood, maybe they bragged to their friends, maybe there's a way to prove they did the killing. He says the cops won't concentrate on that end if they're too busy nailing the lid shut on me.'

I explained that I didn't have any official standing, that I had no license and filed no reports.

'That's okay,' he insisted. 'I told Kaplan what I want is somebody I can trust, and somebody who'll do the job for me. I don't think they're gonna have any kind of case at all, Matt, but the longer this drags on the worse it is for me. I want it cleared up, I want it in the papers that these Spanish assholes did it all and I had nothing to do with anything. You name a fair fee and I'll pay it, me to you, and it can be cash in your hand if you don't like checks. What do you say?'

He wanted somebody he could trust. Had Carolyn from the Caroline told him how trustworthy I was?

What did I say? I said yes.

I met Tommy Tillary and his lawyer in Drew Kaplan's office on Court Street a few blocks from Brooklyn's Borough Hall. There was a Syrian restaurant next door, and at the corner a grocery store specializing in Middle Eastern imports stood next to an antique shop overflowing with stripped oak furniture and brass lamps and bedsteads. Kaplan's office ran to wood panelling and leather chairs and oak file cabinets. His name and the names of two partners were painted on the frosted glass door in old-fashioned gold and black lettering. Kaplan himself looked conservatively up-to-date, with a three-piece striped suit that was better cut than mine. Tommy wore his burgundy blazer and gray flannel trousers and loafers. Strain showed at the corners of his blue eyes and around his mouth. His complexion was off, too, as if anxiety had drawn the blood inward, leaving the skin sallow.

'All we want you to do,' Drew Kaplan said, 'is find a key in one of their pants pockets, Herrera's or Cruz's, and trace it to a locker in Penn Station, and in the locker there's a footlong knife with their prints and her blood on it.'

'Is that what it's going to take?'

He smiled. 'It wouldn't hurt. No, actually we're not in such bad shape. They got some shaky testimony from a pair of Latins who've been in and out of trouble since they got weaned to Tropicana. They got what looks to them like a good motive on Tommy's part.'

'Which is?'

I was looking at Tommy when I talked. His eyes slipped away from mine. Kaplan said, 'A marital triangle, a case of the shorts, and a strong money motive. Margaret Tillary inherited a little over a quarter of a million dollars six or eight months ago. An aunt left a million two and it got cut up four ways. What they don't bother to notice is he loved his wife, and how many husbands cheat? What is it they say? Ninety percent cheat and ten percent lie?'

'That's good odds.'

'One of the killers, Angel Herrera, did some odd jobs at the Tillary house last March or April. Spring cleaning; he hauled stuff out of the basement and attic, a little donkey work for hourly wages. According to Herrera, that's how Tommy knew him to contact him about the burglary. According to common sense, that's how Herrera and his buddy Cruz knew the house and what was in it and how to gain access.'

'The case against Tommy sounds pretty thin.'

'It is,' Kaplan said. 'The thing is, you go to court with something like this and you lose even if you win. For the rest of your life everybody remembers you stood trial for murdering your wife, never mind that you won an acquittal. All that means, some Jew lawyer bought a judge or tricked a jury.'

'So I'll get a guinea lawyer,' Tommy said. 'And they'll think he threatened the judge and beat up the jury.'

'Besides,' the lawyer said, 'you never know which way a jury's going to jump. Tommy's alibi is he was with another lady at the time of the burglary. The woman's a colleague, they could see it as completely above-board, but who says they're going to? What they sometimes do, they decide they don't believe the alibi because it's his girlfriend lying for him, and at the same time they label him a scumbag for screwing around while his wife's getting killed.'

'You keep it up,' Tommy said, 'I'll find myself guilty, the way you make it sound.'

'Plus he's hard to get a sympathetic jury for. He's a big handsome guy, a sharp dresser, and you'd love him in a gin joint but how much do you love him in a courtroom? He's a telephone securities salesman, he's beautiful on the phone, and that means every clown who ever lost a hundred dollars on a stock tip or bought magazine subscriptions over the phone is going to walk into the courtroom with a hard-on for him. I'm telling you, I want to stay the hell *out* of court. I'll *win* in court, I know that, or the worst that'll happen is I'll win on appeal, but who needs it? This is a case that shouldn't be in the first place, and I'd love to clear it up before they even go so far as presenting a bill to the Grand Jury.'

'So from me you want—'

'Whatever you can find, Matt. Whatever discredits Cruz and Herrera. I don't know what's there to be found, but you were a cop and now you're a private, and you can get down in the streets and nose around.'

I nodded. I could do that. 'One thing,' I said. 'Wouldn't you be better off with a Spanish-speaking detective? I know enough to buy a beer in a bodega, but I'm a long ways from fluent.'

Kaplan shook his head. 'Tommy says he wants somebody he can trust,' he said. 'I think he's right. A personal relationship's worth more than a dime's worth of "Me llamo Matteo y como esta usted?".'

'That's the truth,' Tommy Tillary said. 'Matt, I know I can count on you.'

I wanted to tell him all he could count on was his fingers. I didn't really see what I could expect to uncover that wouldn't turn up in a regular police investigation. But I'd spent enough time carrying a shield to know not to push away money when somebody wants to give it to you. I felt comfortable taking a fee. The man was inheriting a quarter of a million dollars, plus whatever insurance she carried. If he was willing to spread some of it around, I was willing to take it.

So I went to Sunset Park and spent some time in the streets and some more time in the bars. Sunset Park is in Brooklyn, of course, on the borough's western edge above Bay Ridge and south and west of Greenwood Cemetery. These days there's a lot of brownstoning going on there, with young urban professionals renovating the old houses and gentrifying the neighborhood. Back then the upwardly mobile young had not yet discovered Sunset Park, and the area was a mix of Latins and Scandinavians, most of the former Puerto Ricans, most of the latter Norwegians. The balance was gradually shifting from Europe to the islands, from light to dark, but this was a process that had been going on for ages and there was nothing hurried about it.

I talked to Herrera's landlord and Cruz's former employer and one of his recent girlfriends. I drank beer in bars and the back rooms of bodegas. I went to the local stationhouse—they hadn't caught the Margaret Tillary murder case, that had been a matter for the local precinct in Bay Ridge and some detectives from Brooklyn Homicide. I read the sheets on both of the burglars and drank coffee with the cops and picked up some of the stuff that doesn't get on the yellow sheets.

I found out that Miguelito Cruz once killed a man in a tavern brawl over a woman. There were no charges pressed; a dozen witnesses reported the dead man had gone after Cruz first with a broken bottle. Cruz had most likely been carrying the knife, but several witnesses insisted it had been tossed to him by an anonymous benefactor, and there hadn't been enough evidence to make a case of weapons possession, let alone homicide.

I learned that Herrera had three children living with their mother in Puerto Rico. He was divorced, but wouldn't marry his current girlfriend because he regarded himself as still married to his ex-wife in the eyes of God. He sent money to his children, when he had any to send.

I learned other things. They didn't seem terribly consequential then and they've faded from memory altogether by now, but I wrote them down in my pocket notebook as I learned them, and every day or so I duly reported my findings to Drew Kaplan. He always seemed pleased with what I told him.

Some nights I stayed fairly late in Sunset Park. There was a dark beery tavern called The Fjord that served as a comfortable enough harbor after I tired of playing Sam Spade. But I almost invariably managed a stop at Armstrong's before I called it a night. Billie would lock the door around two, but he'd keep serving until four and he'd let you in if he knew you.

One night she was there, Carolyn Cheatham, drinking bourbon this time instead of Amaretto, her face frozen with stubborn old pain. It took her a blink or two to recognize me. Then tears started to form in the corners of her eyes, and she used the back of one hand to wipe them away.

I didn't approach her until she beckoned. She patted the stool beside hers and I eased myself onto it. I had coffee with bourbon in it, and bought a refill for her. She was pretty drunk already, but that's never been enough reason to turn down a drink.

She talked about Tommy. He was being nice to her, she said. Calling up, sending flowers. Because he might need to testify that he'd been with her when his wife was killed, and he'd need her to back him up.

But he wouldn't see her because it wouldn't look right, not for a new widower, not for a man who'd been publicly accused of murder.

'He sends flowers with no card enclosed,' she said. 'He calls me from pay phones. The son of a bitch.'

Billie called me aside. 'I don't want to put her out,' he said, 'a nice woman like that, shitfaced as she is. But I thought I was gonna have to. You'll see she gets home?'

I said I would.

First I had to let her buy us another round. She insisted. Then I got her out of there and a cab came along and saved us the walk. At her place, I took the keys from her and unlocked the door. She half sat, half sprawled on the couch. I had to use the bathroom, and when I came back her eyes were closed and she was snoring lightly.

I got her coat and shoes off, put her to bed, loosened her clothing and covered her with a blanket. I was tired from all that and sat down on the couch for a minute, and I almost dozed off myself. Then I snapped awake and let myself out. Her door had a spring lock. All I had to do was close it and it was locked.

Much of the walk back to my hotel disappeared in blackout. I was crossing Fifty-Seventh Street, and then it was morning and I was stretched out in my own bed, my clothes a tangle on the straight-backed chair. That happened a lot in those days, that kind of before-bed blackout, and I used to insist it didn't bother me. What ever happened on the way home? Why waste brain cells trying to remember the final fifteen minutes of the day?

I went back to Sunset Park the next day. I learned that Cruz had been in trouble as a youth. With a gang of neighborhood kids, he used to go into the city and cruise Greenwich Village, looking for homosexuals to beat up. He'd had a dread of homosexuality, probably flowing as it generally does out of a fear of a part of himself, and he stifled that dread by fag-bashing.

'He still doan like them,' a woman told me. She had glossy black hair and opaque eyes, and she was letting me pay for her rum and orange juice. 'He's pretty, you know, and they come on to him, an' he doan like it.'

I called that item in, along with a few others equally earth-shaking. I bought myself a steak dinner at the Slate over on Tenth Avenue that night, then finished up at Armstrong's, not drinking very hard, just coasting along on bourbon and coffee.

Twice the phone rang for me. Once it was Tommy Tillary, telling me how much he appreciated what I was doing for him. It seemed to me that all I was doing was taking his money, but he had me believing that my loyalty and invaluable assistance were all he had to cling to.

The second call was from Carolyn. More praise. I was a gentleman, she assured me, and a hell of a fellow all round. And I should forget that she'd been bad-mouthing Tommy. Everything was going to be fine with them.

I told her I'd never doubted it for a minute, and that I couldn't really remember what she'd said anyway.

I took the next day off. I think I went to a movie, and it may have been *The Sting*, with Newman and Redford achieving vengeance through swindling.

The day after that I did another tour of duty over in Brooklyn. And the day after that I picked up the *News* first thing in the morning. The headline was nonspecific, something like *Kill Suspect Hangs Self in Cell*, but I knew it was my case before I turned to the story on page three.

Miguelito Cruz had torn his clothing into strips, knotted the strips together, stood his iron bedstead on its side, climbed onto it, looped his homemade rope around an overhead pipe, and jumped off the upended bedstead and into the next world.

That evening's six o'clock TV news had the rest of the story. Informed of his friend's death, Angel Herrera had recanted his original story and admitted that he and Cruz had conceived and executed the Tillary burglary on their own. It had been Miguelito who had stabbed the Tillary woman when she walked in on them. He'd picked up a kitchen knife while Herrera watched in horror. Miguelito always had a short temper, Herrera said, but they were friends, even cousins, and they had hatched their story to protect Miguelito. But now that he was dead, Herrera could admit what had really happened.

I was in Armstrong's that night, which was not remarkable. I had it in mind to get drunk, though I could not have told you why, and that *was* remarkable, if not unheard of. I got drunk a lot those days, but I rarely set out with that intention. I just wanted to feel a little better, a little more mellow, and somewhere along the way I'd wind up waxed.

I wasn't drinking particularly hard or fast, but I was working at it, and then somewhere around ten or eleven the door opened and I knew who it was before I turned around. Tommy Tillary, well dressed and freshly barbered, making his first appearance in Jimmy's place since his wife was killed.

'Hey, look who's here!' he called out, and grinned that big grin. People rushed over to shake his hand. Billie was behind the stick, and he'd no sooner set one up on the house for our hero than Tommy insisted on buying a round for the bar. It was an expensive gesture, there must have been thirty or forty people in there, but I don't think he cared if there were three or four hundred.

I stayed where I was, letting the others mob him, but he worked his way over to me and got an arm around my shoulders. 'This is the man,' he announced. 'Best fucking detective ever wore out a pair of shoes. This man's money—' he told Billie '—is no good at all tonight. He can't buy a drink, he can't buy a cup of coffee, if you went and put in pay toilets since I was last there, he can't use his own dime.'

'The john's still free,' Billie said, 'but don't give the boss any ideas.'

'Oh, don't tell me he didn't already think of it,' Tommy said. 'Matt, my boy, I love you. I was in a tight spot, I didn't want to walk out of my house, and you came through for me.'

What the hell had I done? I hadn't hanged Miguelito Cruz or coaxed a confession out of Angel Herrera. I hadn't even set eyes on either man. But he was buying the drinks, and I had a thirst, so who was I to argue?

I don't know how long we stayed there. Curiously, my drinking slowed down even as Tommy's picked up speed. Carolyn, I noticed, was not present, nor did her name find its way into the conversation. I wondered if she would walk in—it was, after all, her neighborhood bar, and she was apt to drop in on her own. I wondered what would happen if she did.

I guess there were a lot of things I wondered about, and perhaps that's what put the brakes on my own drinking. I didn't want any gaps in my memory, any gray patches in my awareness.

After a while Tommy was hustling me out of Armstrong's. 'This is celebration time,' he told me. 'We don't want to sit in one place till we grow roots. We want to bop a little.'

He had a car, and I just went along with him without paying too much attention to exactly where we were. We went to a noisy Greek club, on the East Side I think, where the waiters looked like mob hitmen. We went to a couple of trendy singles joints. We wound up somewhere in the Village, in a dark beery cave that reminded me, I realized after a while, of the Norwegian joint in Sunset Park. The Fjord? Right.

It was quiet there, and conversation was possible, and I found myself asking him what I'd done that was so praiseworthy. One man had killed himself and another had confessed, and where was my role in either incident?

'The stuff you came up with,' he said

'What stuff? I should have brought back fingernail parings, you could have had someone work voodoo on them.'

'About Cruz and the fairies.'

'He was up for murder. He didn't kill himself because he was afraid they'd get him for fag-bashing when he was a juvenile offender.'

Tommy took a sip of Scotch. He said, 'Couple days ago, black guy comes up to Cruz in the chow line. Huge spade, built like the Seagram's Building. "Wait'll you get up to Green Haven," he tells him. "Every blood there's gonna have you for a girlfriend. Doctor gonna have to cut you a brand-new asshole, time you get outta there".'

I didn't say anything.

'Kaplan,' he said. 'Drew talked to somebody who talked to somebody, and that did it. Cruz took a good look at the idea of playin' Drop the Soap for half the jigs in captivity, and the next thing you know the murderous little bastard was dancing on air. And good riddance to him.'

I couldn't seem to catch my breath. I worked on it while Tommy went to the bar for another round. I hadn't touched the drink in front of me but I let him buy for both of us.

When he got back I said, 'Herrera?'

'Changed his story. Made a full confession.'

'And pinned the killing on Cruz.'

'Why not? Cruz wasn't around to complain. Who knows which one of 'em did it, and for that matter, who cares? The thing is, you gave us the lever.'

'For Cruz,' I said. 'To get him to kill himself.'

'And for Herrera. Those kids of his in Santurce. Drew spoke to Herrera's lawyer and Herrera's lawyer spoke to Herrera, and the message was, look, you're going up for burglary whatever you do, and probably for murder, but if you tell the right story you'll draw shorter time and on top of that, that nice Mr Tillary's gonna let bygones be bygones and every month there's a nice check for your wife and kiddies back home in Puerto Rico.'

At the bar, a couple of old men were reliving the Louis–Schmeling fight, the second one, where Louis punished the German champion. One of the old fellows was throwing roundhouse punches in the air, demonstrating.

I said, 'Who killed you wife?'

'One or the other of them. If I had to bet I'd say Cruz. He had those little beady eyes, you looked at him up close and you got that he was a killer.'

'When did you look at him up close?'

'When they came and cleaned the house, the basement and the attic. Not when they came and cleaned me out, that was the second time.'

He smiled, but I kept looking at him until the smile lost its certainty. 'That was Herrera who helped around the house,' I said. 'You never met Cruz.'

'Cruz came along, gave him a hand.'

'You never mentioned that before.'

'Oh, sure I did, Matt. What difference does it make, anyway?'

'Who killed her Tommy?'

'Hey, let it alone, huh?'

'Answer the question.'

'I already answered it.'

'You killed her, didn't you?'

'What, are you crazy? Cruz killed her and Herrera swore to it, isn't that enough for you?'

'Tell me you didn't kill her.'

'I didn't kill her.'

'Tell me again.'

'I didn't fucking kill her. What's the matter with you?'

'I don't believe you.'

'Oh, Jesus,' he said. He closed his eyes, put his head in his hands. He sighed and looked up and said, 'You know, it's a funny thing with me. Over the telephone, I'm the best salesman you could ever imagine. I swear I could sell sand to the Arabs, I could sell ice in the winter, but face to face I'm no good at all. Why do you figure that is?'

'You tell me.'

'I don't know. I used to think it was my face, the eyes and the mouth, I don't know. It's easy over the phone. I'm talking to a stranger, I don't know who he is or what he looks like, and he's not lookin' at me, and it's a cinch. Face to face, especially with someone I know, it's a different story.' He looked at me. 'If we were doin' this over the phone, you'd buy the whole thing.'

'It's possible.'

'It's fucking certain. Word for word, you'd buy the package. Suppose

I was to tell you I did kill her, Matt. You couldn't prove anything. Look, the both of us walked in there, the place was a mess from the burglary, we got in an argument, tempers flared, something happened.'

'You set up the burglary. You planned the whole thing, just the way Cruz and Herrera accused you of doing. And now you wriggled out of it.'

'And you helped me, don't forget that part of it.'

'I won't.'

'And I wouldn't have gone away for it anyway, Matt. Not a chance. I'da beat it in court, only this way I don't have to go to court. Look, this is just the booze talkin', and we can both forget it in the morning, right? I didn't kill her, you didn't accuse me, we're still buddies, everything's fine. Right?'

Blackouts are never there when you want them. I woke up the next day and remembered all of it, and I found myself wishing I didn't. He'd killed his wife and he was getting away with it. And I'd helped him. I'd taken his money, and in return I'd shown him how to set one man up for suicide and pressure another into making a false confession.

And what was I going to do about it?

I couldn't think of a thing. Any story I carried to the police would be speedily denied by Tommy and his lawyer, and all I had was the thinnest of hearsay evidence, my own client's own words when he and I both had a skinful of booze. I went over it for a few days, looking for ways to shake something loose, and there was nothing. I could maybe interest a newspaper reporter, maybe get Tommy some press coverage that wouldn't make him happy, but why? And to what purpose?

It rankled. But I would just have a couple of drinks, and then it wouldn't rankle so much.

Angel Herrera pleaded to burglary, and in return the Brooklyn D.A.'s office dropped all homicide charges. He went upstate to serve five-to-ten.

And then I got a call in the middle of the night. I'd been sleeping a couple of hours but the phone woke me and I groped for it. It took me a minute to recognize the voice on the other end.

It was Carolyn Cheatham.

'I had to call you,' she said, 'on account of you're a bourbon man and a gentleman. I owed it to you to call you.'

'What's the matter?'

'He ditched me,' she said, 'and he got fired out of Tannahill & Co. so he won't have to look at me around the office. Once he didn't need me he let go of me, and do you know he did it over the phone?'

'Carolyn—'

'It's all in the note,' she said. 'I'm leaving a note.'

'Look, don't do anything yet,' I said. I was out of bed, fumbling for my clothes. 'I'll be right over. We'll talk about it.'

'You can't stop me, Matt.'

'I won't try to stop you. We'll talk first, and then you can do anything you want.'

The phone clicked in my ear.

I threw my clothes on, rushed over there, hoping it would be pills, something that took its time. I broke a small pane of glass in the downstairs door and let myself in, then used an old credit card to slip the bolt of her spring lock. If she had engaged the deadbolt lock I would have had to kick the door in.

The room smelled of cordite. She was on the couch she'd passed out on the last time I saw her. The gun was still in her hand, limp at her side, and there was a black-rimmed hole in her temple.

There was a note, too. An empty bottle of Maker's Mark stood on the coffee table, an empty glass beside it. The booze showed in her handwriting, and in the sullen phrasing of the suicide note.

I read the note. I stood there for a few minutes, not for very long, and then I got a dish towel from the pullman kitchen and wiped the bottle and the glass. I took another matching glass, rinsed it out and wiped it, and put it in the drainboard of the sink.

I stuffed the note in my pocket. I took the gun from her fingers, checked routinely for a pulse, then wrapped a sofa pillow around the gun to muffle its report. I fired one round into her chest, another into her open mouth.

I dropped the gun into a pocket and left.

They found the gun in Tommy Tillary's house, stuffed between the cushions of the living-room sofa, clean of prints inside and out. Ballistics got a perfect match. I'd aimed for soft tissue with the round shot into her chest because the bullets can fragment on impact with bone. That was one reason I'd fired the extra shots. The other was to rule out the possibility of suicide.

After the story made the papers, I picked up the phone and called Drew Kaplan. 'I don't understand it,' I said. 'He was free and clear, why the hell did he kill the girl?'

'Ask him yourself,' Kaplan said. He did not sound happy. 'You want my opinion, he's a lunatic. I honestly didn't think he was. I figured maybe he killed his wife, maybe he didn't. Not my job to try him. But I didn't figure he was a homicidal maniac.'

'It's certain he killed the girl?'

'Not much question. The gun's pretty strong evidence. Talk about finding somebody with the smoking pistol in his hand, there it was in Tommy's couch. The idiot.'

'Funny he kept it.'

'Maybe he had other people he wanted to shoot. Go figure a crazy man. No, the gun's evidence, and there was a phone tip, a man called in the shooting, reported a man running out of there and gave a description that fitted Tommy pretty well. Even had him wearing that red blazer he wears, tacky thing makes him look like an usher at the Paramount.'

'It sounds tough to square.'

'Well, somebody else'll have to try to do it,' Kaplan said. 'I told him I can't defend him this time. What it amounts to, I wash my hands of him.'

I thought of this when I read Angel Herrera got out just the other day. He served all ten years because he was as good at getting into trouble inside the walls as he'd been on the outside.

Somebody killed Tommy Tillary with a homemade knife after he'd served two years and three months of a manslaughter stretch. I wondered at the time if that was Herrera getting even, and I don't suppose I'll ever know. Maybe the checks stopped going to Santurce and Herrera took it the wrong way. Or maybe Tommy said the wrong thing to somebody else, and said it face-to-face instead of over the phone.

I don't think I'd do it that way now. I don't drink any more, and the impulse to play God seems to have evaporated with the booze.

But then a lot of things have changed. Billie left Armstrong's not long after that, left New York too; the last I heard he was off drink himself, living in Sausalito and making candles.

I ran into Dennis the other day in a bookstore on lower Fifth Avenue, full of odd volumes on yoga and spiritualism and holistic healing. And Armstrong's is scheduled to close the end of next month. The lease is up for renewal, and I suppose the next you know the old joint'll be another Korean fruit market.

I still light a candle now and then for Carolyn Cheatham and Angel Cruz. Not very often. Just every once in a while.

CHARLES DE LINT is a full-time writer who makes his home in Ottawa, Canada, with his wife, MaryAnn Harris, an artist and program officer in the field of international development who also does the first editing on all of de Lint's fiction.

They're both musicians, specializing in traditional and contemporary Celtic music on a wide variety of acoustic instruments. Performing usually as a duo, they are occasionally found in the line-up of a local band called 'Jump at the Sun'.

De Lint's most recent novels in North America are *The Little Country* and *Spiritwalk*, and in Australia and the UK, *Yarrow*.

Charles de Lint

THE SACRED FIRE

No one lives forever,
and dead men rise up never,
and even the longest river
winds somewhere safe to sea.

from *British folklore* collected by Stephen Gallagher

There were ten thousand maniacs on the radio—the band, not a bunch of lunatics—playing their latest single; Natalie Merchant's distinctive voice rising from the music like a soothing balm.

Trouble me . . .

Sharing your problems . . . sometimes talking a thing through was enough to ease the burden. You didn't need to be a shrink to know it could work. You just had to find someone to listen to you.

Nicky Straw had tried talking. He'd try anything if it would work, but nothing did. There was only one way to deal with his problems and it took him a long time to accept that. But it was hard, because the job was never done. Every time he put one of them down, another of the freaks would come buzzing in his face like a fly on a corpse.

He was getting tired of fixing things. Tired of running. Tired of being on his own.

Trouble me . . .

He could hear the music clearly from where he crouched in the bushes. The boom box pumped out the song from one corner of the blanket on which she was sitting, reading a paperback edition of Christie Riddell's *How to Make the Wind Blow*. She even looked a little like Natalie Merchant. Same dark eyes, same dark hair, same slight build. Better taste in clothes, though. None of those thrift-shop dresses and the like that made Merchant look old before her time; just a nice white Butler U. T-shirt and a pair of bright yellow jogging shorts. White Reeboks with laces to match the shorts, a red headband.

The light was leaking from the sky. Be too dark to read soon. Maybe she'd get up and go.

Nicky sat back on his haunches. He shifted his weight from one leg to the other.

Maybe nothing would happen, but he didn't see things working out that way. Not with how his luck was running.

All bad.

Trouble me . . .

I did, he thought. I tried. But it didn't work out, did it?

So now he was back to fixing things the only way he knew how.

Her name was Luann. Luann Somerson.

She'd picked him up in the Tombs—about as far from the green harbor of Fitzhenry Park as you could get in Newford. It was the lost part of the city—a wilderness of urban decay stolen back from the neon and glitter. Block on block of decaying tenements and run-down buildings. The kind of place to which the homeless gravitated, looking for squats; where the kids hung out to sneak beers and junkies made their deals, hands twitching as they exchanged crumpled bills for little packets of short-lived empyrean; where winos slept in doorways that reeked of puke and urine and the cops only went if they were on the take and meeting the moneyman.

It was also the kind of place where the freaks hid out, waiting for Lady Night to start her prowl. Waiting for dark. The freaks liked her shadows and he did too, because he could hide in them as well as they could. Maybe better. He was still alive, wasn't he?

He was looking for the freaks to show when Luann approached him, sitting with his back against the wall, right on the edge of the Tombs, watching the rush hour slow to a trickle on Gracie Street. He had his legs splayed out on the sidewalk in front of him, playing the drunk, the bum. Three-day stubble, hair getting ragged, scruffy clothes, two dimes in his pocket—it wasn't hard to look the part. Commuters stepped over him or went around him, but nobody gave him a second glance. Their gazes just touched him, then slid on by. Until she showed up.

She stopped, then crouched down so that she wasn't standing over him. She looked too healthy and clean to be hanging around this part of town.

'You look like you could use a meal,' she said.

'I suppose you're buying?'

She nodded.

Nicky just shook his head. 'What? You like to live dangerously or something, lady? I could be anybody.'

She nodded again, a half-smile playing on her lips.

'Sure,' she said. 'Anybody at all. Except you're Nicky Straw. We used to take English 201 together, remember?'

He'd recognized her as well, just hoped she hadn't. The guy she remembered didn't exist anymore.

'I know about being down on your luck,' she added when he didn't respond. 'Believe me, I've been there.'

You haven't been anywhere, he thought. You don't want to know about the places I've been.

'You're Luann Somerson,' he said finally.

Again that smile. 'Let me buy you a meal, Nicky.'

He'd wanted to avoid this kind of thing, but he supposed he'd known all along that he couldn't. This was what happened when the hunt took you into your hometown. You didn't disappear into the background like all the other bums. Someone was always there to remember.

Hey, Nicky. How's it going? How's the wife and that kid of yours?

Like they cared. Maybe he should just tell the truth for a change. You know those things we used to think were hiding in the closet when we were too young to know any better? Well, surprise. One night one of those monsters came out of the closet and chewed off their faces . . .

'C'mon,' Luann was saying.

She stood up, waiting for him. He gave it a heartbeat, then another. When he saw she wasn't going without him, he finally got to his feet.

'You do this a lot?' he asked.

She shook her head. 'First time,' she said.

All it took was one time . . .

'I'm like everyone else,' she said. 'I pretend there's no one there, lying half-starved in the gutter, you know? But when I recognized you, I couldn't just walk by.'

You should have, he thought.

His silence was making her nervous and she began to chatter as they headed slowly down Yoors Street.

'Why don't we just go back to my place?' she said. 'It'll give you a chance to clean up. Chad—that's my ex—left some clothes behind that might fit you . . .'

Her voice trailed off. She was embarrassed now, finally realizing how he must feel, having her see him like this.

'Uh . . .'

'That'd be great,' he said, relenting.

He got that smile of hers as a reward. A man could get lost in its warmth, he thought. It'd feed a freak for a month.

'So this guy,' he said. 'Chad. He been gone long?'

The smile faltered.

'Three and a half weeks now,' she said.

That explained a lot. Nothing made you forget your own troubles so much as running into someone who had them worse.

'Not too bright a guy, I guess,' he said.

'That's . . . Thank you, Nicky. I guess I need to hear that kind of thing.'

'Hey, I'm a bum. We've got nothing better to do than to think up nice things to say.'

'You were never a bum, Nicky.'

'Yeah. Well, things change.'

She took the hint. As they walked on, she talked about the book she'd started reading last night instead.

It took them fifteen minutes or so to reach her apartment on McKennit, right in the heart of Lower Crowsea. It was a walk-up with its own stairwell—a narrow, winding affair that started on the pavement by the entrance of a small Lebanese groceteria and then deposited you on a balcony overlooking the street.

Inside, the apartment had the look of a recent split-up. There was an amplifier on a wooden orange crate by the front window, but no turntable or speakers. The bookcase to the right of the window had gaps where apparently random volumes had been removed. A pair of rattan chairs with bright slipcovers stood in the middle of the room, but there were no end tables to go with them, nor a coffee table. She was making do with another orange crate, this one cluttered with magazines, a couple of plates stacked on top of each other and what looked like every coffee mug she owned squeezed into the remaining space. A small portable black and white Zenith TV stood at the base of the bookcase, alongside a portable cassette deck. There were a couple of rectangles on the wall where paintings had obviously been removed. A couple of weeks' worth of newspapers were in a pile on the floor by one of the chairs.

She started to apologize for the mess, then smiled and shrugged.

Nicky had to smile with her. Like he was going to complain about the place, looking like he did.

She showed him to the bathroom. By the time he came out again, showered and shaved, dressed in a pair of Chad's corduroys and a white linen shirt, both of which were at least a size too big, she had a salad on the table in the kitchen, wine glasses out, the bottle waiting for him to open it, breaded pork chops and potatoes on the stove, still cooking.

Nicky's stomach grumbled at the rich smell that filled the air.

She talked a little about her failed marriage over dinner—sounding sad rather than bitter—but more about old times at the university. As she spoke, Nicky realized that the only thing they had shared back then had been their English class, still he let her ramble on about campus events he only half-remembered and people who'd meant nothing to him then and did even less now.

Because at least they hadn't been freaks.

He corrected himself. He hadn't been able to *recognize* the freaks among them back then.

'God, listen to me,' Luann said suddenly.

They were finished their meal and sitting in her living room having coffee. He'd been wrong; there were still two clean mugs in her cupboard.

'I am,' he said.

She gave him that smile of hers again—this time it had a wistfulness about it.

'I know you are,' she said. 'It's just that all I've been talking about is myself. What about you, Nicky? What happened to you?'

'I . . .'

Where did he start? Which lie did he give her?

That was the one good thing about street people. They didn't ask questions. Whatever put you there, that was your business. But citizens always wanted whys and hows and wherefores.

As he hesitated, she seemed to realize her faux pas.

'I'm sorry,' she said. 'If you don't want to talk about it . . .'

'It's not that.' Nicky told her. 'It's just . . .'

'Hard to open up?'

Try impossible. But oddly enough, Nicky found himself wanting to talk to her about it. To explain. To ease the burden. Even to warn her, because she was just the kind of person the freaks went for.

The fire inside her shimmered off her skin like a high voltage aura, sending shadows skittering. It was a bright shatter of light and a deep golden glow like honey, all at the same time. It sparked in her eyes; blazed when she smiled. Sooner or later it was going to draw a nest of the freaks to her, just as surely as a junkie could sniff out a fix.

'There's these . . . things,' he said slowly. 'They look enough like you or me to walk among us—especially at night—but they're . . . they're not human.'

She got a puzzled look on her face, which didn't surprise him in the least.

'They're freaks,' he said. 'I don't know what they are, or where they came from, but they're not natural. They feed on us, on our hopes and our dreams, on our vitality. They're like . . . I guess the best analogy would be that they're like vampires. Once they're on to you, you can't shake them. They'll keep after you until they've bled you dry.'

Her puzzlement was turning to a mild alarm, but now that he'd started, Nicky was determined to tell it all through, right to the end.

'What . . .' she began.

'What I do,' he said, interrupting her, 'is hunt them down.'

The song by Ten Thousand Maniacs ended and the boom box's speakers offered up another to the fading day. Nicky couldn't name the band this time, but he was familiar with the song's punchy rhythm. The lead singer was talking about burning beds . . .

Beside the machine, Luann put down her book and stretched.

Do it, Nicky thought. Get out of here. Now. While you still can.

Instead, she lay down on the blanket, hands behind her head, and looked into the darkening sky, listening to the music. Maybe she was looking for the first star of the night.

Something to wish upon.

The fire burned in her brighter than any star. Flaring and ebbing to the pulse of her thoughts.

Calling to the freaks.

Nicky's fingers clenched into fists. He made himself look away. But even closing his eyes, he couldn't ignore the fire. Its heat sparked the distance between them as though he lay beside her on the blanket, skin pressed to skin. His pulse drummed, twinning her heartbeat.

This was how the freaks felt. This was what they wanted, what they hungered for, what they fed on. This was what he denied them.

The spark of life.

The sacred fire.

He couldn't look away any longer. He had to see her one more time, her fire burning, burning . . .

He opened his eyes to find that the twilight had finally found Fitzhenry Park. And Luann—she was blazing like a bonfire in its dusky shadows.

'What do you mean, you hunt them down?' she asked.

'I kill them,' Nicky told her.

'But—'

'Understand, they're not human. They just *look* like us, but their faces don't fit quite right and they wear our kind of a body like they've put on an unfamiliar suit of loose clothing.'

He touched his borrowed shirt as he spoke. She just stared at him—all trace of that earlier smile gone. Fear lived in her eyes now.

That's it, he told himself. You've done enough. Get out of here.

But once started, he didn't seem to be able to stop. All the lonely years of the endless hunt came spilling out of him.

'They're out there in the night,' he said. 'That's when they can get away with moving among us. When their shambling walk makes you think of drunks or some feeble old homeless baglady—not of monsters. They're freaks and they live on the fire that makes us human.'

'The . . . the fire . . . ?'

He touched his chest.

'The one in here,' he said. 'They're drawn to the ones whose fires burn the brightest,' he added. 'Like yours does.'

She edged her chair back from the table, ready to bolt. Then he saw her realize that there was no place to bolt to. The knowledge sat there in her eyes, fanning the fear into an ever-more debilitating panic. Where was she going to go that he couldn't get to her first?

'I know what you're thinking,' he said. 'If someone had come to me with this story before I . . . found out about them—'

('Momma! Daddy!' he could her his daughter crying. 'The monsters are coming for me!'

(Soothing her. Showing her that the closet was empty. But never thinking about the window and the fire escape outside it. Never thinking for a minute that the freaks would come in through the window and take them both when he was at work.

(But that was before he'd known about the freaks, wasn't it?)

He looked down at the table and cleared his throat. There was pain in his eyes when his gaze lifted to meet hers again—pain as intense as her fear.

'If someone had told me,' he went on, 'I'd have recommended him for the Zeb, too—just lock him up in a padded cell and throw away the key. But I don't think that way now. Because I can see them. I can recognize them. All it takes is one time and you'll never disbelieve again. And you'll never forget.'

'You . . . you just kill these people . . . ?' she asked.

Her voice was tiny—no more than a whisper. Her mind was tape looped around the one fact. She wasn't hearing anything else.

'I told you—they're not people,' he began, then shook his head.

What was the point? What had he thought was going to happen? She'd go, yeah, right, and jump in to help him? Here, honey, let me hold the stake. Would you like another garlic clove in your lunch?

But they weren't vampires. He didn't know what they were, just that they were dangerous.

Freaks.

'They know about me,' he said. 'They've been hunting me for as long as I've been hunting them, but I move too fast for them. One day, though, I'll make a mistake and then they'll have me. It's that, or the cops'll pick me up and I wouldn't last the night in the cell. The freaks'd be on me so fast . . .'

He let his voice trail off. Her lower lip was trembling. Her eyes looked like those of a small panicked creature, caught in a trap, the hunter almost upon her.

'Maybe I should go,' he said.

He rose from the table, pretending he didn't see the astonished relief in her eyes. He paused at the door that would let him out onto the balcony.

'I didn't mean to scare you,' he said.

'I . . . you . . .'

He shook his head. 'I should never have come.'

'I . . .'

She still couldn't string two words together. Still didn't believe that she was getting out of this alive. He felt bad for unsettling her the way he had, but maybe it was for the best. Maybe she wouldn't bring any more strays home the way she had him. Maybe the freaks'd never get to her.

'Just think about this,' he said, before he left. 'What if I'm right?'

Then he stepped outside and closed the door behind him.

He could move fast when he had to—it was what had kept him alive through all these years. By the time she reached her living-room window, he was down the stairs and across the street, looking back at her from the darkened mouth of an alleyway nestled between a yuppie restaurant and a bookstore, both of which were closed. He could see her, studying the street, looking for him.

But she couldn't see him.

And that was the way he'd keep it.

He came out of the bushes, the mask of his face shifting and unsettled in the poor light. Luann was sitting up, fiddling with the dial on her boom box, flipping through the channels. She didn't hear him until he was almost upon her. When she turned, her face drained of color. She sprawled backwards in her attempt to escape and then could only lie there and stare, mouth working, but no sound coming out. He lunged for her—

But then Nicky was there. The hunting knife that he carried in a sheath under his shirt was in his hand, cutting edge up. He grabbed the freak by the back of his collar and hauled him around. Before the freak could make a move, Nicky rammed the knife home in the freak's stomach and ripped it up. Blood sprayed, showering them both.

He could hear Luann screaming. He could feel the freak jerking in his grip as he died. He could taste the freak's blood on his lips. But his mind was years and miles away, falling back and back to a small apartment where his wife and daughter had fallen prey to the monsters his daughter told him were living in the closet . . .

The freak slipped from his grip and sprawled on the grass. The knife fell from Nicky's hand. He looked at Luann, finally focusing on her. She was on her knees, staring at him and the freak like they were both aliens.

'He . . . his face . . . he . . .'

She could barely speak.

'I can't do it anymore,' he told her.

He was empty inside. Couldn't feel a thing. It was as though all those years of hunting down the freaks had finally extinguished his own fire.

In the distance he could hear a siren. Someone must have seen what went down. Had to have been a citizen, because street people minded their own business, didn't matter what they saw.

'It ends here,' he said.

He sat down beside the freak's corpse to wait for the police to arrive.

'For me, it ends here.'

Late the following day, Luann was still in shock.

She'd finally escaped the endless barrage of questions from both the police and the press, only to find that being alone brought no relief. She kept seeing the face of the man who attacked her. Had it really seemed to *shift* about like an ill-fitting mask, or had that just been something she'd seen as a result of the poor light and what Nicky had told her?

Their faces don't fit quite right . . .

She couldn't get it out of her mind. The face. The blood. The police dragging Nicky away. And all those things he'd told her that night.

They're freaks.

Crazy things.

They live on the fire that makes us human.

They seemed to well up out of some great pain he was carrying around inside him.

They're not human . . . they just look *like us . . .*

A thump on her balcony had her jumping nervously out of her chair until she realized that it was just the paperboy tossing up today's newspaper. She didn't want to look at what *The Daily Journal* had to say, but she couldn't seem to stop herself from going out to get it. She took the paper back inside and spread it out on her lap.

Naturally enough, the story had made the front page. There was a picture of her, looking washed out and stunned. A shot of the corpse being taken away in a body bag. A head and shoulders shot of Nicky . . .

She stopped, her pulse doubling its tempo as the headline under Nicky's picture sank in.

KILLER FOUND DEAD IN CELL—POLICE BAFFLED

'No,' she said.

They know about me.

She pushed the paper away from her until it fell to the floor. But Nicky's picture continued to look up at her from where the paper lay.

They've been hunting me.

None of what he'd told her could be true. It had just been the pitiful ravings of a very disturbed man.

I wouldn't last the night in a cell. The freaks'd be on me so fast . . .

But she'd known him once—a long time ago—and he'd been as normal as anybody then. Still, people changed . . .

She picked up the paper and quickly scanned the story, looking for a reasonable explanation to put to rest the irrational fears that were reawakening her panic. But the police knew nothing. Nobody knew a thing.

'I suppose that at this point, only Nicky Straw knows what really happened,' the police spokesman was quoted as saying.

Nicky and you, a small worried voice said in the back of Luann's mind.

She shook her head, unwilling to accept it.

They're drawn to the ones whose fires burn the brightest.

She looked to her window. Beyond its smudged panes, the night was gathering. Soon it would be dark. Soon it would be night. Light showed a long way in the dark; a bright light would show further.

The ones whose fires burn the brightest . . . like yours does.

'It . . . it wasn't true,' she said, her voice ringing hollowly in the room. 'None of it. Tell me it wasn't true, Nicky.'

But Nicky was dead.

She let the paper fall again and rose to her feet, drifting across the room to the window like a ghost. She just didn't seem to feel connected to anything anymore.

It seemed oddly quiet on the street below. Less traffic than usual—both vehicular and pedestrian. There was a figure standing in front of the bookstore across the street, back to the window display, leaning against the glass. He seemed to be looking up at her window, but it was hard to tell because the brim of his hat cast a shadow on his face.

Once they're on to you, you can't shake them.

That man in the park. His face. Shifting. The skin seeming too loose.

They'll keep after you until they bleed you dry.

It wasn't real.

She turned from the window and shivered, hugging her arms around herself as she remembered what Nicky had said when he'd left the apartment last night.

What if I'm right?

She couldn't accept that. She looked back across the street, but the figure was gone. She listened for a footstep on the narrow, winding stairwell that led up to her balcony. Waited for the movement of a shadow across the window.

JULIE SMITH is the author of eight mysteries and the winner of the 1991 Edgar Allen Poe Award for best novel, given by the Mystery Writers of America. She decided to become a mystery writer at about age twelve, but later, on giving it further thought, chose a parallel career in journalism. She reported on everything from cults to murders during her time with the *Times-Picayune* in New Orleans then for nine years with the *San Francisco Chronicle*. She is creator of the two sleuths Rebecca Schwartz and Paul McDonald. Titles include *Death Turns a Trick*, *The Sourdough Wars*, *Tourist Trap*, *True-Life Adventure* and *Huckleberry Fiend*. *New Orleans Mourning* introduces Officer Skip Landon and was followed by *The Axeman's Jazz*.

Julie Smith

Blood Types

'Refresh my recollection, counsellor. Are holographic wills legal in California?'

Though we'd hardly spoken in seven years or more, I recognized the voice on the phone as easily if I'd heard it yesterday. I'd lived with its owner once. 'Gary Wilder. Aren't you feeling well?'

'I feel fine. Settle a bet, OK?'

'Unless you slept through more classes than I thought, you know perfectly well they're legal.'

'They used to be. It's been a long time, you know? How are you, Rebecca?'

'Great. And you're a daddy, I hear. How's Stephanie?'

'Fine.'

'And the wee one?'

'Little Laurie-bear. The best thing that ever happened to me.'

'You sound happy.'

'Laurie's my life.'

I was sorry to hear it. That was a lot of responsibility for a ten-month-old.

'So about the will,' Gary continued. 'Have the rules changed since we were at Boalt?'

'A bit. Remember how it could be invalidated by anything pre-printed on it? Like in the case where there was a date stamped on the paper the woman used, and the whole thing was thrown out?'

'Yeah. I remember someone asked whether you could use your own letterhead.'

'That was you, Gary.'

'Probably. And you couldn't, it seems to me.'

'But you probably could now. Now only the 'materially relevant' part has to be handwritten. And you don't have to date it.'

'No? That seems odd.'

'Well, you would if there were a previous dated will. Otherwise just write it out, sign it, and it's legal.'

Something about the call, maybe just the melancholy of hearing a voice from the past, put me in a gray and restless mood. It was mid-December and pouring outside—perfect weather for doleful ruminations on a man I hardly knew any more. I couldn't help worrying that if Laurie was Gary's whole life, that didn't speak well for his marriage. Shouldn't Stephanie at least have gotten a small mention? But she hadn't and the Gary I knew could easily have fallen out of love with her. He was one of life's stationary drifters—staying in the same place, but drifting from one mild interest to another, none of them very consuming and none very durable. I hoped it would be different with Laurie; it wouldn't be easy to watch your dad wimp out on you.

But I sensed it was already happening. I suspected that phone call meant little Laurie, who was his life, was making him feel tied down and he was sending out feelers to former and future lady friends.

The weather made me think of a line from a poem Gary used to quote:

Il pleure dans mon coeur
Comme il pleut sur la ville.

He was the sort to quote Paul Verlaine. He read everything, retained everything, and didn't do much. He had never finished law school, had sold insurance for a while and was now dabbling in real estate I'd heard, though I didn't know what that meant, exactly. Probably trying to figure out a way to speculate with Stephanie's money, which, out of affection for Gary, I thanked heaven she had. If you can't make up your mind what to do with your life, you should at least marry well and waffle in comfort.

Gary died that night. Reading about it in the morning *Chronicle*, I shivered, thinking the phone call was one of those grisly coincidences. But the will came the next day.

The *Chronicle* story said Gary and Stephanie were both killed instantly when their car went over a cliff on a twisty road in a blinding rainstorm. The rains were hellish that year. It was the third day of a five-day flood.

Madeline Bell, a witness to the accident, said Gary had swerved to avoid hitting her Mercedes as she came round a curve. The car had exploded and burned as Bell watched it roll off a hill near San Anselmo, where Stephanie and Gary lived.

Even in that moment of shock I think I felt more grief for Laurie than I did for Gary, who had half-lived his life at best. Only a day before, when I'd talked to Gary, Laurie had had it made—her mama was rich and her daddy good-looking. Now she was an orphan.

I wondered where Gary and Stephanie were going in such an awful storm. To a party, probably, or home from one. It was the height of the holiday season.

I knew Gary's mother, of course. Would she already be at the Wilder house, for Hanukkah, perhaps? If not, she'd be coming soon; I'd call in a day or two.

In the meantime, I called Rob Burns, who had long since replaced Gary in my affections, and asked to see him that night. I hadn't thought twice of Gary in the past five years, but something was gone from my life and I needed comfort. It would be good to sleep with Rob by my side and the sound of rain on the roof—life-affirming, as we say in California. I'd read somewhere that Mark Twain, when he built his mansion in Hartford, installed a section of tin roof so as to get the best rain sounds. I could understand the impulse.

It was still pouring by mid-morning the next day, and my throat was feeling slightly scratchy, the way it does when a cold's coming on. I was rummaging for vitamin C when Kruzick brought the mail in—Alan Kruzick, incredibly inept but inextricably installed secretary for the law firm of Nicholson and Schwartz, of which I was a protesting partner. The other partner, Chris Nicholson, liked his smart-ass style, my sister Mickey was his girlfriend, and my mother had simply laid down the law—hire him and keep him.

'Any checks?' I asked.

'Nope. Nothing interesting but a letter from a dead man.'

'What?'

He held up an envelope with Gary Wilder's name and address in the upper left corner. 'Maybe he wants you to channel him.'

The tears that popped into my eyes quelled even Kruzick.

The will was in Gary's own handwriting, signed, written on plain paper, and dated December 17, the day of Gary's death. It said:

'This is my last will and testament, superseding all others. I leave everything I own to my daughter, Laurie Wilder. If my wife and I die before her 21st birthday, I appoint my brother, Michael Wilder, as her legal guardian. I also appoint my brother as executor of this will.'

My stomach clutched as I realized that Gary had known when we talked that he and Stephanie were in danger. He'd managed to seem his usual happy-go-lucky self, using the trick he had of hiding his feelings that had made him hard to live with.

But if he knew he was going to be killed, why hadn't he given the murderer's identity? Perhaps he had, I realized. I was a lawyer, so I'd gotten the will. Someone else might have gotten a letter about what was happening. I wondered if my old boyfriend had gotten involved with the dope trade. After all, he lived in Marin County, which had the highest population of coke dealers outside the greater Miami area.

I phoned Gary's brother at his home in Seattle, but was told he'd gone to San Anselmo. I had a client coming in five minutes, but after that, nothing pressing. And so by two o'clock I was on the Golden Gate Bridge, enjoying a rare moment of foggy overcast, the rain having relented for a while.

It was odd about Gary's choosing Michael for Laurie's guardian. When I'd known him well he'd had nothing but contempt for his brother. Michael was a stockbroker and a go-getter; Gary was a mooner-about, a romantic, and a rebel. He considered his brother boring, stuffy, a bit crass and utterly worthless. On the other hand, he adored his sister, Jeri, a free-spirited dental hygienist married to a good-natured sometime carpenter.

Was Michael married? Yes, I thought. At least he had been. Maybe fatherhood had changed Gary's opinions on what was important—Michael's money and stability might have looked good to him when he thought of sending Laurie to college.

I pulled up in front of the Wilder–Cooper house, a modest redwood one that had probably cost nearly half a million. Such were real estate values in Marin County—and such was Stephanie's bank account.

At home were Michael Wilder—wearing a suit—and Stephanie's parents, Mary and Jack Cooper. Mary was a big woman, comfortable and talkative; Jack was skinny and withdrawn. He stared into space, almost sad, but mostly just faraway, and I got the feeling watching TV was his great passion in life, though perhaps he drank as well.

The idea, it appeared, was simply to leave the room without anyone noticing, the means of transportation being entirely insignificant.

It was a bit awkward, my being the ex-girlfriend and showing up unexpectedly. Michael didn't seem to know how to introduce me, and I could take a hint. It was no time to ask to see him privately.

'I'd hoped to see your mother,' I said.

'She's at the hospital,' said Mary. 'We're taking turns now that . . .' she started to cry.

'The hospital!'

'You don't know about Laurie?'

'She was in the accident?'

'No. She's been very ill for the last two months.'

'Near death,' said Mary. 'What that child has been through shouldn't happen to an animal. Tiny little face just contorts itself like a poor little monkey's. Screams and screams and screams; and *rivers* flow out of her little bottom. *Rivers*, Miss Schwartz!'

Her shoulders hunched and began to shake. Michael looked helpless. Mechanically, Jack put an arm around her.

'What's wrong?' I asked Michael.

He shrugged. 'They don't know. Can't diagnose it.'

'Now, Mary,' said Jack. 'She's better. The doctor said so last night.'

'What hospital is she in?'

'Marin General.'

I said to Michael: 'I think I'll pop by and see your mother—would you mind pointing me in the right direction? I've got a map in the car.'

When we arrived at the curb, I said, 'I can find the hospital. I wanted to give you something.'

I handed him the will. 'This came in today's mail. It'll be up to you as executor to petition the court for probate.'

As he read, a look of utter incredulity came over his face. 'But . . . I'm divorced. I can't take care of a baby.'

'Gary didn't ask in advance if you'd be willing?'

'Yes, but . . . I didn't think he was going to die!' His voice got higher as reality caught up with him. 'He called the day of the accident. But I thought he was just depressed. You know how people get around the holidays.'

'What did he say exactly?'

'He said he had this weird feeling, that's all . . . like something bad might happen to him. And would I take care of Laurie if anything did.'

'He didn't say he was scared? In any kind of trouble?'

'No . . . just feeling weird.'

'Michael, he wasn't dealing, was he?'

'Are you kidding? I'd be the last to know.' He looked at the ground a minute. 'I guess he could have been.'

Ellen Wilder was cooing to Laurie when I got to the hospital. 'Ohhhh, she's much better now. She just needed her Grandma's touch, that's all it was.'

She spoke to the baby in the third person, unaware I was there until I announced myself, whereupon she almost dropped the precious angel-wangel. We had a tearful reunion, Gary's mother and I. We both missed Gary and we both felt for poor Laurie.

Ellen adored the baby more than breath, to listen to her, and not only that, she possessed the healing power of a witch. She had spent the night Gary and Stephanie were killed with Laurie, and all day the next day, never even going home for a shower. And gradually, the fever had broken, metaphorically speaking. With Grandma's loving attention, the baby's debilitating diarrhea had begun to ease off and little Laurie had seemed to come back to life.

'Look, Rebecca.' She tiptoed to the sleeping baby. 'See those cheeks? Roses in them. She's getting her pretty color back, widdle Waurie is, yes, her is.' She seemed not to realize she'd lapsed into babytalk.

She came back and sat down beside me. 'Stephanie stayed with her nearly round the clock, you know. She was the best mother anyone ever . . . ' Ellen teared up for a second and glanced around the room, embarrassed.

'Look. She left her clothes here. I'll have to remember to take them home. The *best* mother . . . She and Gary were invited to a party that night. It was a horrible rainy, rainy night, but poor Stephanie hadn't been anywhere but the hospital in weeks.'

'How long had you been here?'

'Oh, just a few days. I came for Hanukkah—and to help out if I could. I knew Stephanie had to get out, so I offered to stay with Laurie. I was just dying to have some time with the widdle fweet fing anyhow . . . ' This last was spoken more or less in Laurie's direction. Ellen seemed to have developed a habit of talking to the child while carrying on other conversations.

'What happened was Gary had quite a few drinks before he brought me over. Oh, God, I should never have let him drive! We nearly had a wreck on the way over—you know how stormy it was. I kept telling him he was too drunk to drive, and he said I wanted it that way, just like I always wanted him to have strep throat when he was a kid. He said he felt fine then and he felt fine now.'

I was getting lost. 'You *wanted* him to have strep throat?'

She shrugged. 'I don't know what he meant. He was just drunk, that's all. Oh, God, my poor baby!' She sniffed, fumbled in her purse, and blew her nose into a tissue.

'Did he seem okay that afternoon—except for being drunk?'

'Fine. Why?'

'He called me that afternoon—about his will. And he called Michael to say he—well, I guess to say he had a premonition about his death.'

'His will? He called you about a will?'

'Yes.'

'But he and Stephanie had already made their wills. Danny Goldstein drew them up.' That made sense, as Gary had dated his holograph. Danny had been at Boalt with Gary and me. I wondered briefly if it hurt Ellen to be reminded that all Gary's classmates had gone on to become lawyers just like their parents would have wanted.

A fresh-faced nurse popped in and took a look at Laurie. 'How's our girl?'

'Like a different baby.'

The nurse smiled. 'She sure is. We were really worried for a while there.' But the smile faded almost instantly. 'It's so sad. I never saw a more devoted mother. Laurie never needed us at all—Stephanie was her nurse. One of the best I ever saw.'

'I didn't know Stephanie was a nurse.' The last I'd heard she was working part-time for a caterer, trying to make up her mind whether to go to chef's school. Stephanie had a strong personality, but she wasn't much more career-minded than Gary was. Motherhood, everyone seemed to think, had been her true calling.

'She didn't have any training—she was just good with infants. You should have seen the way she'd sit and rock that child for hours, Laurie having diarrhea so bad she hardly had any skin on her little butt, crying her little heart out. She must have been in agony like you and I couldn't imagine. But finally Stephanie would get her to sleep. Nobody else could.'

'Nobody else could breast-feed her,' I said, thinking surely I'd hit on the source of Stephanie's amazing talent.

'Stephanie couldn't either. Didn't have enough milk.' The nurse shrugged. 'Anyone can give a bottle. It wasn't that.'

When she left, I said, 'I'd better go. Can I do anything for you?'

Ellen thought a minute. 'You know what you could do? Will you be going to Gary's again?'

'I'd be glad to.'

'You could take some of Stephanie's clothes and things. They're going to let Laurie out in a day or two and there's so much stuff here.' She looked exasperated.

Glad to help, I gathered up clothes and began to fold them. Ellen found a canvas carry-all of Stephanie's to pack them in. Zipping it open, I saw a bit of white powder in the bottom, and my stomach flopped over. I couldn't get the notion of drugs out of my mind. Gary had had a 'premonition' of death, the kind you might get if you burned someone and they threatened you—and now I was looking at white powder.

I found some plastic bags in a drawer that had probably once been used to transport diapers or formula and lined the bottom of the carry-all with them, to keep the powder from sticking to Stephanie's clothes.

But instead of going to Gary's, I dropped in at my parents' house in San Rafael. It was about four o'clock and I had some phoning to do before five.

'Darling!' said Mom. 'Isn't it awful about poor Gary Wilder?'

Mom had always liked Gary. She had a soft spot for ne'er-do-wells, as I knew only too well. She was the main reason Kruzick was currently ruining my life. The person for whom she hadn't a minute was the one I preferred most—the blue-eyed and dashing Mr Rob Burns, star reporter for the San Francisco *Chronicle*.

Using the phone in my dad's study, Rob was the very person I rang up. His business was asking questions that were none of his business, and I had a few for him to ask.

Quickly explaining the will, the odd phone call to Michael, and the white powder, I had him hooked. He smelled the same rat I smelled and, more important, he smelled a story.

While he made his calls, I phoned Danny Goldstein.

'Becky baby!'

'Don't call me that.'

'Terrible about Gary, isn't it? Makes you *think*, man.'

'Terrible about Stephanie too.'

'I don't know. She pussy-whipped him.'

'She was better than Melissa.'

Danny laughed unkindly, brayed you could even say. Everyone knew Gary had left me for Melissa, who was twenty-two and a cutesy-wootsy dollbaby who couldn't be trusted to go to the store for a six-pack. Naturally, everyone thought *I* had Gary pussy-whipped when the truth was, he wouldn't brush his teeth without asking my advice about it. He was a man desperate for a woman to run his life and I was relieved to be rid of the job.

But still, Melissa had hurt my pride. I thought Gary's choosing her meant he'd grown up and no longer needed me. It was a short-lived maturity, however—within two years Stephanie had appeared on the scene. I might not see it exactly the way Danny did, but I had to admit if he'd had any balls, she was the one to bust them.

'I hear motherhood mellowed her,' I said.

'Yeah she was born for it. Always worrying was the kid too hot, too cold, too hungry—one of those poo-poo moms.'

'Huh?'

'You know. Does the kid want to go poo-poo? Did the kid already go poo-poo? Does it go poo-poo enough? Does it go poo-poo too much? Is it going poo-poo *right now*? She could discuss color and consistency through a whole dinner party, salmon mousse to kiwi tart.'

I laughed. Who didn't know the type? 'Say listen, Danny,' I said, 'Did you know Laurie's been in the hospital?'

'Yeah. Marina, my wife, went to see Stephanie—tried to get her to go out and get some air while she took care of the baby, but Stephanie wouldn't budge.'

'I hear you drew up Gary and Stephanie's wills.'

'Yeah. God, I never thought—poor little Laurie. They asked Gary's sister to be her guardian—he hated his brother and Stephanie was an only child.'

'Guess what? Gary made another will just before he died, naming the brother as Laurie's guardian.'

'I don't believe it.'

'Believe it. I'll send you a copy.'

'There's going to be a hell of a court fight.'

I wasn't so sure about that. The court, of course, wouldn't be bound by either parent's nomination. Since Stephanie's will nominated Jeri as guardian, Jeri and Michael might choose to fight it out, but given Michael's apparent hesitation to take Laurie, I wasn't sure there'd be any argument at all.

'Danny,' I said, 'you were seeing a lot of him, right?'

'Yeah. We played racquetball.'

'Was he dealing coke? Or something else?'

'Gary? No way. You can't be a dealer and be as broke as he was.'

The phone rang almost the minute I hung up. Rob had finished a round of calls to what he called his 'law enforcement sources'. He'd learned that Gary's brakes hadn't been tampered with, handily blowing my murder theory.

Or seemingly blowing it. Something was still very wrong, and I wasn't giving up till I knew what the powder was. Mom asked me to dinner, but I headed back to the city—Rob had said he could get someone to run an analysis that night.

It was raining again by the time I'd dropped the stuff off, refused Rob's dinner invitation (that was two) and gone home to solitude and split pea soup that I make up in advance and keep in the freezer for nights like this. It was the second night after Gary's death; the first night I'd need to reassure myself I was still alive. Now I needed to mourn. I didn't plan anything fancy like sackcloth and ashes, just a quiet night home with a book, free to let my mind wander and my eyes fill up from time to time.

But first I had a message from Michael Wilder. He wanted to talk. He felt awful, calling me like this, but there was no one in his family he felt he could talk to. Couldn't we meet for coffee or something?

Sure we could—at my house. Not even for Gary's brother was I going out in the rain again.

After the soup, I showered and changed into jeans. Michael arrived in wool slacks and a sportscoat—not even in repose, apparently, did he drop the stuffy act. Maybe life with Laurie would loosen him up. I asked if he'd thought any more about being her guardian.

It flustered him. 'Not really,' he said, and didn't meet my eyes.

'I found out the original wills named Jeri as guardian. If Stephanie didn't make a last-minute one too, hers will still be in effect. Meaning Jeri could fight you if you decide you want Laurie.'

'I can't even imagine being a father,' he said. 'But Gary must have had a good reason . . . ' he broke off. 'Poor little kid. A week ago everyone thought *she* was the one who was going to die.'

'What's wrong with her—besides diarrhea?' I realized I hadn't had the nerve to ask either of the grandmothers because I knew exactly what would happen—I'd get details that would give *me* symptoms and two hours later, maybe three or four, I'd be backing towards the door, nodding, with a glazed look on my face, watching matriarchal jaws continue to work.

But Michael only grimaced. 'That's all I know about it, just life-threatening diarrhea.'

'*Life-threatening*?'

'Without an IV, a dehydrated baby can die in fifteen minutes. Just ask my mother.' He shrugged. 'Anyway, the doctors talked about electrolyte abnormalities, whatever they may be, and did every test in the book. But the only thing they found was what they called 'high serum sodium levels'. He shrugged again, as if to shake something off. 'Don't ask—especially don't ask my mom or Stephanie's.'

We both laughed. I realized Michael had good reasons for finding sudden parenthood a bit on the daunting side.

I got us some wine and when I came back, he'd turned deadly serious. 'Rebecca, something weird happened today. Look what I found.' He held out a paper signed by Gary and headed 'Beneficiary Designation'. 'Know what that is?'

I shook my head.

'I used to be in insurance—as did my little brother. It's the form you use to change your life insurance beneficiary.'

The form was dated December 16, the day before Gary's death. Michael had been named beneficiary and Laurie contingent beneficiary. Michael said, 'Pretty weird, huh?'

I nodded.

'I also found both Gary's and Stephanie's policies—each for half a million dollars and each naming the other as beneficiary, with Laurie as contingent. For some reason, Gary went to see his insurance agent the day before he died and changed his. What do you make of it?'

I didn't at all like what I made of it. 'It goes with the will,' I said. 'He named you as Laurie's guardian, so he must have wanted to make sure you could afford to take care of her.'

'I could afford it. For Christ's sake!'

'He must have wanted to compensate you.' I stopped for a minute. 'It might be his way of saying thanks.'

'You're avoiding the subject, aren't you?'

I was. 'You mean it would have made more sense to leave the money to Laurie directly.'

'Yes. Unless he'd provided for her some other way.'

'Stephanie had money.'

'I don't think Gary knew how much, though.'

I took a sip of wine and thought about it, or rather thought about ways to talk about it, because it was beginning to look very ugly. 'You're saying you think,' I said carefully, 'that he knew she was going to inherit the half million from Stephanie's policy. Because she was going to die and he was the beneficiary and he was going to die and his new will left his own property to Laurie.'

Michael was blunt: 'It looks like murder–suicide, doesn't it?'

I said, 'Yeah,' unable to say any more.

Michael took me over ground I'd already mentally covered: 'He decided to do it in a hurry, probably because it was raining so hard—an accident in the rain would be much more plausible. He made the arrangements. Then he called me and muttered about a premonition, to give himself some sort of feeble motive for suddenly getting his affairs in order; he may have said the same thing to other people as well. Finally, he pretended to be drunk, made a big show of almost having an accident on the way to the hospital, picked up Stephanie and drove her over a cliff.'

Still putting things together, I mumbled, 'You couldn't really be sure you'd die going over just any cliff. You'd have to pick the right cliff, wouldn't you?' And then I said, 'I wonder if the insurance company will figure it out.'

'Oh, who cares! He probably expected they would but wanted to make a gesture. And he knew I didn't need the money. That's not the point. The point is why?' He stood up and ran his fingers through his hair, working off excess energy. 'Why kill himself, Rebecca? And why take Stephanie with him?'

'I don't know,' I said. But I hadn't a doubt that that was what he'd done. There was another why—why make Michael Laurie's guardian? Why not his sister as originally planned?

The next day was Saturday and I would have dozed happily into mid-morning if Rob hadn't phoned at eight. 'You know the sinister white powder?'

'Uh-huh.'

'Baking soda.'

'That's all?'

'That's it. No heroin, no cocaine, not even any baby talc. Baking soda. Period.'

I thanked him and turned over, but the next couple of hours were full of vaguely disquieting dreams. I woke upset, feeling oddly tainted, as if I'd collaborated in Gary's crimes. It wasn't till I was in the shower—performing my purification ritual if you believe in such things—that things came together in my conscious mind. The part of me that dreamed had probably known all along.

I called a doctor friend to find out if what I suspected made medical sense. It did: to a baby Laurie's age, baking soda would be a deadly poison. Simply add it to the formula, and the excess sodium would cause her to develop severe dehydrating diarrhea; it might ultimately lead to death. But she would be sick only as long as someone continued to doctor her formula. The poisoning was not cumulative; as soon as it stopped, she would begin to recover and in only a few days she would be dramatically better.

In other words, he described Laurie's illness to a T. And Stephanie, the world's greatest mother, who was there round the clock, must have fed her—at any rate would have had all the opportunity in the world to doctor her formula.

It didn't make sense. Well, part of it did. The part I could figure out was this: Gary saw Stephanie put baking soda in the formula, already knew about the high sodium reports, put two and two together, may or may not have confronted her . . . no, definitely didn't confront her. Gary never confronted anyone.

He simply came to the conclusion that his wife was poisoning their child and decided to kill her, taking his own aimless life as well. That would account for the hurry—to stop the poisoning without having to confront Stephanie. If he accused her, he might be able to stop her, but things would instantly get too messy for Gary-the-conflict-avoider. Worse, the thing could easily become a criminal case and if Stephanie were convicted, Laurie would have to grow up knowing her mother had deliberately poisoned her. If she were acquitted, Laurie might always be in danger. I could follow his benighted reasoning perfectly.

But I couldn't, for all the garlic in Gilroy, imagine why Stephanie would want to kill Laurie. By all accounts, she was the most loving of mothers, would probably even have laid down her own life for her child's. I called a shrink friend, Elaine Alvarez.

'Of course she loved the child,' Elaine explained. 'Why shouldn't she? Laurie perfectly answered her needs.' And then she told me some things that made me forget I'd been planning to consume a large breakfast in a few minutes. On the excuse of finally remembering to take Stephanie's clothes, I drove to Gary's house.

The family was planning a memorial service in a day or two for the dead couple; Jeri had just arrived at her dead brother's house; friends had dropped by to comfort the bereaved; yet there was almost a festive atmosphere in the house. Laurie had come home that morning.

Michael and I took a walk. 'Bullshit!' he said. 'Dogcrap! No one could have taken better care of that baby than Stephanie. Christ, she martyred herself. She stayed up night after night . . . '

'Listen to yourself. Everything you're saying confirms what Elaine told me. The thing even has a name. It's called Munchausen Syndrome by Proxy. The original syndrome, plain old Munchausen, is when you hurt or mutilate yourself to get attention.

'"By proxy" means you do it to your nearest and dearest. People say, "Oh, that poor woman. God, what she's been through. Look how brave she is! Why, no one in the world could be a better mother." And Mom gets off on it. There are recorded cases of it, Michael, at least one involving a mother and baby.'

He was pale. 'I think I'm going to throw up.'

'Let's sit down a minute.'

In fact, stuffy, uptight Michael ended up lying down in the dirt on the side of the road, nice flannel slacks and all, taking breaths till his color returned. And then, slowly, we walked back to the house.

Jeri was holding Laurie, her mother standing over her, Mary Cooper sitting close on the couch. 'Oh, look what a baby-waby. What a darling girly-wirl. Do you feel the least bit hot? Laurie-baurie, you're not running a fever, are you?'

The kid had just gotten the thumbs-up from a hospital and she was wrapped in half a dozen blankets. I doubted she was running a fever.

Ellen leaned over to feel the baby's face. 'Ohhh, I think she might be. Give her to Grandma. Grandma knows how to fix babies, doesn't she, Laurie girl? Come to Grandma and Grandma will sponge you with alcohol, Grandma will.'

She looked like a hawk coming in for a landing, ready to snare its prey and fly up again, but Mary was quicker still. Almost before you saw it happening, she had the baby away from Ellen and in her own lap. 'What you need is some nice juice, don't you Laurie-bear? And then Meemaw's going to rock you and rock you . . . oh, my goodness, you're burning up.' Her voice was on the edge of panic. 'Listen, Jeri, this baby's wheezing! We've got to get her breathing damp air . . . '

She wasn't wheezing, she was gulping, probably in amazement. I felt my own jaw drop and, looking away, unwittingly caught the eye of Mary's husband, who hadn't wanted me to see the anguish there. Quickly, he dropped a curtain of blandness. Beside me, I heard Michael whisper, 'My God!'

I knew we were seeing something extreme. They were all excited to have Laurie home and they were competing with each other, letting out what looked like their scariest sides if you knew what we did. But a Stephanie didn't come along every day. Laurie was in no further danger, I was sure of it. Still, I understood why Gary had had the sudden change of heart about guardianship.

I turned to Michael. 'Are you going to try and get her?'

He plucked at his sweater sleeve, staring at his wrist as if it had a treasure map on it. 'I haven't decided.'

An image from my fitful morning dreams came back to me: a giant in a forest, taller than all the trees and built like a mountain; a female giant with belly and breasts like boulders, dressed in white robes and carrying, draped across her outstretched arms, a dead man, head dangling on its flaccid neck.

In a few days Michael called. When he got home to Seattle, a letter had been waiting for him—a note, rather, from Gary, postmarked the day of his death. It didn't apologize, it didn't explain—it didn't even say, 'Dear Michael.' It was simply a quote from *Hamlet* typed on a piece of paper, not handwritten, Michael thought, because it could be construed as a confession and there was the insurance to think about.

This was the quote:

Diseases desperate grown
By desperate appliance are relieved,
Or not at all.

I didn't ask Michael again whether he intended to take Laurie. I was too furious, at the moment, with one passive male, to trust myself to speak civilly with another.

Instead, I simmered inwardly, thinking how like Gary it was to confess to murder with a quote from Shakespeare. Thinking that, as he typed it, he probably imagined grandly that nothing in his life would become him like the leaving of it. The schmuck.

JOE R. LANSDALE has published more than three hundred short stories in a variety of genres including mystery, suspense, horror, western, and science fiction. Lansdale has published four suspense novels—*Act of Love* (1981), *The Nightrunners* (1987), *Cold in July* (1989), and *Savage Season* (1990). He is also the author of *Dead in the West* (1986), *The Magic Wagon* (1986), *The Drive-In: A B-Movie with Blood and Popcorn* (1988), *The Drive-In 2: Not Just One of them Sequels* (1990) and *Batman: Captured by the Engines* (1991). He has also edited anthologies including *Best of the West* (1986), *New Frontiers* (1989) and *Razored Saddles* (1989). A book-length collection of Lansdale's short fiction, *By Bizarre Hands*, was published in 1989, and included *Night they Missed the Horror Show*, Lansdale's masterful story which won a Bram Stoker Award for Best Short Story. Lansdale lives with his wife, Karen, and their two children in Nacogdoches, Texas.

Joe R. Lansdale

Night They Missed The Horror Show

For Lew Shiner, a story that doesn't flinch

If they'd gone to the drive-in like they'd planned, none of this would have happened. But Leonard didn't like drive-ins when he didn't have a date, and he'd heard about *Night of the Living Dead*, and he knew a nigger starred in it. He didn't want to see no movie with a nigger star. Niggers chopped cotton, fixed flats, and pimped nigger girls, but he'd never heard of one that killed zombies. And he'd heard too that there was a white girl in the movie that let the nigger touch her, and that peeved him. Any white gal that would let a nigger touch her must be the lowest trash in the world. Probably from Hollywood, New York, or Waco, some god-forsaken place like that.

Now Steve McQueen would have been all right for zombie killing and girl handling. He would have been the ticket. But a nigger? No sir.

Boy, that Steve McQueen was one cool head. Way he said stuff in them pictures was so good you couldn't help but think someone had written it down for him. He could sure think fast on his feet to come up with the things he said, and he had that real cool, mean look.

Leonard wished he could be Steve McQueen, or Paul Newman even. Someone like that always knew what to say, and he figured they got plenty of bush too. Certainly they didn't get as bored as he did. He was so bored he felt as if he were going to die from it before the night was out. Bored, bored, bored. Just wasn't nothing exciting about being in the Dairy Queen parking lot leaning on the front of his '64 Impala looking out at the highway. He figured maybe old crazy Harry who janitored at the high school might be right about them flying saucers. Harry was always seeing something. Bigfoot, six-legged weasels, all manner of things. But maybe he was right about the saucers. He said he'd seen one a couple nights back hovering over Mud Creek and it was shooting down those rays that looked like wet peppermint sticks. Leonard figured if Harry really had seen the saucers and the rays, then those rays were boredom rays. It would be a way for space critters to get at earth folks, boring them to death. Getting melted down by heat rays would have been better. That was at least quick, but being bored to death was sort of like being nibbled to death by ducks.

Leonard continued looking at the highway, trying to imagine flying saucers and boredom rays, but he couldn't keep his mind on it. He finally focused on something in the highway. A dead dog.

Not just a dead dog. But a DEAD DOG. The mutt had been hit by a semi at least, maybe several. It looked as if it had rained dog. There were pieces of that pooch all over the concrete and one leg was lying on the curbing on the opposite side, stuck up in such a way that it seemed to be waving hello. Doctor Frankenstein with a grant from Johns Hopkins and assistance from NASA couldn't have put that sucker together again.

Leonard leaned over to his faithful, drunk companion, Billy—known among the gang as Farto, because he was fart-lighting champion of Mud Creek—and said, 'See that dog there?'

Farto looked where Leonard was pointing. He hadn't noticed the dog before, and he wasn't nearly as casual about it as Leonard. The puzzle-piece hound brought back memories. It reminded him of a dog he'd had when he was thirteen. A big, fine German Shepherd that loved him better than his Mama.

Sonofabitch dog tangled its chain through and over a barbed wire fence somehow and hung itself. When Farto found the dog its tongue looked like a stuffed, black sock and he could see where its claws had just been able to scrape the ground, but not quite enough to get a toe hold. It looked as if the dog had been scratching out some sort of coded message in the dirt. When Farto told his old man about it later, crying as he did, his old man laughed and said, 'Probably a goddamn suicide note.'

Now, as he looked out at the highway, and his whiskey-laced Coke collected warmly in his gut, he felt a tear form in his eyes. Last time he'd felt that sappy was when he'd won the fart-lighting championship with a four-inch burner that singed the hairs of his ass and the gang awarded him with a pair of colored boxing shorts. Brown and yellow ones so he could wear them without having to change them too often.

So there they were, Leonard and Farto, parked outside the DQ, leaning on the hood of Leonard's Impala, sipping Coke and whiskey, feeling bored and blue and horny, looking at a dead dog and having nothing to do but go to a show with a nigger starring in it. Which, to be up front, wouldn't have been so bad if they'd had dates. Dates could make up for a lot of sins, or help make a few good ones, depending on one's outlook.

But the night was criminal. Dates they didn't have. Worse yet, wasn't a girl in the entire high school would date them. Not even Marylou Flowers, and she had some kind of disease.

All this nagged Leonard something awful. He could see what the problem was with Farto. He was ugly. Had the kind of face that attracted flies. And though being fart-lighting champion of Mud Creek had a certain prestige among the gang, it lacked a certain something when it came to charming the gals.

But for the life of him, Leonard couldn't figure his own problem. He was handsome, had some good clothes, and his car ran good when he didn't buy that old cheap gas. He even had a few bucks in his jeans from breaking into washaterias. Yet his right arm had damn near grown to the size of his thigh from all the whacking off he did. Last time he'd been out with a girl had been a month ago, and as he'd been out with her along with nine other guys, he wasn't rightly sure he could call that a date. He wondered about it so much, he'd asked Farto if he thought it qualified as a date. Farto, who had been the fifth in line, said he didn't think so, but if Leonard wanted to call it one, wasn't no skin off his dick.

But Leonard didn't want to call it a date. It just didn't have the feel of one, lacked that something special. There was no romance to it.

True, Big Red had called him Honey when he put the mule in the barn, but she called everyone Honey—except Stoney. Stoney was Possum Sweets, and he was the one who talked her into wearing the grocery bag with the mouth and eye holes. Stoney was like that. He could sweet-talk the camel out from under a sand nigger. When he got through chatting Big Red down, she was plumb proud to wear that bag.

When finally it came his turn to do Big Red, Leonard had let her take the bag off as a gesture of good will. That was a mistake. He just hadn't known a good thing when he had it. Stoney had had the right idea. The bag coming off spoiled everything. With it on, it was sort of like balling the Lone Hippo or some such thing, but with the bag off, you were absolutely certain what you were getting, and it wasn't pretty.

Even closing his eyes hadn't helped. He found that the ugliness of that face had branded itself on the back of his eyeballs. He couldn't even imagine the sack back over her head. All he could think about was that puffy, too-painted face with the sort of bad complexion that began at the bone.

He'd gotten so disappointed, he'd had to fake an orgasm and get off before his hooter shriveled up and his Trojan fell off and was lost in the vacuum.

Thinking back on it, Leonard sighed. It would certainly be nice for a change to go with a girl that didn't pull the train or had a hole between her legs that looked like a manhole cover ought to be on it. Sometimes he wished he could be like Farto, who was as happy as if he had good sense. Anything thrilled him. Give him a can of Wolf Brand Chili, a big moon pie, Coke and whiskey and he could spend the rest of his life fucking Big Red and lighting the gas out of his asshole.

God, but this was no way to live. No women and no fun. Bored, bored, bored. Leonard found himself looking overhead for spaceships and peppermint-colored boredom rays, but he saw only a few moths fluttering drunkenly through the beams of the DQ's lights.

Lowering his eyes back to the highway and the dog, Leonard had a sudden flash. 'Why don't we get the chain out of the back and hook it up to Rex there? Take him for a ride.'

'You mean drag his dead ass around?' Farto asked.

Leonard nodded.

'Beats stepping on a tack,' Farto said.

They drove the Impala into the middle of the highway at a safe moment and got out for a look. Up close the mutt was a lot worse. Its innards had been mashed out of its mouth and asshole and it stunk something awful. The dog was wearing a thick, metal-studded collar and they fastened one end of their fifteen-foot chain to that and the other to the rear bumper.

Bob, the Dairy Queen manager, noticed them through the window, came outside and yelled, 'What are you fucking morons doing?'

'Taking this doggie to the vet,' Leonard said. 'We think this sumbitch looks a might peeked. He may have been hit by a car.'

'That's so fucking funny I'm about to piss myself,' Bob said.

'Old folks have that problem,' Leonard said.

Leonard got behind the wheel and Farto climbed in on the passenger side. They maneuvered the car and dog around and out of the path of a tractor-trailer truck just in time. As they drove off, Bob screamed after them, 'I hope you two no-dicks wrap that Chevy piece of shit around a goddamn pole.'

As they roared along, parts of the dog, like crumbs from a flakey loaf of bread, came off. A tooth here. Some hair there. A string of guts. A dew claw. And some unidentifiable pink stuff. The metal-studded collar and chain threw up sparks now and then like fiery crickets. Finally they hit seventy-five and the dog was swinging wider and wider on the chain, like it was looking for an opportunity to pass.

Farto poured him and Leonard up Cokes and whiskey as they drove along. He handed Leonard his paper cup and Leonard knocked it back, a lot happier now than he had been a moment ago. Maybe this night wasn't going to turn out so bad after all.

They drove by a crowd at the side of the road, a tan station wagon and a wreck of a Ford up on a jack. At a glance they could see that there was a nigger in the middle of the crowd and he wasn't witnessing to the white boys. He was hopping around like a pig with a hotshot up his ass, trying to find a break in the white boys so he could make a run for it. But there wasn't any break to be found and there were too many to fight. Nine white boys were knocking him around like he was a pinball and they were a malicious machine.

'Ain't that one of our niggers?' Farto asked. 'And ain't that some of the White Tree football players that's trying to kill him?'

'Scott,' Leonard said, and the name was dogshit in his mouth. It had been Scott who had outdone him for the position of quarterback on the team. That damn jig could put together a play more tangled than a can of fishing worms, but it damn near always worked. And he could run like a spotted-ass ape.

As they passed, Farto said. 'We'll read about him tomorrow in the papers.'

But Leonard drove only a short way before slamming on the brakes and whipping the Impala around. Rex swung way out and clipped off some tall, dried sunflowers at the edge of the road like a scythe.

'We gonna go back and watch?' Farto asked. 'I don't think them White Tree boys would bother us none if that's all we was gonna do, watch.'

'He may be a nigger,' Leonard said, not liking himself, 'but he's our nigger and we can't let them do that. They kill him, they'll beat us in football.'

Farto saw the truth in this immediately. 'Damn right. They can't do that to our nigger.'

Leonard crossed the road again and went straight for the White Tree boys, hit down hard on the horn. The White Tree boys abandoned beating their prey and jumped in all directions. Bullfrogs couldn't have done any better.

Scott stood startled and weak where he was, his knees bent in and touching one another, his eyes as big as pizza pans. He had never noticed how big grillwork was. It looked like teeth there in the night and the headlights looked like eyes. He felt like a stupid fish about to be eaten by a shark.

Leonard braked hard, but off the highway in the dirt it wasn't enough to keep from bumping Scott, sending him flying over the hood and against the glass where his face mashed to it then rolled away, his shirt snagging one of the windshield wipers and pulling it off.

Leonard opened the car door and called to Scott who lay on the ground, 'It's now or never.'

A White Tree boy made for the car, and Leonard pulled the taped hammer handle out from beneath the seat and stepped out of the car and hit him with it. The White Tree boy went down to his knees and said something that sounded like French but wasn't. Leonard grabbed Scott by the back of the shirt and pulled him up and guided him around and threw him into the open door. Scott scrambled over the front seat and into the back. Leonard threw the hammer handle at one of the White Tree boys and stepped back, whirled into the car behind the wheel. He put the car in gear again and stepped on the gas. The Impala lurched forward, and with one hand on the door Leonard flipped it wider and clipped a White Tree boy with it as if he were flexing a wing. The car bumped back on the highway and the chain swung out and Rex cut the feet out from under two White Tree boys as neatly as he had taken down the dried sunflowers.

Leonard looked in his rear view mirror and saw two White Tree boys carrying the one he had clubbed with the hammer handle to the station wagon. The others he and the dog had knocked down were getting up. One had kicked the jack out from under Scott's car and was using it to smash the headlights and windshield.

'Hope you got insurance on that thing,' Leonard said.

'I borrowed it,' Scott said, peeling the windshield wiper out of his T-shirt. 'Here, you might want this.' He dropped the wiper over the seat and between Leonard and Farto.

'That's a borrowed car?' Farto said. 'That's worse.'

'Nah,' Scott said. 'Owner don't know I borrowed it. I'd have had that flat changed if that sucker had him a spare tire, but I got back there and wasn't nothing but the rim, man. Say, thanks for not letting me get killed, else we couldn't have run that ole pig together no more. Course, you almost run over me. My chest hurts.'

Leonard checked the rear view again. The White Tree boys were coming fast. 'You complaining?' Leonard said.

'Nah,' Scott said, and turned to look through the back glass. He could see the dog swinging in short arcs and pieces of it going wide and far. 'Hope you didn't go off and forget your dog tied to the bumper.'

'Goddamn,' said Farto, 'and him registered too.'

'This ain't so funny,' Leonard said, 'them White Tree boys are gaining.'

'Well speed it up,' Scott said.

Leonard gnashed his teeth. 'I could always get rid of some excess baggage, you know.'

'Throwing that windshield wiper out ain't gonna help,' Scott said.

Leonard looked in his mirror and saw the grinning nigger in the back seat. Nothing worse than a comic coon. He didn't even look grateful. Leonard had a sudden horrid vision of being overtaken by the White Tree boys. What if he were killed with the nigger? Getting killed was bad enough, but what if tomorrow they found him in a ditch with Farto and the nigger? Or maybe them White Tree boys would make him do something awful with the nigger before they killed him. Like making him suck the nigger's dick or some such thing. Leonard held his foot all the way to the floor; as they passed the Dairy Queen he took a hard left and the car just made it and Rex swung out and slammed a light pole then popped back in line behind them.

The White Tree boys couldn't make the corner in the station wagon and they didn't even try. They screeched into a car lot down a piece, turned around and came back. By that time the tail lights of the Impala were moving away from them rapidly, looking like two inflamed hemorrhoids in a dark asshole.

'Take the next right coming up,' Scott said, 'then you'll see a little road off to the left. Kill your lights and take that.'

Leonard hated taking orders from Scott on the field, but this was worse. Insulting. Still, Scott called good plays on the field, and the habit of following instructions from the quarterback died hard. Leonard made the right and Rex made it with them after taking a dip in a water-filled bar ditch.

Leonard saw the little road and killed his lights and took it. It carried them down between several rows of large tin storage buildings, and Leonard pulled between two of them and drove down a little alley lined with more. He stopped the car and they waited and listened. After about five minutes, Farto said, 'I think we skunked those father rapers.'

'Ain't we a team?' Scott said.

In spite of himself, Leonard felt good. It was like when the nigger called a play that worked and they were all patting each other on the ass and not minding what color the other was because they were just creatures in football suits.

'Let's have a drink,' Leonard said.

Farto got a paper cup off the floorboard for Scott and poured him some warm Coke and whiskey. Last time they had gone to Longview, he had peed in that paper cup so they wouldn't have to stop, but that had long since been poured out, and besides, it was for a nigger. He poured Leonard and himself drinks in their same cups.

Scott took a sip and said, 'Shit, man, that tastes kind of rank.'

'Like piss,' Farto said.

Leonard held up his cup. 'To the Mud Creek Wildcats and fuck them White Tree boys.'

'You fuck 'em,' Scott said. They touched their cups, and at that moment the car filled with light.

Cups upraised, the Three Musketeers turned blinking toward it. The light was coming from an open storage building door and there was a fat man standing in the centre of the glow like a bloated fly on a lemon wedge. Behind him was a big screen made of a sheet and there was some kind of movie playing on it. And though the light was bright and fading out the movie, Leonard, who was in the best position to see, got a look at it. What he could make out looked like a gal down on her knees sucking this fat guy's dick (the man was visible only from the belly down) and the guy had a short, black revolver pressed to her forehead. She pulled her mouth off of him for an instant and the man came in her face then fired the revolver. The woman's head snapped out of frame and the sheet seemed to drip blood, like dark condensation on a window pane. Then Leonard couldn't see anymore because another man had appeared in the doorway, and like the first he was fat. Both looked like huge bowling balls that had been set on top of shoes. More men appeared behind these two, but one of the fat men turned and held up his hand and the others moved out of sight. The two fat guys stepped outside and one pulled the door almost shut, except for a thin band of light that fell across the front seat of the Impala.

Fat Man Number One went over to the car and opened Farto's door and said, 'You fucks and the nigger get out.' It was the voice of doom. They had only thought the White Tree boys were dangerous. They realized now that they had been kidding themselves. This was the real article. This guy would have eaten the hammer handle and shit a two-by-four.

They got out of the car and the fat man waved them around and lined them up on Farto's side and looked at them. They boys still had their drinks in their hands, and sparing that, they looked like cons in a line up.

Fat Man Number Two came over and looked at the trio and smiled. It was obvious the fatties were twins. They had the same bad features in the same fat faces. They wore Hawaiian shirts that varied only in profiles and color of parrots and had on white socks and too-short black slacks and black, shiny, Italian shoes with toes sharp enough to thread needles.

Fat Man Number One took the cup away from Scott and sniffed it. 'A nigger with liquor,' he said. 'That's like a cunt with brains. It don't go together. Guess you was getting tanked up so you could put the old black snake to some chocolate pudding after awhile. Or maybe you was wantin' some vanilla and these boys were gonna set it up.'

'I'm not wanting anything but to go home,' Scott said.

Fat Man Number Two looked at Fat Man Number One and said, 'So he can fuck his mother.'

The fatties looked at Scott to see what he'd say but he didn't say anything. They could say he screwed dogs and that was all right with him. Hell, bring one on and he'd fuck it now if they'd let him go afterwards.

Fat Man Number One said, 'You boys running around with a jungle bunny makes me sick.'

'He's just a nigger from school,' Farto said. 'We don't like him none. We just picked him up because some White Tree boys were beating on him and we didn't want him to get wrecked on account of he's our quarterback.'

'Ah,' Fat Man Number One said, 'I see. Personally, me and Vinnie don't cotton to niggers in sports. They start taking showers with white boys the next thing they want is to take white girls to bed. It's just one step from one to the other.'

'We don't have nothing to do with him playing,' Leonard said. 'We didn't integrate the schools.'

'No,' Fat Man Number One said, 'that was ole Big Ears Johnson, but you're running around with him and drinking with him.'

'His cup's been peed in,' Farto said. 'That was kind of a joke on him, you see. He ain't our friend, I swear it. He's just a nigger that plays football.'

'Peed in his cup, huh?' said the one called Vinnie. 'I like that, Pork, don't you? Peed in his fucking cup.'

Pork dropped Scott's cup on the ground and smiled at him. 'Come here, nigger. I got something to tell you.'

Scott looked at Farto and Leonard. No help there. They had suddenly become interested in the toes of their shoes; they examined them as if they were true marvels of the world.

Scott moved toward Pork, and Pork, still smiling, put his arms around Scott's shoulders and walked him toward the big storage building. Scott said, 'What are we doing?'

Pork turned Scott around so they were facing Leonard and Farto who still stood holding their drinks and contemplating their shoes. 'I didn't want to get it on the new gravel drive,' Pork said and pulled Scott's head in close to his own and with his free hand reached back under his Hawaiian shirt and brought out a short, black revolver and put it to Scott's temple and pulled the trigger. There was a snap like a bad knee going out and Scott's feet lifted in unison and went to the side and something dark squirted from his head and his feet swung back toward Pork and his shoes shuffled, snapped, and twisted on the concrete in front of the building.

'Ain't that somethin',' Pork said as Scott went limp and dangled from the thick crook of his arm, 'the rhythm is the last thing to go.'

Leonard couldn't make a sound. His guts were in his throat. He wanted to melt and run under the car. Scott was dead and the brains that had made plays twisted as fishing worms and commanded his feet on down the football field were scrambled like breakfast eggs.

Farto said, 'Holy shit.'

Pork let go of Scott and Scott's legs split and he sat down and his head went forward and clapped on the cement between his knees. A dark pool formed under his face.

'He's better off, boys,' Vinnie said. 'Nigger was begat by Cain and the ape and he ain't quite monkey and he ain't quite man. He's got no place in this world 'cept as a beast of burden. You start trying to train them to do things like drive cars and run with footballs it ain't nothing but grief to them and the whites too. Get any on your shirt, Pork?'

'Nary a drop.'

Vinnie went inside the building and said something to the men that could be heard but not understood, then he came back with some crumpled newspapers. He went over to Scott and wrapped them around the bloody head and let it drop back on the cement. 'You try hosing down that shit when it's dried, Pork, and you wouldn't worry none about that gravel. The gravel ain't nothing.'

Then Vinnie said to Farto, 'Open the back door of that car.' Farto nearly twisted an ankle doing it. Vinnie picked Scott up by the back of the neck and the seat of his pants and threw him onto the floorboard of the Impala.

Pork used the short barrel of his revolver to scratch his nuts, then put the gun behind him, under his Hawaiian shirt. 'You boys are gonna go to the river bottoms with us and help us get shed of this nigger.'

'Yes, sir,' Farto said. 'We'll toss his ass in the Sabine for you.'

'How about you?' Pork asked Leonard. 'You trying to go weak sister?'

'No,' Leonard croaked, 'I'm with you.'

'That's good,' Pork said. 'Vinnie, you take the truck and lead the way.'

Vinnie took a key from his pocket and unlocked the building door next to the one with the light, went inside, and backed out a sharp-looking gold Dodge pickup. He backed it in front of the Impala and sat there with the motor running.

'You boys keep your place,' Pork said. He went inside the lighted building for a moment. They heard him say to the men inside, 'Go on and watch the movies. And save some of them beers for us. We'll be back.' Then the light went out and Pork came out, shutting the door. He looked at Leonard and Farto and said, 'Drink up, boys.'

Leonard and Farto tossed off their warm Coke and whiskey and dropped the cups on the ground.

'Now,' Pork said, 'you get in the back with the nigger, I'll ride with the driver.'

Farto got in the back and put his feet on Scott's knees. He tried not to look at the head wrapped in newspaper, but he couldn't help it. When Pork opened the front door and the overhead light came on Farto saw there was a split in the paper and Scott's eye was visible behind it. Across the forehead the wrapping had turned dark. Down by the mouth and chin was an ad for a fish sale.

Leonard got behind the wheel and started the car. Pork reached over and honked the horn. Vinnie rolled the pickup forward and Leonard followed him to the river bottoms. No one spoke. Leonard found himself wishing with all his heart that he had gone to the outdoor picture show to see the movie with the nigger starring in it.

The river bottoms were steamy and hot from the closeness of the trees and the under and over-growth. As Leonard wound the Impala down the narrow, red clay roads amidst the dense foliage, he felt as if his car were a crab crawling about in a pubic thatch. He could feel from the way the steering wheel handled that the dog and the chain were catching brush and limbs here and there. He had forgotten all about the dog and now being reminded of it worried him. What if the dog got tangled and he had to stop? He didn't think Pork would take kindly to stopping, not with the dead burrhead on the floorboard and him wanting to get rid of the body.

Finally they came to where the woods cleared out a spell and they drove along the edge of the Sabine River. Leonard hated water and always had. In the moonlight the river looked like poisoned coffee flowing there. Leonard knew there were alligators and gars big as little alligators and water moccasins by the thousands swimming underneath the water, and just the thought of all those slick, darting bodies made him queasy.

They came to what was known as Broken Bridge. It was an old worn-out bridge that had fallen apart in the middle and it was connected to the land on this side only. People sometimes fished off it. There was no one fishing tonight.

Vinnie stopped the pickup and Leonard pulled up beside it, the nose of the Chevy pointing at the mouth of the bridge. They all got out and Pork made Farto pull Scott out by the feet. Some of the newspapers came loose from Scott's head exposing an ear and part of the face. Farto patted the newspaper back into place.

'Fuck that,' Vinnie said. 'It don't hurt if he stains the fucking ground. You two idgits find some stuff to weight this coon down so we can sink him.'

Farto and Leonard started scurrying about like squirrels, looking for rocks or big, heavy logs. Suddenly they heard Vinnie cry out. 'Godamighty, fucking A. Pork. Come look at this.'

Leonard looked over and saw that Vinnie had discovered Rex. He was standing looking down with his hands on his hips. Pork went over to stand by him, then Pork turned around and looked at them. 'Hey, you fucks, come here.'

Leonard and Farto joined them in looking at the dog. There was mostly just a head now, with a little bit of meat and fur hanging off a spine and some broken ribs.

'That's the sickest fucking thing I've ever fucking seen,' Pork said.

'Godamighty,' Vinnie said.

'Doing a dog like that. Shit, don't you got no heart? A dog. Man's best fucking goddamn friend and you two killed him like this.'

'We didn't kill him,' Farto said.

'You trying to fucking tell me he done this to himself? Had a bad fucking day and done this.'

'Godamighty,' Vinnie said.

'No sir,' Leonard said. 'We chained him on there after he was dead.'

'I believe that,' Vinnie said. 'That's some rich shit. You guys murdered this dog. Godamighty.'

'Just thinking about him trying to keep up and you fucks driving faster and faster makes me mad as a wasp,' Pork said.

'No,' Farto said. 'It wasn't like that. He was dead and we were drunk and we didn't have anything to do, so we—'

'Shut the fuck up,' Pork said, sticking a finger hard against Farto's forehead. 'You just shut the fuck up. We can see what the fuck you fucks did. You drug this here dog around until all his goddamn hide came off . . . What kind of mothers you boys got anyhow that they didn't tell you better about animals?'

'Godamighty,' Vinnie said.

Everyone grew silent, stood looking at the dog. Finally Farto said, 'You want us to go back to getting some stuff to hold the nigger down?'

Pork looked at Farto as if he had just grown up whole from the ground. 'You fucks are worse than niggers, doing a dog like that. Get on back over to the car.'

Leonard and Farto went over to the Impala and stood looking down at Scott's body in much the same way they had stared at the dog. There, in the dim moonlight shadowed by trees, the paper wrapped around Scott's head made him look like a giant papier-mâché doll. Pork came up and kicked Scott in the face with a swift motion that sent newspapers flying and sent a thonking sound across the water that made frogs jump.

'Forget the nigger,' Pork said. 'Give me your car keys, ball sweat.' Leonard took out his keys and gave them to Pork and Pork went around to the trunk and opened it. 'Drag the nigger over here.'

Leonard took one of Scott's arms and Farto took the other and they pulled him over to the back of the car.

'Put him in the trunk,' Pork said.

'What for?' Leonard asked.

'Cause I fucking said so,' Pork said.

Leonard and Farto heaved Scott into the trunk. He looked pathetic lying there next to the spare tire, his face partially covered with the newspaper. Leonard thought, if only the nigger had stolen a car with a spare he might not be here tonight. He could have gotten that flat changed and driven on before the White Tree boys even came along.

'All right, you get in there with him,' Pork said, gesturing to Farto.

'Me?' Farto said.

'Nah, not fucking you, the fucking elephant on your fucking shoulder. Yeah, you, get in the trunk. I ain't got all night.'

'Jesus, we didn't do anything to that dog, mister. We told you that. I swear. Me and Leonard hooked him up after he was dead . . . It was Leonard's idea.'

Pork didn't say a word. He just stood there with one hand on the trunk lid looking at Farto. Farto looked at Pork, then the trunk, then back to Pork. Lastly he looked at Leonard, then climbed into the trunk, his back to Scott.

'Like spoons,' Pork said, and closed the lid. 'Now you, whatsit, Leonard? You come over here.' But Pork didn't wait for Leonard to move. He scooped the back of Leonard's neck with a chubby hand and pushed him over to where Rex lay at the end of the chain with Vinnie still looking down at him.

'What you think, Vinnie?' Pork asked. 'You got what I got in mind?'

Vinnie nodded. He bent down and took the collar off the dog. He fastened it on Leonard. Leonard could smell the odor of the dead dog in his nostrils. He bent his head and puked.

'There goes my shoeshine,' Vinnie said, and he hit Leonard a short one in the stomach. Leonard went to his knees and puked some more of the hot Coke and whiskey.

'You fucks are the lowest pieces of shit on this earth, doing a dog like that,' Vinnie said. 'A nigger ain't no lower.'

Vinnie got some strong fishing line out of the back of the truck and they tied Leonard's hands behind his back. Leonard began to cry.

'Oh shut up,' Pork said. 'It ain't that bad. Ain't nothing that bad.'

But Leonard couldn't shut up. He was caterwauling now and it was echoing through the trees. He closed his eyes and tried to pretend he had gone to the show with the nigger starring in it and had fallen asleep in his car and was having a bad dream, but he couldn't imagine that. He thought about Harry the janitor's flying saucers with the peppermint rays, and he knew if there were any saucers shooting rays down, they weren't boredom rays after all. He wasn't a bit bored.

Pork pulled off Leonard's shoes and pushed him back flat on the ground and pulled off the socks and stuck them in Leonard's mouth so tight he couldn't spit them out. It wasn't that Pork thought anyone was going to hear Leonard, he just didn't like the noise. It hurt his ears.

Leonard lay on the ground in the vomit next to the dog and cried silently. Pork and Vinnie went over to the Impala and opened the doors and stood so they could get a grip on the car to push. Vinnie reached in and moved the gear from park to neutral and he and Pork began to shove the car forward. It moved slowly at first, but as it made the slight incline that led down to the old bridge, it picked up speed. From inside the trunk, Farto hammered lightly at the lid as if he didn't really mean it. The chain took up slack and Leonard felt it jerk and pop his neck. He began to slide along the ground like a snake.

Vinnie and Pork jumped out of the way and watched the car make the bridge and go over the edge and disappear into the water with amazing quietness. Leonard, pulled by the weight of the car, rustled past them. When he hit the bridge, splinters tugged at his clothes so hard they ripped his pants and underwear down almost to his knees.

The chain swung out once toward the edge of the bridge and the rotten railing, and Leonard tried to hook a leg around an upright board there, but that proved wasted. The weight of the car just pulled his knee out of joint and jerked the board out of place with a screech of nails and lumber.

Leonard picked up speed and the chain rattled over the edge of the bridge, into the water and out of sight, pulling its connection after it like a pull toy. The last sight of Leonard was the soles of his bare feet, white as the bellies of fish.

'It's deep there,' Vinnie said. 'I caught an old channel cat there once, remember? Big sucker. I bet it's over fifty feet deep down there.'

They got in the truck and Vinnie cranked it.

'I think we did them boys a favor,' Pork said. 'Them running around with niggers and what they did to that dog and all. They weren't worth a thing.'

'I know it,' Vinnie said. 'We should have filmed this, Pork, it would have been good. Where the car and that nigger lover went off in the water was choice.'

'Nah, there wasn't any women.'

'Point,' Vinnie said, and backed around and drove onto the trail that wound its way out of the bottoms.

ANDREW VACHSS has worked as a federal investigator (tracking chains of sexually-transmitted disease), social caseworker, community organizer, and director of numerous agencies including a re-entry center for former convicts and a maximum-security institution for violent youth. His experience also includes various forms of manual labor, taxi driving, and a stint in Africa during the Biafran war. Vachss is the author of several novels in the 'Burke' series including *Blossom* and *Sacrifice* (Pan), which appears in more than a dozen languages—literary prizes include the Grand Prix de Litterature Policiere (France), the Deutschen Krimi Preis (Germany), and the Falcon Award (Japan). He has published numerous works of non-fiction and his short stories are collected in the *Hard Looks* ('graphic novel') anthology by Dark Horse Comics (USA). For the past fifteen years he has worked as a lawyer, with a practice limited to representation of children and youth. Asked to describe his work, Vachss replied: 'Crime, violence, child abuse . . . and the inextricably intertwined connections between them.'

Andrew Vachss

Treatment

I

The prosecutor was a youngish man, better dressed than his government salary would warrant, ambition shining on his clean-shaven face. He held a sheaf of papers in his hand, waving them about for emphasis as though the jury were still in the courtroom.

'Doctor, are you trying to tell this court that it should leave a convicted child molester free in the community? Is that what you're saying?'

I took a shallow breath through my nose, centering myself, reaching for calm. 'No, Mr Montgomery, that is what *you* are saying. The defendant suffers from pedophilia. That is, he is subject to intense, recurrent sexual urges and sexually arousing fantasies involving sexual activity with prepubescent children.'

'Fancy words, doctor, but they all come down to the same thing, don't they? The defendant is a homosexual who preys on little boys . . . isn't that right?'

'No, it is *not* right. In fact, your statement is rather typical of the ignorance of the law enforcement community when it comes to any of the paraphilias. A homosexual is an individual whose sexual preference is for those of his or her own gender. Such a preference is not a disorder, unless such feelings are dystonic to the individual . . . and that is relatively rare. You would not call a man who engaged in sexual activity with young girls a *heterosexual* offender, would you? Of course not. The root of much of the hostility against pedophiles is, actually, nothing more than thinly-veiled homophobia.'

The prosecutor's face flushed angrily. 'Are you saying the State has prosecuted this offender because of *homophobia*, doctor?'

'It is surely a factor in the equation. Isn't it true that you personally believe homosexuals are"sick," sir?'

'They are! I . . . I'll ask the questions here, if you don't mind.'

'I don't mind. I was trying to answer your questions more fully, to give the court a better understanding of the phenomena involved. If you check the *Diagnostic and Statistical Manual of the American Psychiatric Association*, you will see that homosexuality is not listed as a disorder. Pedophilia is. The specific code, for your information, is 302.20. Homosexuality is present at birth. Hard-wired, if you will. Sexual activity with children is, on the other hand, volitional conduct.'

'And they're not born that way?'

'No. There is no bio-genetic code for pedophilia. The essential etiology is an early sexual experience—those you would call perpetrators began as those you would call victims. Once infected, the victim learns to wear a mask. They are capable of the most complex planning, often with great patience.'

'So every child who is molested becomes a molester?'

'Certainly not. Some do, some don't. As I explained, it essentially comes down to a matter of choice. No matter what a person's circumstances, he always owns his own behavior.'

'So, then . . . what does this manual of yours say about recidivism, doctor?'

'That's a good question. The course of the disorder is usually chronic, especially among pedophiles fixated upon the same sex. Recidivism, however, fluctuates with psychosocial stress—the more intense the stress, the more likely there will be a recurrence.'

'So you admit offenders like Mr Wilson here are more likely to commit new crimes?'

'All things being equal, yes. However, we don't treat such individuals with conventional psychotherapy. We understand the chronicity of their behavior, and it is the goal of treatment to interdict that behavior. To control their conduct, not their thoughts. I am completing my research for a journal entry now, but all the preliminary data indicate an extremely high rate of success. That is, with proper treatment.'

'This "treatment" of yours, doctor . . . it doesn't include prison, does it?'

'No, it does not. Incarceration is counter-indicated for pedophiles. The sentences, as you know, are relatively short. And the degree of psychosocial stress in prison for such individuals is incalculable. In fact, studies show the recidivism rate for previously-incarcerated pedophiles is extraordinarily high.'

'But he wouldn't be molesting children in prison, would he?'

'I understand your question to be rhetorical, sir, but the real issue is long-term protection of the community, not temporary incapacitation. Even when therapy is offered in prison, and it rarely is, it is an axiom of our profession that coercive therapy is doomed to failure. No treatment is perfect, but we know this: the patient must be a participant in the treatment, not a mere recipient of it.'

The judge leaned down from the bench. With his thick mane of white hair and rimless glasses, he looked like Central Casting for the part.

'Doctor, so what you're saying is that motivation is the key?'

'Yes I am, your honor. And Mr Wilson has displayed a high level of such motivation. In fact, he consulted our program before he was ever arrested, much less convicted.'

The prosecutor slapped the table in front of him. 'Sure! But he knew he was about to be indicted, didn't he, doctor?'

'I have no way of knowing what was in his mind,' I replied mildly. 'And the source of the motivation is far less significant than its presence.'

'So what's this "cure", doctor? What's this wonderful "treatment" of yours?'

'The treatment is multi-modality. Not all pedophiles respond to the same inputs. We use groupwork, confrontation, aversive therapy, insight-orientation, conditioning, even libido-reducing drugs when indicated.'

'How much were you paid for your testimony today, doctor?'

The defense attorney leaped to his feet. 'Objection! That isn't relevant.'

'Oh, I think I'll allow it,' the judge said. 'You may answer the question, doctor.'

'I was paid nothing for my testimony today, sir. I evaluated Mr Wilson, provided a report to his attorney, a copy of which has been furnished to you. I charge my time at seventy-five dollars an hour. I haven't sent in a bill yet, but I imagine the total will come to around fifteen hundred dollars.'

'No further questions,' the prosecutor snarled.

II

'You're as good as they say you are,' the defense attorney told me, shaking my hand in his paneled office. 'Nobody knows those people like you do.'

I nodded, waiting patiently.

'It's just amazing . . . the way you predicted everything the prosecution would do. Hell, I thought we were dead in the water on this one. Told Wilson he could expect to do about five years in the pen. And here the judge hands him probation on a platter.'

'Psychiatric probation,' I reminded him.

'Yeah, I know. He has to stay in treatment with you for the full term or he goes inside. But so what? It's a better deal than he would have gotten in the joint.'

'I kept my word?' Watching him carefully.

'You surely did, my friend. And don't think I've forgotten about our arrangement, either. Here you are, just like I promised.'

The check was drawn on his escrow account. Fifteen hundred dollars. I put it in my attaché case along with the ten thousand in cash lying next to it on his teakwood desk.

III

Wilson sat across from me in my private office, his face a study in eager anticipation.

'This won't be easy,' I told him. 'We have to remake you, start from the beginning. And we begin with honesty, all right?'

'Yes, that's what I want. Honesty. I didn't see much of it during my trial.'

'Tell me about that.'

'Well, the boys lied. I don't mean about . . . what we did. But about how they felt about it. You know what I'm saying? I didn't force them . . . *any* of them. It was love. A special love. All I wanted to do was be something special to them. A loving, special friend. That D.A., he turned it into something ugly. The jury never heard my side of it.'

'How did it start?'

'With that boy Wesley . . . the first one to testify. When I first met him, he was eight years old. And you never met a more seductive little boy, always wanting to be cuddled. He doesn't have a father, you know. I mean, it's natural for a boy to seek love.'

'I know.'

'And I loved him. Why should that be a crime? I never used force, never hurt him even once.'

'How do you feel . . . about being prosecuted?'

'I feel like *I'm* the victim. I did nothing wrong—it's the laws that are wrong. And, someday, you'll see, the laws will change. I mean, kids have rights too, don't they? What good is the right to say "no" if they don't have the right to say "yes"?'

'The law says they're too young to consent to sex.'

'That's a lot of crap. Kids know what they want. You know how willful they can get, how demanding. I've been around kids all my life. That's the way they are.'

'Okay, look. Your problem is a simple one, isn't it?'

'What do you mean?'

'You got caught.'

'But . . .'

'That's your problem, Mr Wilson. You got caught. And our treatment here, it's to guarantee it doesn't happen again.'

Suspicion glazed his eyes. 'How could you do that?'

'First of all, we set the stage. You'll get therapy for a while, learn how to talk the talk. Then, eventually, you'll be relocated. You'll never be able to live around here after what happened. Never get a job working around kids. But, after a while, you'll be able to move to a new town. And start over.'

'Is this a trick?'

'No trick. I know my business. And I'm smart enough to know it's all a matter of packaging. This is America. Whatever we *call* things, that's what they become. And what they're going to call you is "cured", understand?'

He nodded, dry-washing his hands, still apprehensive. 'You said something in court . . . about drugs . . .'

'Don't worry about it. Sometimes a court insists on depo-provera . . . so-called "chemical castration". But that's not a problem here. And even if it were, we could give you one of the androgen group, reverse it almost instantly.'

'My lawyer said it would be real expensive.'

'Oh yes. We're the only clinic in the country that provides this range of services, but look what you're getting for your money . . .

no victim confrontation, no shock treatments, no encounter groups, no drugs. Just preparation for how you're going to . . . successfully . . . live the rest of your life. And you don't spend a day in jail. Pretty good, isn't it?'

'How did you . . . ?'

'Get into this? It's easy enough to understand. While I was still in medical school, I realized that pedophile treatment is the growth industry of the 90s. The money's great, the malpractice premiums are low, and there are other benefits too.'

'Like being paid in cash,' he said, smiling the sociopath's smile.

'Like that,' I said, holding out my hand for the money.

IV

'Okay Mr Wilson, you're about ready for discharge. Our records will show you've completed intensive individual psychotherapy, participated in group, undergone aversive conditioning. All satisfactory. I can truthfully say you're ready to live without probation supervision. Have you made plans?'

'I sure have. In fact, I've been corresponding with a few boys in an orphanage in Florida. You know, counselling them about their problems. I've been offered a job down there, and I'll be leaving as soon as my lawyer gets me released from probation.'

'Good. There's just one more thing. You've never really apologized to the boys, and most therapists think that's a key element in treatment.'

'I don't want to . . .'

'No, of course you won't have to see them. What would really help persuade the court is a letter from you to the boys . . . just telling them you understand what you did, how you take full responsibility. Like we taught you, remember? Urge them to go on with their lives, and promise they'll never see you again, okay?'

'You think it'll work?'

'I'm sure it will work. I know these people. Write me out a couple of drafts, and I'll stop by tonight when I'm done with the last group and look them over. Then we'll pick the best one.'

'Thanks, doc. You saved my life again.'

V

Wilson lived in a modern highrise right near the city line. I rang his bell around 11.30. He buzzed me in. The lobby was deserted—the place is mostly a retirement community. I insisted he move from his old address to a place where there were few children around. To reduce the temptation.

I took the steps to the 26th floor, not even breathing hard. I don't get to work out at the dojo anymore, but I like to stay in shape.

Wilson had a half-dozen samples ready for me, all in his educated handwriting on personalized blue stationery. He stepped out onto the balcony to smoke a cigarette while I read them through. Finally, I found one that was suitable.

> I'm sorry for everything I did. I know now that no excuse, no rationalization will ever make things right. I've been learning about myself, and now I know the truth. You are the victims, not me. I know why I did what I did, and I'm sorry for all the pain I caused. It's better this way. You will never see me again. I hope you grow up to be good citizens, and always stay true to yourselves. Goodbye.

His signature was strong, self-assured. I left the letter I selected on his desk. Then I went outside to join him on the balcony.

The night was warm, velvety dark. City lights winked below, quiet and peaceful.

'Was that what you wanted, doc?' he asked.

'Perfect,' I said, patting him gently on the back.

'Look out there, Mr Wilson . . . see your future.'

He leaned over the balcony. I knife-edged my right hand, swept it into a perfect power-arc to the back of his neck, followed through with the blow, spinning on my right foot and sweeping him over the side with my left hand.

He didn't scream on the way down.

I stepped back inside, dialed 911, told them he had jumped. While I waited, I tore the other letters into small bits and flushed them down the toilet.

JOYCE HARRINGTON When your first attempt at writing a story gets published, and then goes on to win an Edgar, what do you do for an encore?

Joyce Harrington has been struggling with this dilemma since 1973 when she went home with an Edgar for *The Purple Shroud*. She has since been nominated three more times, and has more than 50 published stories and three novels to her credit.

An advertising and public relations executive in New York City, Joyce has raised two sons who often serve as inspiration and character studies for her fiction. Her stories range from sweetly sinister rural tales to the tough, gritty urban street scene. And always, character is the key to plot. 'With me,' she says, 'action always springs from my characters' needs, desires and compulsions.'

Joyce Harrington

ANDREW, MY SON

'Do you hear the cats?' Andrew asks me. He is standing by the window, peering out into the deep winter darkness.

I have heard no cats, but I listen carefully. If I could make my ears twitch, I would. It's always best, with Andrew, to put on a good show.

I make a noncommittal sound, 'Um-hum,' which could mean yes. Or no. A mistake. Andrew can't abide inattention or ambivalence.

'Listen, will you!' he shouts. 'They're out there yowling. I'll put poison out. I swear I will.' He paces in front of the fireplace. The flickering logs light his narrow face from below. His eyes are fierce, feral. This is my son.

'Alley cats,' I murmur. 'A female in heat. They're fighting over her. It's what they do.' I still haven't heard them.

'Disgusting.' He bends over me to spit the words into my face. 'You're disgusting. To even think such a thing.' He flings himself away and into the tall armchair opposite mine. Then he simply sprawls and stares at me. I wonder what he's thinking.

Andrew was a pretty child—fine golden curls, an angelic smile, huge eyes of a deep indigo verging on purple. Now he is a handsome young man. The golden curls have thickened and burnished; the eyes have narrowed with intelligence and temperament.

The smile is still angelic, but wasn't Lucifer once an angel?

I do not like my son.

I rise from my chair. My neglected book falls on the floor, face down, its pages crumpled. 'Good night, Andrew,' I say. 'Sleep well.'

'Pleasant dreams, Mother,' he says. His tone conveys unmistakably that he wishes me nothing of the kind. It was a mistake telling him of the nightmares that have begun to plague me. I am always making mistakes with Andrew. Do all mothers make mistakes with their sons?

I stoop to pick up my book. His foot extends to kick it out of my reach. I straighten to gaze sorrowfully down at him, lolling and smirking in his chair.

'You shouldn't read such trash,' he says.

'It's harmless. It helps me sleep.' Once again, I bend and reach for it.

He swoops to pick it up and tosses it into the fire.

It's only a paperback, a romance of other times and of people engaged in passion and adventure. It can be replaced. I stand and watch the flames flirt with its pages. When it is fully ablaze, I turn and stride from the room. My shoulders are straight and my head erect.

Andrew's merry laughter follows me.

In the morning, the house is cold and Andrew is gone. He hasn't slept in his bed. He's turned the thermostat down. Another of his tricks. I turn it up and get back into bed and wait for the heat to rise. It would be nice to have a cup of hot tea, but I lack the energy to go down to the kitchen to make it. Or am I afraid?

Alone in the darkened bedroom, waiting for the heat and daylight, I argue the point with myself. What is there to be afraid of? That he has left surprises for me? Constructed booby traps? In many ways, Andrew is still a child, dependent on me for what little love there is in his life. And like a child, reaching for independence, he resents me. I try to make allowances for that.

Often, I wish that he would marry. I dream of a lovely young woman for him and sons of his own. The little family would live nearby, but not too near. They would visit occasionally, but not too often. Christmas, Thanksgiving, the Fourth of July. We would have laughter and feasting. I would make the peach cobbler that Andrew's father loved so well.

There are tears on my cheeks and I wipe them away with the back of my hand. The radiator clanks and pale gray daylight shows outside my window. Bare branches gleam with a frosting of ice.

It's silly to be afraid of the kitchen. I get up and wrap my fleecy robe over my flannel nightgown. My slippers are lined with lambswool. I will drink my cup of tea and go about my business until Andrew returns. Today will be a good day to work on the sweater I am secretly knitting for his birthday.

And then there is my appointment this afternoon.

The doctor sits as usual in his wheelchair, his fat legs and little feet hanging motionless down. I wonder, as I always do, why his legs are so fat if they are paralyzed. But I don't know what disease confines him to the chair, and I would never dream of asking. He probably wouldn't tell me, not about him.

He waits, with infinite patience, for me to begin.

I tell him about Andrew burning my book.

'Was it a good book?' he asks.

'It was just a book.' I know I am being evasive.

'Were you enjoying it?'

'Ummm. Yes.'

'Is that why Andrew burned it?'

'I suppose so. We hadn't talked about it. He couldn't know whether I was enjoying it or not.'

There is a long pause.

Then I tell him about Andrew turning the thermostat down.

'I think he's trying to freeze me to death.' I laugh a little to show I don't mean it literally.

But the doctor doesn't laugh. 'Do you think Andrew would kill you?' he asks.

'No!' I exclaim. 'What would he do without me?'

'Exactly,' says the doctor.

There is another long pause. Long enough for the doctor to start the next round.

'Tell me about the accident,' he says.

'I've told you about that. Many times.'

'Yes. But each time, we learn somethng new. Isn't it so?'

I nod. And then I begin. 'It was winter. This time of year. The anniversary is in a few weeks. Twenty years ago. Andrew was eight years old. Carl had sprained his ankle, so I was driving him to the station. He was taking a later train that morning. The roads were icy.' My voice tapers off. This part is always so difficult.

'Go on,' the doctor prompts.

'The roads were very icy. I was supposed to have had the snow tires put on, but hadn't got around to it yet. I was in the early months of pregnancy and not very energetic. Lazy, I suppose. Andrew was leaning over the back seat with his arms around my neck. I had told him to sit down, but he wouldn't. Carl started scolding him. I couldn't bear for anyone to scold Andrew, not even his father. We began to argue. Carl said I was pampering the boy, making a sissy out of him. Andrew was crying. His arms tightened around my neck. I couldn't breathe. I took my hands off the steering wheel to loosen his grip. We were cresting a hill. The car swerved into the other lane just as another car came up from the other side. We crashed. That's all.'

I had been speaking rapidly, repeating the facts as I had repeated them so many times in this heavy room. I am out of breath and sitting bolt upright in my chair, reliving the moment. This doctor does not use a couch. I think he likes to watch the faces of his patients. Sometimes, I think he lives their lives in these tormented moments. In that wheelchair, he can't have much of a life of his own.

'Relax now,' he says softly. 'There is more.'

'More,' I murmur. 'Yes. Of course there's more. The aftermath. Carl died. I lost the baby.'

'And Andrew?'

'Andrew was . . . seriously injured. He flew over my shoulder and went through the windshield. His head . . . '

'Yes?'

'He has scars to this day. Fortunately, his hair is thick and they can't be seen.'

The doctor sighs. I don't blame him. It's a sad story.

'Do you blame yourself?' he asks.

'I guess I do. I was driving.'

'Do you blame Andrew?'

'No. How could I? He was only a child.'

'His arms around your neck, choking you?'

'He was frightened. His father was angry with him.'

'Do you blame Carl?'

'How can you blame a dead man?'

The doctor sighs again. 'It's hard work,' he says. 'It goes slowly. But you must try to be honest. For your own sake. So Andrew . . . he was seriously hurt?'

'I thought he would die.'

'And . . . ?'

'He didn't.'

'He didn't,' the doctor repeats. 'He got well and went back to school?'

I have to think about that. 'He got well and . . . and I had a teacher come to the house.'

'What was her name?'

'It wasn't a woman. It was a man.'

'What was his name?'

'I can't remember. It was a long time ago.'

The doctor rolls his wheelchair behind his desk, a sign that our time is up. 'Will you try to remember for next time? Perhaps there are some records you could look up.'

'Yes,' I promise earnestly. 'I'll try. I'll look.'

His attention is on his desk calendar and I know I am dismissed. Somehow, I feel he is disappointed with me. I leave the dark cave of his office, wondering if I will return next week. What began as something to cure my nightmares has suddenly turned threatening.

Andrew doesn't like his dinner. He sits at the table, moodily pushing his food around on his plate. 'Why don't we ever have fish?' he whines. 'Don't you know that red meat is bad for you?'

'You don't like fish,' I tell him. 'You've always liked rare roast beef, just like your father.'

'You killed my father. If you hadn't killed him in the car, you would have killed him with roast beef.' He picks up his plate and dumps his dinner into my lap.

I sit there with gravy soaking through the skirt of my green wool jersey dress. It brings a heat and a wetness to my thighs, a mockery of the ancient act of love. Carefully, I gather the mess into my napkin and carry it into the kitchen. The dress may not be ruined. I sponge it off as best I can, and then go upstairs to change. There is no point in being angry with Andrew. He will not listen. I think it's better not to provoke him. Tomorrow, I'll get some nice fillet of sole.

Instead of going downstairs to sit with Andrew in the living room, I climb on a chair to reach into the top of the closet. There, in an old suitcase, I know are papers, old photographs. I had promised the doctor to look. The suitcase is dusty. I wipe it off before putting it on the bed. I have not looked into this suitcase for many years. My hands fumble reluctantly with the latches. Before I can open them, Andrew appears in the doorway.

'Having a nostalgia trip?' he sneers.

'I thought I'd look,' I mumble.

'Want to twine my innocent baby curls around your finger? I'll bet you saved each tooth I put under my pillow. Go ahead and open it. I'd like to see too.'

'You've seen already.' I know I am accusing him, but suddenly, I don't care. 'You've been snooping into this. How dare you?'

'Snooping, Mother?' He is sly, self-righteous. 'But it's my life too. Isn't it? Isn't that what you've got stored away in there? My brief life?'

'What are you talking about?' I realize I am shrieking like a madwoman. I say it again, softly and reasonably. 'What are you talking about, Andrew?'

'You don't really want me to say it. Come downstairs and have some coffee. I've made it. It's all ready and waiting for you.'

I am overcome by his sudden kindness. Perhaps we can have a pleasant evening together. We'll talk about the future. He'll tell me of his fiancée, his secret fiancée, whom I've never met. He'll ask me if she may come to dinner, and we'll plan together for a wedding in the summer.

He has gotten out the silver coffee service and my best china cups and saucers. 'Andrew! How nice!' I exclaim. I can smell the fragrant fresh-brewed coffee.

Andrew, solicitous, takes my arm and ushers me to my chair. He pours a cup of coffee and brings it to me. He smiles benignly as I lift the cup to my lips. I sip. And the cup flies out of my hand, my lips sting, my tongue is seared. 'Water!' I gasp.

Andrew laughs. His bitter laughter rings in my ears as I run to the kitchen and rinse my mouth directly under the faucet. When the awful burning in my mouth recedes to a prickling, stinging pain, I raise my head and turn the water off. There on the counter is an open can of Drano.

'What's wrong, Mother? Don't you like my coffee?' He is hovering nearby, his face a mask of solicitude.

I cannot speak. My lips will crack. I walk past him and go back upstairs to my room. I lock the door. In the mirror, I see that my mouth and tongue are blistered. I also see the reflection of the old suitcase, just where I left it on the bed. I turn and stare at it. Is it time to open it? Now? After all these years?

I sit on the bed and remember a trip when the suitcase was new. Yes, it was our honeymoon. Carl's and mine. We had no knowledge then of Andrew. We were only and selfishly together, the two of us. We went to San Francisco, a city neither of us had seen and we both had dreamed of. We thought of living there, if Carl could arrange a transfer. But he couldn't and so that part of our dream faded. San Francisco does not have icy roads. I have often thought that Andrew was conceived in a room at the Palace Hotel. The timing was right. We should never have left that room. Or, perhaps, never have found it.

I open the suitcase. It's not so difficult after all to release the latches and raise the lid. Inside, I find old rags, shreds of yellowed newspapers, broken toys. No documents. No photographs. Ah, Andrew.

For a week I have been left in peace. Andrew does this from time to time. Usually after one of his more outrageous pranks. I don't know where he goes, nor do I ever ask. Some things, it's better not to know. He will return filthy and repentant. He will say, 'Mother, I'm sorry.'

And I will forgive him. What else can I do?

The blisters on my mouth are almost healed, but the doctor notices immediately. I tell him about Andrew's coffee. I tell him I could find no papers.

'Would you like to take a rest?' he says. 'I can get you a room.'

'A rest? You mean in a hospital?' I am shocked that he would suggest such a thing. And yet, I am tempted. Yes, very tempted.

'It's not a hospital. It's a private facility. For people who just need a little time out from their worries. I would like you to consider it.' His voice is so soothing. It seems like such a good idea.

'Oh, no,' I hear myself saying. 'I couldn't do that. Andrew needs me. He'll be coming home soon. I've bought him new clothes. I've almost finished his sweater. His birthday will be soon. He'll be home for that.'

The doctor is silent. Waiting.

I try to wait him out, in silence. But I can't do it. I've become too accustomed to the luxury of talking. I haven't told Andrew of my visits to the doctor. In the beginning, the doctor wanted to speak to Andrew, but I told him that would be dangerous. He believed me.

At last, I am forced to ask the question that has troubled me for years. 'Why does he do these things? I've been so good to him. I've tried so hard to make up to him for all that he's lost.'

'What has he lost?' the doctor asks in that quiet, insistent voice of his.

'Why, you know. I've told you.'

'Tell me again.'

It's not possible that he doesn't remember. He just wants to torture me by going over and over it. I shake my head. I simply cannot do it again.

'What has Andrew lost?' He is implacable. Cruel.

'His father,' I mutter.

'What else?'

'I don't know.' I seldom perspire, but now my hands, my face, my entire body, even my feet are slick and damp. My whispered words reverberate in the hazy room.

'You know,' the doctor insists.

I try to get out of the chair. I don't have to stay and submit to this. I can get into my car and drive home. I have a feeling that Andrew will come home tonight. I can't get up. Something keeps me nailed to the chair.

'Try to say it. I know it's difficult for you. But you'll feel so much better. What has Andrew lost?'

I remain mute. The words will not come. And yet, the thought is there. Oh, yes. The thought. It's always been there. Hasn't it? Yes.

The doctor is giving up. I can see it in his eyes. He's losing interest. A patient who will not speak is useless. I hate to feel useless. I begin to chatter. I intend to use up my hour. After all, I'm paying for it.

He listens, not interrupting, until I've exhausted my store of trifles. Then he says, 'Will you come in tomorrow? I think it's important. We've reached a crucial point.'

'Tomorrow? I don't know. It depends.' But I am flattered by this attention. I make a show of consulting my date book. There is nothing written on tomorrow's page, yet I frown over it as if I had appointments of great moment. 'Yes, all right,' I allow. 'I can make it. Same time?'

As I am driving away from the medical center where the doctor has his office, I see Andrew walking toward me along the street. This is an unpleasant part of town, old and seedy, inhabited by riffraff. He is walking with a woman. She is not young. She wears too much makeup to compensate for her loss of youth. She teeters along on extravagantly high heels, and she is wrapped in an imitation fur coat. I drive on past them, hoping that Andrew has not seen me or recognized the car. He has given no sign, but Andrew wouldn't. Why is he here? What has Andrew lost?

'Hello, Mother.'

He has caught me by surprise, my knitting in my lap. I try to hide it under a magazine. Even from across the room, I can smell the liquor on him and the cheap perfume. 'Would you like some shrimp salad?' I ask. I'll never risk roast beef again.

Andrew makes a rude, gagging noise like a child rejecting a dish he does not like. Then he asks, 'What were you doing in town today, Mother? Spying on me?'

'No, of course not. I had an appointment.'

'Oh, an appointment. Not with a doctor, by any chance?'

'No. I . . . I went to see a decorator. Don't you think it's time I redid this room?'

He strolls around the living room, examining the wallpaper, kicking at the chairs. 'Don't change it,' he says. 'I like it this way. Just the way it was twenty years ago.' Then he swings on me, his face contorted with fury. 'And don't lie to me! Don't ever lie to me. You went to see a psychiatrist. A nut doctor. Are you crazy, Mother?'

I remain outwardly calm, but my hands clutching my knitting are clammy. 'I am not crazy, Andrew. And *you* have been spying on *me*.'

He laughs at that. 'Don't you know by now that you have no secrets from me? That thing in your lap, for instance. It's a sweater, isn't it? To keep your little boy warm and cozy. Too bad he'll never wear it. I wouldn't be caught dead in that ugly piece of trash.'

It's so hard to keep from crying, but I've learned that that's the biggest mistake of all. To let Andrew see my weakness. 'Go take a bath,' I tell him. 'You smell.'

'Ah, but I smell of life, Mother. Something you know nothing about.' Nevertheless, he disappears up the stairs and I am left alone.

I pick up my knitting and try to concentrate, but it's useless. I might as well rip it all up and make pot holders out of the yarn.

The next day, Andrew is repentant. He brings me breakfast in bed. Two soft-boiled eggs, buttered toast, fresh orange juice, a pot of tea. The white wicker bed tray is one I used during Andrew's long recuperation after the accident.

'How lovely!' I exclaim. 'Andrew, you can be so thoughtful.'

He sits at the foot of the bed and smiles at me. 'You're the only mother I have.' Angelic. 'I don't know why I do the things I do.'

'Let's forget all that,' I tell him. 'We'll go on from here, this moment. You have your whole life ahead of you.'

'Yes,' he broods. 'And yours is almost over. I haven't given you much joy.'

'Oh, yes, you have. Why, I remember . . .'

'Please, Mother. Don't remember. It makes me sad.' But then he grins impishly and says, 'Let's do something special today. Let's start redoing the living room. You were right about that. It's old and gloomy. I'd like to tear that old wall-paper right off the walls. It's peeling off anyway. Come on, Mom. Put on your working clothes and let's get busy.' He leaps off the bed and dashes out the door.

'Wait!' I call after him. 'We can't do it all ourselves.'

'Yes, we can!' he shouts back as he goes thundering down the stairs.

By the time I am dressed, he has already torn long strips of wallpaper off the wall. He has taken the draperies off the windows, and the room, in the cold winter daylight, looks shabbier than I realized it was.

'You'd better make a list,' he tells me. 'New draperies, new furniture; the piano can stay but only if you play it for me.'

'I haven't played for years,' I tell him. 'I don't know if I can remember how. You always said it made you nervous.'

'Sit down and play,' he commands, 'while I get on with the wallpaper. It's all got to go. Every scrap of it.'

I sit on the bench and open the lid covering the keys. 'It's probably out of tune,' I murmur. But I tentatively finger the keys and begin with something simple. Carl always liked me to play 'Smoke Gets in Your Eyes.'

'That's right, Mom.' Andrew is on top of the ladder, scraping away at the wallpaper near the ceiling. 'Sing for me. I want to hear you sing.'

'Oh, no,' I protest. 'I never could sing. Even your father had to admit that.'

Andrew turns and stares down at me. 'Sing,' he says softly.

And I do. I can't remember all the words and my voice creaks and cracks, but it seems to please Andrew. He hums along and works steadily. Soon one entire wall of the living room is bare, down to the plaster, except for some places where the paper refuses to peel away.

'I'll have to get a blowtorch,' he says. 'That's the only way. And I can use it to strip the old paint off the woodwork. Oh, we're going to have fun. This room is going to look wonderful! And then we can start in on the rest of the house.'

'I don't know,' I whisper weakly. 'Isn't a blowtorch dangerous?'

'Not if you know how to use it.'

And then he is gone.

Maybe he won't come back. I have spent the past two hours waiting for him. I have missed my appointment with the doctor, but I can't leave with the house in such a mess and Andrew not back yet. I know I should be doing something, but I don't know what to do. I haven't even washed my breakfast dishes. I want to be happy that Andrew is finally taking an interest in the house and I am, really, but all this sudden change is making me uneasy. I prowl the dishevelled living room, fingering the dusty old draperies, crackling the torn wallpaper under foot, remembering when it was all new and gleaming and I was young and proud.

The phone rings, but I can't bring myself to answer it. It might be the doctor, wanting to know why I didn't show up. How can I tell him that I don't need him anymore? That Andrew has changed and we are going to be all right now, a family. I won't have any more nightmares. The phone stops ringing.

He's back, carrying a blowtorch and a big greasy can of some kind of fuel.

'Don't put it on the rug,' I warn him.

'It doesn't matter,' he says. 'The rug has got to go. We'll have a new one. Pale green, I think. Like the grass in springtime.' And he smiles.

'What took you so long?' I ask.

'You weren't supposed to ask,' he says, 'but since you did, I might as well tell you. I was getting a surprise for you.' He reaches into his pocket and pulls out a small white box. 'This is for you,' he says. 'Because I've been such a bad boy.' He hands me the box.

I am thunderstruck. It is the first time Andrew has ever given me a gift.

'Open it,' he urges.

I open it and there on a bed of soft blue velvet lies a gold heart-shaped locket on a thin gold chain. 'Andrew!' I exclaim. 'How pretty!'

'Open the locket,' he says.

My hands can hardly manage the delicate latch, but at last the locket springs open. On one side, there is a picture of me as I was twenty years ago. On the other, Andrew's baby face beams up at me, golden curls, huge eyes, sweet innocent smile. 'Oh, Andrew!' is all I can say before the tears gush forth.

'Now, Mom,' he says. 'It's nothing to cry about. Here, let me put it on for you.'

While he fastens the golden chain around my neck, I wipe my eyes and try to compose myself. When he finishes, he is all business once again. 'Back to work for me,' he says, 'and back to the piano for you. Music makes the time fly.'

I am in an ecstasy of delight and I try to play the old songs as best I can. I am dimly aware of Andrew doing something with the blowtorch and the can of fuel. I play on, one song after another. Andrew goes quietly about his work. For the first time in years, we are happy with each other. What more could a mother ask?

The doorbell rings, but I can't stop to answer it. I don't want anyone to interrupt this precious time. There is a pounding at the door and I hear voices calling my name. 'Go away!' I shout, before starting another song.

The flames are licking at the torn wallpaper now. And Andrew is smiling. Somehow he seems younger, as if the years are rolling back and he is becoming a boy again. The rug is smoldering. Andrew was never a gawky adolescent. He was a handsome teenager, never a spot of acne, never an awkward moment. The smoke brings tears to my eyes, but after so many years of not crying, I don't mind. Andrew looks about twelve years old, but that could be an illusion caused by the smoke. It's very warm in the room. The old sofa is burning now. The piano is near the picture window and hasn't caught fire yet.

Andrew stands in the flames and smiles at me. He beckons to me, this ten-year-old boy. 'Mommy, Mommy,' he calls. 'Isn't this fun?'

On the other side of the picture window, I can see agitated faces. The doctor is there, in his wheelchair. And the woman from his office. I am astonished and secretly pleased that he's come all this way just for me. Sirens wail in the distance, coming closer.

Andrew's eyes are closing. Blood gushes from his head and cascades down his pale face. He crumples and falls to the floor. I have seen him this way before. It is the way he was after the accident. I rise from the piano bench. This time I am determined I will save him.

But before I can reach him, there is a tremendous crash of glass behind me. Two tall men leap through the broken window and pick me up. 'My son! My son! Andrew, my son! Save him first.'

But they pay no attention. It is all so undignified. They bundle me into an ambulance, but not before I notice the great hoses they are aiming into my house. I can hear my doctor talking to the ambulance attendants. 'Suicidal,' he says. 'But I never thought she'd do something like this.'

How little he understands. Andrew will be back. Andrew *always* comes back. The fire is a good thing. It has burned away the past. Now we'll really fix up the house, make it better than new, with no memories. Andrew and I will be happy together. Forever.

NEAL BARRETT, JR's work spans the field from science fiction, Westerns, and historical novels to 'off the wall' mainstream fiction. He has been honored by the Science Fiction Writers of America, the Western Writers of America, and is a recipient of a Theodore Sturgeon Memorial Award. His mystery/suspense novel, *Pink Vodka Blues*, will be published in July of 1992. He is currently completing another mystery/suspense, *Dead Dog Blues*.

Twilight Zone called his 1986 novel, *Through Darkest America*, 'a book of astonishing power.' *The Washington Post* hailed *The Hereafter Gang* (1991) as 'one of the great American novels.'

Barrett recently completed eight adaptations of the shorter works of writer Andrew Vachss for *Dark Horse Comics*, plus an adaptation of Vachss' novel, *Blue Belle*. He is currently adapting Joe Lansdale's novel, *Dead in the West*, for Dark Horse.

Neal Barrett, Jr, his wife, Ruth, and their cat, Sue Jean, live in Fort Worth, Texas.

Neal Barrett, Jr
TONY RED DOG

Tony learns purely by accident the Scozarri brothers have taken out a girl he liked a lot then dumped her at a pet-food plant. The brothers work for the Tranalone family which is heavy into stuff like dog food and packing plants and anything that has to do with meat, so the guys who do legwork for Dominic Tranalone can drop off a stiff without driving out of town. Everybody on the street knows this is what they do, and anybody in the know buys their sausage and salami out of state. Tony figures what the brothers probably did was use the girl real bad before that. Leo and Lenny have warped ideas about social situations. Leo is mean, but Lenny's flat crazy in the head.

So Tony is mad as hell and out for blood. Nothing has pissed him off this much since the last remake of *Geronimo.* That girl was real fine and she treated Tony nice. She didn't ever tell an Indian joke or call him chief. She had a smile on her face and her hair smelled good all the time. She didn't have to end up like that.

Tony thinks about the girl all day. He can't keep his mind on the job. It isn't right. A thing like that is all wrong and he's got to set it straight. What he ought to do is drop everything and do it now. Find those assholes and get it off his mind. If he does, though, Sal will flat shit because it isn't authorized, and Mickey Ric will come down on Tony like a safe, and Tony doesn't need that. So he'll have to see Sal and Sal will have to go to Ric and Ric will have to ask the old man. Which he won't, because Mickey Ric wouldn't help Tony on a bet. If Tony Red Dog was on fire, Mickey Ricca wouldn't piss and put him out. Besides that, Bennie Fischetti's sent the word down he doesn't want any trouble with the Tranalone family right now, he doesn't want to rock the boat.

Which leaves Tony right where he is which is nowhere at all, and the Scozarri brothers are laughing up their sleeves. Tony gets so wound up in all this he boosts a sky-blue Caddy instead of the black he's supposed to get, which fucks up his orders for the day.

Tony finds Sal where anybody can, which is at the back table of the Donut Shoppe where Sal presides twenty-two hours every day. Sal doesn't do without sleep, but at three-hundred-sixty-two pounds it is easier to nap where he is than go to bed, and there's donuts and coffee close by.

Vinnie D. and Bobby Gallo are there, and Tony says hello. Bobby and Vinnie are never real far from Sal, and Tony sees they're getting fat too. All you got to do is look at Sal, you put on maybe two or three pounds.

'I got to talk to you, Sal,' Tony says. 'Something's happened.'

'I heard,' Sal says.

'I want to do 'em,' Tony says, getting right to the point. 'Those bastards got it coming.'

'Don't take everything personal,' Sal says.

This is what Tony figured that he'd say. 'Sal, I got a right. The Scozarri brothers knew I was seeing that girl. This is an embarrassment to me.'

Sal blinks like an owl and licks sugar off his lips. 'That's it right there,' he tells Tony. 'It's an embarrassment to you. It ain't business. It's a personal thing with you. You got the word same as me. No trouble. No hassle with the Tranalones.'

'You could ask,' Tony says, knowing how much good this will do. 'It isn't just me. It's a reflection on the family. Tell Mickey Ricca that.'

Sal pretends he's thinking this over, like he's making some real big decision in his head. He knows that's what a *capo* ought to do, that it lets the soldiers see he's on the ball. Sal 'Hippo' Galiano is a *capo* without a lot of clout, since boosting cars and hijacking trucks now and then isn't all that big a family deal. It's not like he's Nick Cannatella who's the *caporegime* for dope, a guy even Mickey Ricca respects.

So Sal finally blinks and says, 'Okay, I'll make a call. I'll check it out with Ric. I ain't making no promises, you understand.'

'Right,' Tony says, 'I appreciate it, Sal.' He knows what he did before he walked in the shop. That even if Sal gets the nerve to make the call, Mickey Ricca's going to turn him down flat, that right here's as far as it's going to go. That if something gets done, Tony's got to do it on his own.

Sal is watching Tony close and he knows what's in his head. 'Don't do anything stupid,' he says. 'You got a good job. Don't go and fuck it up. Find another broad. Take the day off. Have a little fun.'

'Sure,' Tony says, and even Vinnie D. can see that Tony doesn't mean that at all.

Sal looks Tony up and down. Takes in the alligator boots and the jeans, the black hair down to Tony's shoulders and the bandanna wrapped around his head. His mouth curls up like he's tasted something bad.

'Tony, listen,' he says, 'no fucking offense, okay? You got to dress like that? I mean, it's okay you're out in the sticks. You're attackin' the fucking wagontrain, fine. You're walking down the street here, nobody dresses like that, they got a suit. Vinnie and Bobby here, they got a suit. Anyone you see they got a suit.'

Tony looks at Sal. 'I'm not Vinnie D., I'm me, Sal. I got my blood. I got native ethnic pride.'

'Shit, I'm an ethnic too,' Sal says. 'You don't see me wearing no toga and a sword, I got a suit. Everybody's got a suit.' He digs in his vest and finds a bill and drops it on the table. 'Here's a C, okay? Get a suit. Get a nice suit. See Harry down at Gold's and do something with the hair. Tell him that the hair's on me.'

Tony picks up the bill, and Sal knows he's just tossed money down the drain, that Tony's not about to get a suit.

'Thanks,' Tony says. 'Ask Ric. Just ask him, okay?'

'I ain't promising a thing,' Sal says.

Tony's wrong about Sal. Sal calls Ric because he knows Tony's got a short fuse. He knows if Tony does something dumb that it's Sal Galiano that Ricca's going to see. So the call is to cover Sal's ass, and this tells Ric what he already knew, which is Sal can't cut it anymore. He's got to call and check, he can't handle it himself. Sal's a stand-up guy; he's got a lot of friends who moved up while Sal stayed where he was, and Ricca's got to think about that. He makes a note to find a club where Sal can put his name outside and someone else can do the work.

Tony's wrong about Mickey Ricca too. Ricca gives a lot of thought to what Tony wants to do. He knows he isn't going to let Tony make a hit. Not while the boss is trying to work this scam with the Tranalone family, which is mostly Mickey Ricca's idea. What Bennie Fischetti's telling Dominic Tranalone is they ought to squeeze the South Side blacks and split the territory up. That the black guys are getting too big and cutting into everybody's take, and not working through the families like they should. Dominic Tranalone hates blacks, so he's willing to talk to Bennie about that. What Tranalone doesn't know is that Bennie's been talking to the blacks on the side. He's going to use the blacks to squeeze the Tranalones out, and when he gets that done he'll put the black guys out of business too. So this is no time to start knocking off Tranalone guys, when everybody's supposed to be friends.

What Mickey Ricca's thinking is there ought to be a way to put Tony in the scam and also get the Indian off his back. He's got to be smart about this because it's Mickey Ricca's fault in a way that Tony Red Dog's where he is. Tony worked for Jackie Pinelli out in Phoenix, and did a favor Mickey couldn't overlook. What happened is, Charlie Franzone, who is Mickey Ricca's asshole brother-in-law, steals a car one night and rides around buck naked blowing coke. There's maybe three naked broads in the car which doesn't help. When the cops run him down, it turns out the car belongs to some big cheese up in vice. They throw the book at Charlie, and Mickey Ricca's wife is like crying all night and driving Mickey Ricca nuts. So Ricca calls Jackie Pinelli and Jackie talks to Tony Red Dog. Tony flies out to LA and boosts a bottle-green Jag and gets the papers and the numbers all straight, and drives back to Phoenix the next day. The Jag goes to a guy in the DA's office Jackie knows and the case against Charlie kind of falls in a hole and disappears. Ricca's wife stops crying and Ricca sends Charlie off to Texas somewhere and buys him a car-wash place, which he figures even Charlie Franzone can't possibly fuck up a whole lot. He sends Jackie five grand and asks Tony what he wants. Tony wants to come back east, he's tired of working in the sticks, and Ricca says fine, come ahead.

When he sees this guy he nearly shits, but he knows he can't send the guy back. Ricca owes Tony one and a debt is a debt. Which is partly why he hates Tony's guts and wants him out. Besides that, it's embarrassing to have a fucking Apache Indian working for the family. It don't look right. Ricca sees some guy, he goes to eat, this guy makes a fucking war whoop, or sticks a couple of fingers up for feathers on his head. It's a flat humiliation is what it is, and Ricca wants to put an end to that.

So he thinks about this then he thinks a little more, and then something starts working in his head. Thinking's what got him where he is—thinking sideways and inside out until he's got every angle covered right. Now he thinks he's got something worthwhile. Something he can use. The old man doesn't like to talk a whole lot, but Ricca thinks he'll want to talk about this.

Tony spends the morning boosting cars then takes the day off. With Sal's hundred bucks he buys a white leather jacket with a six-inch fringe. There's even fringe on the sleeves and some beadwork on the chest. The beadwork's Jersey Navajo but what the fuck. The jacket's worth five bills if you bought it in a store.

The rest of the day he drives around, hitting all the spots he knows where the sleazeball Scozarris might be. He drives real slow past the meat-packing plants and the dives that the Tranalones own. He hits the porno shops and a string of strip joints because he knows the Scozarris have a little piece of that.

It comes to him then that he's wasting all his time. It just hits him like that and he nearly rams a cab. What a fucking dope! He's driving all over sucking gas and these guys are somewhere in the sack. There's daytime business and there's stuff you do at night. Leo and Lenny are into night, and that's when Tony's going to find them on the street. What he needs to do now is go home and sleep himself. Get a drink and a steak and go to bed. Start out again about ten.

Before he goes home he makes one more pass along the streets. He doesn't see the Scozarris but he sees something else. At a place where the Tranalone family likes to eat, he sees a black stretch limo at the curb. Tinted glass and guys in black suits, and stepping out is Tommy 'Horse' Calise himself. Tony's impressed. Calise is *consigliere* to Dominic Tranalone, and one of the smartest guys around. You don't have to like a guy to admire the way he works.

Tony only gets a quick look and then Calise's inside, but he knows he's seen the Horse. You could go to a game there's maybe sixty thousand guys, you'd see the Horse right away. About six-foot-four, maybe one-forty-five soaking wet, and these eyes jammed up around his nose. Jesus, what a nose—it's a nose that could edge out any fucking nag at the track. Tony gets a look at a cute little number trailing right after Horse and he's got to laugh at that, because the nose isn't the only part that gave the Horse his name.

Bennie Fischetti is sitting in the dark. The room looks like a museum, the way Ricca figures that a museum ought to look. It's maybe ninety-six inside and the old man's got a sweater and a shawl. Ricca wonders what'll happen when he dies. Bennie's son Joey is the underboss now but he don't know shit about the business. The title makes Joey feel good. What Joey knows about is girls maybe twelve or thirteen. He's forty-three, he wears a suit and tennis shoes. So what's Bennie Fischetti going to do? Who's going to run the family when he's gone? Ricca knows it's got to be him, but he can't read the old man's mind. There isn't nobody on earth can do that.

'Don Fischetti, I don't wish to take your time,' Ricca says, 'but I feel this is something you ought to know. We've got this *soldato* works for Sal, his name's Tony Red Dog. You seen the guy once, he's got his hair down to here.'

The old man looks like he's awake, but Ricca isn't sure. He tells Fischetti how the Scozarris offed the girl and what Tony wants to do.

'The thing is,' Ricca says, 'this bimbo isn't really Tony's girl except maybe in his head. Tony sees a broad on the street he falls in love, that's his girl. What she was is a waitress turns tricks on the side out at Fatso DiCarlo's place, which is run by the Tranalone family. So the Scozarris, they were where they ought to be, and Tony's got no business in the place. What he's doing in there is sniffing after this broad. There's maybe two, three hundred places he could be, he's hanging out in a Tranalone dive. The guy's nuts.'

The old man looks at Ric. He doesn't move, he just looks. 'So why you bring this to me,' he wants to know. 'You are *consigliere*. I need to hear about an Indian? I don't need to hear about an Indian and a whore.'

'Right,' Ricca says quickly, 'this ain't about that but it is. What I got's an idea, and that's the thing you got to hear. It's a business idea is what it is.'

The old man seems to pay attention now. 'Maybe I will listen,' he says. 'Maybe I will hear this business thing.'

Tony drives around all night. He wonders if Leo and Lenny are laying low. Tony doesn't think they got the sense to do that. He asks a few questions, but he can't do a whole lot of that. The guys who got answers are the guys he can't ask. He drives by the strip joints and doesn't see a thing. He tries the packing plants again. He drives by diners and cafes, and it's light when he gets into bed. Okay fine, he'll try again. There's no big rush. They got to turn up, and he'll be there when they do.

It's after noon when he drops by again to see Sal. Sal doesn't ask why he isn't on the job. He sees the white jacket with the beads and he doesn't say a thing about that. He doesn't want to work Tony up, he wants to keep Tony cool.

'Hey, Tony,' Sal says, 'you're looking sharp. You had anything to eat? Vinnie, get Tony a couple of glazed.'

'I'm fine,' Tony says, and shakes his head no to Vinnie D. 'So you call Ric or what?'

'I said I'd call, right?' Sal says. 'So I called. Ricca says he fully understands. He says he knows how you feel.'

'So it's okay or not?'

Sal forgets he's trying to be nice. Fuck it, you can't be nice to this prick. 'Just listen, okay? You got no fucking manners. You got to talk, you don't listen to nobody else. Ric says he's going to get back. He says he knows you understand this ain't a good time. He says he don't like to see the Scozarris get away with this shit. He says he'll see what he can do.'

'When?' Tony says.

'When what?'

'When's he going to get back?'

This burns Sal up. He doesn't like Tony's attitude at all. 'Mickey Ricca gets back to you, pal, when Mickey Ricca wants to get back,' he tells Tony. 'That is fucking good enough for you. In the meantime, you keep your nose clean. You boost some cars for me like you're supposed to be doing right now. You don't do nothing else but that. You got that, Tony?'

'I got it, Sal.'

'Fine. You got it. I'm glad to hear you got it. I'm glad I'm getting through.'

'Maybe you should ought to try a smoke signal, Sal,' grins Vinnie D.

'Maybe I got a signal for you,' Tony says. He looks right at Vinnie D., and Vinnie doesn't smile anymore.

'Both of you, just shut the fuck up,' Sal says. He flips Tony a white envelope. 'From Ric. He wants you to have it.'

'What is it?'

'It's a Easter card,' Sal says. 'What you think it is? Go on, get some work done. You got a whole half a day.'

Sal watches Tony leave. He doesn't like what's going on at all. He wishes Indians would stay on the tube. He likes to watch them on the tube. They can't cause him any grief in there, they got their hands full with the Duke. What Mickey Ricca said to Sal was, 'Sal, you keep that crazy Indian on ice. Give him five bills from me. Make godamn sure he doesn't do something me and the old man don't want to hear. I'll be in touch. You stay where I can get you on the phone.'

Sal wonders where Ricca thinks he'll go. He never goes anywhere at all. So maybe Ricca thinks that's funny, it's a joke. So go fuck yourself, Sal thinks, but he doesn't think it aloud.

What Sal doesn't like about this is he knows who Ric is going to call if Tony gets out of line, and he figures that's exactly what Tony's going to do. So what's Sal going to do about that? Chase him down the street? The truth is, Tony Red Dog scares the shit out of Sal, and he figures maybe Tony knows it too.

Tony doesn't go back to work. He goes to a movie instead then walks down to Otto's for a steak. The envelope he's got has three hundred bucks from Mickey Ric. Which means Mickey Ric told Sal to give him five. Tony knows what it's for. Mickey Ricca's tossing him a bone. He's not going to do shit. He's going to tell him that he can't make the hit.

On one side of the coin, he sees maybe Mickey Ricca's right. Tony keeps his eyes open all the time. He knows more about the family business than a guy like Vinnie D. Sal sent him on a hijack deal once or twice with Daddy Jones, who's pretty high in the South Side blacks. Tony got along fine with Daddy Jones, who said he'd never seen a greaseball Indian before and even bought Tony a beer. So Tony knows the family's getting friendly with the blacks, and he knows there's got to be a reason why. Whatever that is, Tony figures the old man will end up on the top, and everyone else under that.

Tony understands all this and maybe Ricca's got a point, but it doesn't get Tony what he wants. He can't get the girl off his mind. That was an awful thing to do. About as bad as you can get. He can't let guys say the Indian's a real easy touch. You want to grind up his girl it's okay, he won't do a damn thing. Guys are talking like that, you can't show your face on the street. And if he waits for Mickey Ric, that's the way it's going to be.

While Tony is finishing off his steak, he looks up and spots a great looking broad across the room. He likes what he sees because the broad is looking right at him, too. He raises up his glass like he's seen in the movies and the girl seems to like that a lot. She likes it so much she leaves the bar and starts her way across the room. Tony likes the way she moves. She's built just right but she doesn't look cheap. She's taller than he thought and her dress is all black with no jewelry at all, like a girl in a fashion magazine. Her hair is classy too, real light blond and flipping up kind of cute on the ends.

She walks right up to his table. Just stands there and smiles. Doesn't say a thing. It hits Tony then and he stands up quick and gets her chair.

'I'm Jill,' the girl says.

'Right, I'm Tony,' Tony says. 'What do you like to drink?'

'White wine will be fine.'

Class, Tony thinks, and says, 'Hey, I'll have one of those too.'

She's got a little black purse like the dress. The purse is so little it couldn't hold a quarter and a dime.

'You're an Indian, right?' Jill says, this coming right out of left field. The way she says it, though, it doesn't turn him off.

'Yeah, I guess I am,' Tony says.

'What kind?'

'Mescalero Apache.'

'No kidding.'

'Hey, I ever lie to you before?'

The girl laughs. She's got kind of blue eyes, and one side of her mouth turns up like she's telling some joke to herself.

'I'm nuts about the jacket,' Jill says.

'It's nothin',' Tony says. 'I got better stuff than this. I go somewhere nice, I got a closet full of stuff. I bet I got a hundred shirts.'

'So you do that a lot?'

'Do what?'

'Go somewhere nice.'

Tony's getting the message straight. This doll is saying let's make a deal.

'Yeah,' Tony says. 'I been known to go out. I'm a fun kinda guy.'

'So what do you do?' Jill says.

'I'm in cars.'

'Buying or selling?'

'Just selling. No buying. And what about you?'

'I'm an actress,' Jill says.

'Oh, yeah?' This is maybe going to cost a little more, Tony thinks. A girl says 'actress' she isn't some hooker walks the street, she's got a place somewhere and the price is going to go through the roof.

'So look,' Tony says, 'you want to take off now, you want another drink, what?'

The little smile around her mouth disappears. 'Sorry,' she says, 'I guess I made a big mistake.'

'What? How come?' Tony doesn't get this at all.

'I shouldn't ever ought to do it,' Jill says. 'I mean you see a guy you like and say hello, that isn't going to work. You do that, the guy's for sure going to get the wrong idea. A girl can't do that 'cause the guy's going to think something else which is just what you're thinking right now.'

She reaches in her purse and gets a little gold pen and writes something on the napkin by her drink.

'Listen, I think you're a real nice guy,' she tells Tony with a smile. 'You change your mind, you want to think about me like you're not thinking now, you got my number there to call.'

She gets up and plants a kiss on his cheek, and Tony feels her hair brush his nose. He gets a little whiff of perfume then she's gone before he knows what to do.

Jesus, what kind of broad is this? Tony follows her out the door with his eyes. The most terrific looking girl he's ever seen and now she's gone. He feels kind of dizzy and he knows he didn't drink enough for that, he knows how to hold his booze. That's a crock about an Indian can't hold his booze, he can drink as good as anyone around. So he knows what it is, he doesn't have to think about it twice. It isn't just her bod, there's that too, but it's something more than that. He loves this girl is what it is. He doesn't even know her last name, but he knows he's got it bad.

First thing in the morning, Mickey Ricca's in the old man's Caddy, wishing he was still at home in bed. Don Fischetti doesn't hardly ever sleep, so when he's got to go out which is maybe twice a year, he's up and out at six. He's got a meet at noon he doesn't care. Drive around, he tells Danny, and Danny drives around.

The Caddy's all green outside and in. The old man likes green. Fischetti and Ric are in the back. Danny Fusco drives, and Bennie's son Joey's next to him. Joey's got egg on the back of his shirt. Egg, and a little crumb of toast. How did the dummy do that? Ricca thinks. How the fuck can a guy get breakfast on his back?

'The thing with Tranalone,' Bennie says, 'the thing with him, he likes to talk. Dominic likes to talk. Listen, let him say what he's got to say. It don't mean a thing, you got to listen all the same.'

'That's the way he is,' Ric agrees. 'I seen him do it all the time. He'll start on something, he's off on something else. He gets done, you don't know what he said.'

'Horse,' Bennie says. 'Horse is the guy you want to watch. What Horse Calise says, Dominic is thinking in his head. Tranalone talks an hour and a half. Horse says maybe two words. Two words, that's all you got to know.'

'The Horse is smart,' Ricca says. 'You got to give him that. I wouldn't put the guy down.'

'You do, and you make a big mistake,' Bennie says. 'Anyone sees through the scam that's Horse. Dominic, he isn't going to see. You talk, you don't have the time to think.'

The old man leans back and takes a nap. Danny drives around. The Caddy gets six, maybe seven miles a gallon, so Ric figures he's got to stop for gas. Joey likes to ride; he sees some grade-school girl on a bike, and watches till she gets out of sight.

'The thing with the Indian,' Bennie says.

'It's okay,' Ricca says.

'I don't need a problem,' Bennie says. 'You got a guy he's black or maybe red. Maybe he's a Chink. You got a problem's what you got.'

'You got my word, Don Fischetti,' Ricca says.

'That Joey,' Bennie says, giving Ric a nudge. 'Always got his nose in a book. He don't read no junk he's reading high-class stuff. He's reading something all the time.'

Ricca's seen Joey read. Joey's got a stack of *Classic Comics* on the seat.

'Hey, you gotta be proud,' Ricca says.

Tony doesn't sleep at all. He knows he ought to look for the Scozarris but he sits around the room. He can't watch TV. He doesn't want to eat. What he wants to do is call up the girl but it's the middle of the night. He wants to call her up now and tell her how he knows he's been a jerk. They can go somewhere and talk. Eat anywhere she wants. He won't try nothing funny, he won't even touch her till they know each other for a week. Jesus, he hopes she won't hold him to that.

He gets out early on the job. If he's working, he won't have to think about calling up the girl. He's afraid if he does she'll turn him down. She said he could call, but that doesn't mean she won't turn him down.

He's got a special order he's got to fill—Porsches, and they got to be showroom new. This kind of car's not as common as your Chevys or your Fords, but Tony gets the job done quick. Cars are like people, Tony knows; they like to hang around their own kind. So he hits some classy tennis courts and a couple of country clubs, and by noon he's got five stashed in Dio's garage, ready for the guys to go to work. Even Dio's impressed, but Tony doesn't care about that. What he cares about is calling up the girl.

Jill doesn't say no she says yes. Tony can't believe his luck. She says fine, she'll go out tonight if Tony wants, if Tony's got his act together and intends to treat her right. Tony says great, that's the way it's going to be. Jill tells him that she'll meet him at eight and tells him where.

Tony thinks about an hour what to wear. He wants to wear the white jacket with the beads but she's seen that before. He wears that, she'll think he don't have nothing else. He goes through everything he's got and ends up in his blue ostrich boots and a western-cut suit. The suit's kind of off-yellow white and there's a rattlesnake stitched on the back. The snake's got a genuine rattle sewn on with simulated ruby eyes. He looks in the mirror and he figures this will knock her on her ass.

The place where Jill says to meet her is a bar called 'A Streetcar Named Michelle'. Tony doesn't care much for bars with funny names. They usually got funny-looking people inside. Fags in tight pants and broads with purple hair. So he's glad to see this isn't that kind of place at all. There are people here in jeans and running shoes, and people in businessman suits. A girl in a waitress outfit and a guy in greasy coveralls, like the guys down at Dio's garage. There's maybe a couple of fags but not a lot of funny hair.

Jill spots him and makes her way through the crowd, and Tony goes weak in the knees. Christ, she looks great. A white woolly sweater and a skirt and nice heels. She's got something sparkly in her hair and her eyes are bright as Christmas tree lights.

'Hi,' Jill says, 'say, I *love* those boots. Tony, you look *out*standing.'

'Hey, so do you,' Tony says. 'Listen, you ain't seen the back of the suit.' Tony turns around and Jill lets out a kind of shriek and says she's never seen anything like that before, and Tony's glad he had the sense to dress right.

Jill pulls him through the crowd and introduces him to everyone she knows, which includes some terrific looking broads. Everyone there is an actor or an actress, Jill says, only mostly they're doing something else. Tony has a few drinks, and starts to like everyone he meets. They don't talk like real people do but he likes them all the same.

And later on when they're out in the car trying to figure where to eat, Jill scoots in close and leans her head on his arm and Tony figures this is going to work. The girl's high class but she's got to come around. A nice dinner and that wine she likes to drink he's going to have her in the sack.

'So tell me about yourself,' Jill says.

'There isn't anything to tell,' Tony says.

'Come on, sure there is.' She gives him a little toy hit that warms his heart. 'Like, where'd you grow up?'

Tony doesn't like to talk about this but he does. 'Arizona. On the Fort Apache Indian Reservation.'

'Not good, huh?' She can tell that easy by his voice.

'It was okay, I guess.'

'I don't think it was.'

'Yeah, well you're right.'

'So you got out of that.'

'When I was fourteen, maybe fifteen. Something like that. Worked on a couple of ranches and other stuff.'

'Then you got into cars.'

'Right. Tucson and Phoenix. All over.'

'And then you came here.'

'Yeah. And then up here.' Tony figures maybe that's about enough. 'Look, what do you like to eat? Steak, seafood. You name it.'

'Seafood's fine,' Jill says.

'Terrific,' Tony says, glad to talk on something that's not about him. 'There's a place over on the east side, they got lobster they ship in fresh. They got 'em swimming in a tank.'

'Hey, great,' Jill says. 'I haven't had a—*Jesus*, Tony!'

Jill has to slam her hands on the dash because Tony's suddenly turned the car around in the middle of the street. Guys are honking and yelling but Tony don't hear anyone at all. He just pulls up and stops because right there's the cream-colored Buick Lenny drives, parked at a Rodeway Inn. Christ, what's he going to do? He's got Jill in the car and everything's going real fine. If he dumps her off now he isn't going to get her back. If he waits and comes back, the Scozarris are going to maybe be gone.

'Look,' he tells Jill. 'I'll be right back. Sit tight, it's okay.'

'What's going on?' Jill says. 'What're you going to do?' She maybe looks a little scared.

Tony puts on an easy smile. 'I seen a car back there. A guy owes me for the car. The guy's a deadbeat. You got to get these guys when you can.'

'Yeah, right,' Jill says, and doesn't look like she's buying this at all.

Tony gives her a wink and gets out and shuts the door. He stops for a minute at the trunk and gets a sawed-off pump and an old potato sack and puts the gun in the sack and walks back to the Rodeway Inn.

He doesn't know if they parked the car right before their door but his luck is running good. Leo opens up the door when Tony knocks and Tony jams the shotgun in his face.

Leo looks sick, like he might throw up.

'Inside,' Tony says, and looks around fast to find Lenny. He can hear the shower going and that's another lucky break.

'It's about that fuckin' girl,' Leo says.

'Sit down,' Tony says, and Leo sits.

'So let's talk,' Leo says.

'Let's not,' Tony says. He picks up a cushion from the couch and tosses it in Leo's lap. Leo grabs the cushion and looks surprised and Tony jams the shotgun up against the cushion and there isn't hardly any noise at all. Tony pockets the empty shell and peeks in the bathroom door and the room is full of steam. He goes in and opens up the shower door. Lenny is all lathered up. He's hairy as a dog. There's a little more noise this time but not much because Lenny's pretty fat. Tony turns off the water and makes sure he's got both empties in his pocket. He wipes down the gun with a towel and leaves it on the sink and takes a look at his watch. Three, maybe four minutes. He's sorry Lenny didn't get to see who it was but Tony can't complain. One more thing to do and he's gone. Hey, the night's turning out great.

It's not hardly morning when the phone wakes him up. He grabs it without even looking and Sal says, 'Listen, I got a message from Ric you're going to like. Ric says it ain't a good time but he thinks you got a right. This is a personal favour from Mickey Ric is what it is.'

Tony sees Jill's kicked off the covers and the sun's making stripes across her back, but Sal's got his full attention now.

'You're saying Ric don't mind,' Tony says. 'It's okay.'

'What the fuck you think,' Sal says. 'I gotta say it twice? A couple of the guys, they seen the car. It's at a Rodeway Inn past the loop. You get off your ass you'll catch 'em cold.'

It's warm in the room, but Tony feels a chill. 'Right,' he says, trying to keep what he's thinking to himself. 'That's great, Sal. I appreciate the call.'

'So get it done,' Sal says. 'Do it now. I don't want to hear you complaining no more. Get it done. And hey, I want to see you here at three-forty-five.'

'Why three-forty-five?' Tony says.

'Why the fuck not?' Sal says, and hangs up.

Tony sits on the bed and looks at the phone. Like maybe Sal will say something else. Something that will stop the empty feeling in his gut.

Jill sits up and stretches and looks at her watch. 'My God, I got to get to work,' she says. 'Who was that on the phone?'

'Get up,' Tony says. 'Get dressed.' He's still looking at the phone.

'Huh? What's with you?'

'Just do it. Hurry up.' Tony's pulling on his pants and looking for his boots. Jill is standing there naked still looking half asleep. She looks great. Tony wonders why you got to do stuff that you don't want to do when you'd rather be doing something else.

'You mind telling me what?' Jill says. She looks even better with her hands on her hips.

'Let's go,' Tony says. 'Get somethin' on.'

'Last night it was get something off.'

'Last night ain't today,' Tony says, and starts picking up her clothes off the floor.

Tony's slamming gears and Jill is still complaining. She's got the mirror down, and trying to get her lipstick straight and Tony's taking corners like he might make the Indy this year.

'I don't care for your lousy driving style,' Jill says.

'I'm driving just fine,' Tony says.

'I lose my job I am moving in with you,' Jill says. 'I got to have some breakfast, Tony. I'm no good I don't eat. Just let me out here. Let me out I'll get a cab.'

'Listen, I got a problem,' Tony says. 'What I got is deep shit. I got to think. I don't got the time to eat.'

'Okay, fine. That's fine,' JIll says. The way Tony looks, the way he talks, says now is a real good time to keep quiet and hope Tony doesn't run into a truck.

In a minute Tony stops and makes a call. Twenty minutes after that he pulls up behind the South Side Bowl-O-Lot and stops. There's another car there, a red Caddy with a lot of extra chrome. Tony doesn't say a thing to Jill. He takes the keys and gets out and walks across to the other car.

Daddy Jones is standing by the Caddy. He looks like a spider in a Panama suit. Big shades, and a lot of white teeth.

'Listen, I got trouble,' Tony says.

'I expect you do,' says Daddy Jones. 'Going to happen, you working for the white-eyes, man. Them treaties don't mean shit.'

'You want to hear this or not?' Tony says. Daddy Jones is too cool. Nothing bothers Daddy Jones and that irritates Tony a lot.

'My meter running, babe,' says Daddy Jones.

Tony talks. Daddy Jones listens. After a while, Daddy Jones listens real good. When Tony's through, Daddy Jones thinks a long time.

'Keemo-sahby, this real heavy shit,' says Daddy Jones.

'Tell me about it,' Tony says.

'Got to talk to my man. Won't tell you a thing before I do.'

'I know that. I know you got to do that.'

Daddy Jones takes off his shades and looks Tony in the eye. 'Man, you best be hittin' me straight. This better not be no jive.'

'I am in enough shit without messing around with you,' Tony says.

'I hear that,' says Daddy Jones. He gives Tony a card with a number on the back. Tony goes back to his car.

Jill doesn't say a thing. She smokes and takes turns crossing one leg over the next. Tony drives a few blocks and then finds another phone. He calls Bennie Fischetti at his home. He knows Bennie doesn't take any calls, but some guy will give the old man his name.

Tony gets back in the car. He doesn't drive and he doesn't look at Jill.

'Okay, look,' Tony says. 'Who you doing this for? Who you supposed to call?'

For a minute Jill doesn't say a thing. Then she looks at Tony real surprised. 'Tony, what are you talking about? You lost me there, hon.'

Tony reaches over and holds her chin straight, not hard or anything, just enough so she doesn't turn away. 'Listen,' he says, 'I'm not a bad guy, and maybe you'd have come on to me anyway, okay? Maybe not. But too much funny shit is happening to me, and I figure it's got to be you. I like you a lot. I'm not going to do nothing to you, all right? I ain't even mad. But you're going to have to tell me how it is.'

'Oh, Jesus, Tony.' Jill looks like she's going to cry. Tony lets her go.

'Sal or Mickey Ricca?' Tony says.

'Sal,' Jill says. Her eyes are getting wet and she reaches up with a finger and wipes her cheek. 'I hate this shit, you know? I had to. He didn't give me any choice.'

'I know that,' Tony says. 'So what are you supposed to do?'

'Sal said it was a joke.'

'Yeah it is. It's on me.'

'Sal, he—all I know is he's supposed to call you this morning and tell you something to do. I don't know what. I don't know a thing about that. I guess that was him on the phone.'

'He knew you'd be at my place.'

Jill looks at her hands. 'I wanted to be there anyway, Tony. You don't have to believe that but it's true.'

'So what else?'

'He's going to call me at home. About noon. I'm supposed to tell him what I think you're going to do, anything I heard you say, which is nothing, by the way.' She looks at Tony now. She's glad this is over, and Tony doesn't have to prompt her anymore. 'Tomorrow night Sal says I hit these clubs and bars and like I'm supposed to be all swacked out, you know? Boozed up. And I let on as how I was with you today and I saw you—do something. I don't even know what. Sal's supposed to tell me that.'

'Jesus . . . ' Tony lets out a breath. It's about like he figured only worse. That godamn Ricca's thought the whole thing out. Even down to Jill spreading the word at some Tranalone bar that he's hit the Scozarris. Just a little extra insurance which is Ric all the way.

Whatever, the guy is going to nail it down and you got to give him that. And then Jill sort of drops out of sight like forever, only Jill doesn't know about that, which is something Sal sort of left out. Everything's falling into place and he knows why Sal said 3.45, and this burns Tony up, because this is the time Mickey Ricca gets a shave and a shine every day down at Gold's, which is close to the donut shop. The son of a bitch wants to watch. He wants to sit in his barber chair and watch Tony go, he wants the fun of doing that.

Tony thinks for a minute but he knows this is what he's got to do, that he's got to trust the girl, and he's not too worried once he tells her how Ricca don't exactly plan to keep her around.

'Okay, look,' Tony says, 'I'm going to lay this out on the line. Don't ask a bunch of dumb questions, just listen.'

Tony tells her how he works for Sal and Ric and the Bennie Fischetti family, which he figures that she already knows, and how he had this beef with the Scozarris only Ric wouldn't let him work it out.

'So when Sal calls this morning and says fine, go ahead,' Tony says, 'I know right off I been fucked. If Ric says fine I'm set up and I know what Ric's going to do. I hit the Scozarris then Ric hits me. See, this makes the old man look good. The hit ain't business, so Bennie makes it up to the Tranalones and they figure how Bennie's getting old and ain't strong anymore and really wants to make peace. So the Tranalone family gets sucked in good and goes to sleep while Bennie makes a deal with the blacks. What you gotta understand is I ain't even a big player in this. What I am is a little extra angle for Mickey Ric. He looks good with the boss and he gets me out of his hair. Which is what he's been wanting all along because he don't want an Indian working for the family. This is no big news to me. This I already know.'

'Oh, my God.' Jill bites her lip and looks as if she might cry again. 'So what are you going to do? I mean, there's got to be—' Her face brightens up like she's just had a great idea. 'Tony. Tony, look—if you *don't* do anything to these Scozarri people, Ricca's plan won't work! Don't you see?' She reaches out and holds his hand tight. 'I mean, you get out of town right now, Tony, we could do that together, we do that and nothing's going to happen at all. Tony, I'd really like that. Honest. I really would.'

'Yeah, well we got a little problem there,' Tony says. He tells her how this is maybe not such a good idea since he's already done the

Scozarris only nobody knows about that so it's going to be hard to back out.

'You what?' Jill looks kind of white. 'When—when did you do that?'

Tony tells her when and she looks like she might get sick, either that or maybe hit him in the face.

'My God, what the hell kind of thing is that to do you got a date,' she wants to know. 'You take a girl out, the very first date you do that. I cannot *believe* this.'

'Listen, it kind of came up,' Tony says. 'Something comes up that's what you got to do.'

Jill doesn't want to talk. She turns away and looks out the front and does things with her lips, and Tony knows a broad does that there's no use trying to make her talk.

Tony gets her calmed down and then stops at a drive-in spot and gets her a breakfast to go. Jill feels better after that, so he tells her what it is they've got to do. Jill listens and it's clear she doesn't like this at all. What she'd really like to do is pack a bag and leave town. Catch a plane to LA or Mexico and dye her hair. Change her name to Mary Smith. She knows that's not how it's going to be. If she goes along with Sal which she doesn't want to do she's got a real short weekend ahead. With Tony Red Dog she's got a chance. Not a whole lot because Tony's full of crazy ideas that won't work but it's too late to think about that.

Tony lets her off at her apartment and makes sure he's got her phone number right.

'Take it easy,' he says. 'Do what you got to do you'll be fine. You're going to be just fine.'

Jill gives him a look. 'Don't you tell me I'll be fine. Don't you say that to me.'

'Okay I won't.'

Tony starts to drive off, and Jill leans in the window and plants a nice kiss on his mouth. 'You're going to be just fine,' Jill says.

'Yeah, right,' Tony says.

He leaves her there and goes half a mile and stops at a booth to call Bennie Fischetti again. The old man won't talk, but the word will get through that he called. Now he's got to wait. It isn't even noon, he's got to wait. Drive around and get back to Jill and check in with Daddy Jones and then drive around some more. He thinks about Sal and Mickey Ric and how this is going to go down, but mostly he thinks about Jill. She's got a smile that won't quit and she's great in the sack but he isn't much in love anymore. Some but not a lot. She really set him up good and he can understand that, but this kind of takes the shine off of things. Like they maybe can't really hit it off. This really brings him down and he doesn't want to think about that, he's got a lot of shit to do.

Tony pulls up at the donut shop right at 3.45. Everything looks fine. It looks like an ordinary day. Inside, Sal is sitting in the back. He's got donut powder on his mouth, he's got coffee down his shirt. Bobby Gallo and Vinnie are there too. Bobby Gallo gives Tony a grin. Vinnie D. tries to look like there's nothing going down, but Vinnie's not smart enough for that.

'Hey, Tony,' Sal says, and even Sal's got a smile. 'Have a seat, you want a glazed?'

Tony sits. He knows he's okay, it's not going to happen here.

'So listen,' Sal says, and leans as close to the table as he can. 'How'd it go, you get it done?'

'Right after breakfast,' Tony says.

Sal gets a kick out of this. He's shaking all over which is something else to see.

'Jesus. Right after breakfast,' Sal says. He's spitting donut powder on his shirt. 'Leo and Lenny. Like brushing your teeth, huh, Tony? Huh? Huh?'

Sal laughs and looks at Bobby and Vinnie D., and they think this is the funniest thing they ever heard. Boy, everyone's having a lot of fun, Tony thinks, and he sees how Bobby and Vinnie D. are kind of edging past Sal, Vinnie pretending he's got to sneeze, and Bobby going back for more glazed, which puts them both right behind Tony's chair. These guys are smooth, Tony thinks. These guys are slick as Goofy and Donald Duck.

Now Sal's not laughing anymore. Nothing's funny now that Vinnie and Bobby Gallo are where they ought to be.

'Tony, we got to talk,' Sal says.

'Fine,' Tony says. 'You told me to be here, Sal, so here I am.'

Sal shakes his head. 'Not here.'

'Not here what?'

'I mean this ain't where you and me got to talk.'

Tony tries to look puzzled and surprised. 'Sal, just what the fuck is this? You want to tell me what? I'm not any good at playing games.'

Sal looks at Tony, serious and kind of sad, only Tony knows the sad isn't real.

'You carrying, Tony?' Sal wants to know.

'No I'm not carrying,' Tony says. 'Should I be?'

Sal looks at Bobby Gallo, and Bobby says, 'Stand up, Tony, okay?' He says it real nice.

Tony stands and lets Bobby shake him down.

'Jesus Christ, Sal,' Tony tries to look scared. 'You're not gonna do me. Listen, what the hell for?'

'Nothing personal, Tony,' Sal says. 'It's business. It's just business is all.'

'Fuck that,' Tony says. 'Hey. Whatever this is we can work something out.'

'If I could do that, Tony, I would,' Sal says. 'There ain't nothing I can do.'

And then Tony sees something that he's never seen before. He can't hardly believe what he sees which is Sal Galiano getting up. Jesus, it's worth getting hit to see that. There probably aren't four or five guys ever seen this before. This is not your plain everyday standing up. This is a major operation. This is a dumb Jap movie where the lips and the sound don't match; this thing's coming up from the mud, it's going to fuck up Tokyo good, it's going to dump a bunch of donuts on the Japs. Tony knows it wasn't Sal's idea, that Mickey Ric told Sal he had to handle this himself, but Tony feels pretty good. How many guys have got Sal Galiano on his feet?

When they get in Sal's car, Tony in back with Bobby Gallo, Sal up front with Vinnie D., Tony feels a little lump in his gut. He's felt okay until now. Now he don't feel right at all. He's thinking how he's screwed himself good. He's thinking maybe half a dozen things can go wrong, and he'll have to try to grab Bobby's piece, which Bobby's not about to let him do. He's thinking maybe Jill had the right idea: Get out of town and don't fuck with Mickey Ric. Instead here he is watching Sal take up the front seat and squeezing Vinnie out the door.

'Sal, listen' Tony says, 'I got to make a call. You got to let me make a call.'

This gets a laugh from up front. 'You got to be kidding,' Sal says.

'I'm kidding, a time like this? Sal, I got to make a call. I got to talk to Bennie Fischetti. That's who I gotta call.'

'You're stalling,' Sal says. 'Shit, I'd do the same thing if I was you. I'd do the same thing. Tony, the old man ain't going to help. You got to learn to relax. That's what you want to do. Don't think about nothing at all. It won't take a minute, it's over like that.'

'Relax,' Tony says.

'That's the thing to do. That's the best thing to do.'

Tony sees they're going up First, past the pawn shops and the bum hotels toward the freeway east and out of town. He knows where they're going, he knows the way they got to take. He and Bobby Gallo and Vinnie have been out there once before, when Eddie Pliers got greedy with the skim. The Tranalone family's got their meat packing plants; Bennie Fischetti's got a marsh. The Minellis had the marsh before that, which means there's stiffs out there from like 1922, and it's not a good place to stop and fish, you don't know what you'll maybe catch.

'You got to let me call,' Tony says. 'Fuck, it's not going to cost you a thing, I'm paying for the call. Sal, I got to talk to the old man. I got to do that.'

'What for?' Sal wants to know. Or maybe he doesn't care, he's got nothing else to do.

'I can't say what for.'

'So don't.'

Tony seems to think about that. 'Okay. It's about Mickey Ricca. That's what it's about.' They're passing Eighth. They're passing through a neighborhood's going to the dogs, half the buildings empty, a few sleazy bars, stores going out of business every day.

Sal turns his neck around as far as it will go, which is maybe half an inch. 'What you want to do back there is relax,' Sal says. 'You don't want to be thinking up shit because it isn't going to do you no good. Okay? Just shut the fuck up. Think about a broad. Something. Don't talk.'

'You hear what I gotta say,' Tony says, 'you're not going to say don't talk. You're going to thank me is what you're going to do. You're going to say, hey, thanks, Tony. This is what you're going to do.'

'Shut the fuck up,' Sal says.

'Yeah, right.'

'So what about Ric?'

'Forget it. It's got to be the old man.'

'Fuck you,' Sal says. 'We'll do a seance thing. Bobby knows a gypsy broad. You can talk to the old man then.'

Vinnie thinks this is a riot, and Bobby does too. They're coming up on Seventeenth and the Freeway's six, maybe seven blocks away, and Tony's thinking, shit, this is it, it isn't coming down and I'm feeding the fish. I been set up twice, and both times by the same fucking broad. And then they pass Nineteenth and here's a Caddy pulled up by a cigar store with a window patched up with silver tape, and coming out of this store is Daddy Jones. Daddy Jones and Tommy 'Horse' Calise. Daddy Jones, the Horse, and Mickey Ric.

'Holy shit, look at that!' Vinnie says, and slows the car and stares at what he sees.

'Jesus,' Sal says, 'keep driving. Don't stop the fucking car.' Sal looks at Mickey Ric and Mickey Ric looks back, and it's hard to say who's staring harder at who. Daddy Jones ducks his head. Horse tries to turn away, tries to get back in the store, but there's no mistaking Horse. Now the car's past and there's nothing else to see and nobody says a thing. There isn't anything to say except the two *consiglieres* of the two biggest families in town are standing back there together with the number two South Side black. Standing there like asshole buddies which is not the kind of thing you want to see.

'I'm talking, you don't listen.' Tony says. 'I got to make a call, you say, Tony, you ain't making any call.'

'Call,' Sal says. 'Vinnie, find a phone. The guy's got to make a call.'

Mickey Ricca tells the old man this is all a bunch of crap. It wasn't Horse at all it was some other guy, and anyway the colored had a piece in his hand all the time. He had a piece in his hand and Ricca couldn't do a thing. The fuckers pick him up, he's on the way to get a shine, he can't do a damn thing, and this Indian's behind all this is who it is.

Bennie Fischetti's old, he's not dumb. It could happen just the way Ricca says and it looks kind of fishy, hell it stinks is what it does, Sal and these guys are passing by and there's Calise and the black and Mickey Ric, they just happen to walk out of this store, and who's going to buy something like that?

Only Bennie can't see how the Indian could be that stupid, he sets up a deal like this any kid could see through. An Indian's smart, he's got cunning in his blood. A deer shits somewhere he can follow it for miles. An Indian can sneak up on a fort. You don't even know he's there. And the Indian tried to call. He tried to call him all day. Bennie knows about that. And Sal Galiano, he saw the whole thing, Sal swears it was the Horse, how's a guy mistake the Horse?

And of course that's the thing, Bennie can't check it out with the Horse, he can't ask. The Horse wouldn't give Bennie the time of day. Anything's wrong in the Fischetti family, fine. That's fine with Horse Calise and Dominic Tranalone. And he can't ask the colored. What a colored's going to do he's going to lie. That's what your colored's got to do.

So Bennie don't know, he's got no way to get to the truth. What he knows is if Ric's talking straight he's let the Indian set him up. A guy fucks up once he can maybe do it twice and Bennie doesn't like to wait for that. A guy gets careless, he can bring you down quick. So maybe Ric's clean this time, he's maybe not. He's clean today so tomorrow's something else. Mickey Ric's a good man and Mickey's smart, but a guy that smart doesn't like to stay down he likes to move, and the way he likes to move is up. Besides, Bennie's thinking how Ric hasn't ever treated Joey good at all. Benny knows the kid's not bright, but Ric could show him some respect. Ric laughs at Joey and this is something Ric shouldn't ought to do.

Bennie calls in Nick Cannatella who's the *caporegime* for dope. He gives Nick a glass of wine and has a talk; when Nick leaves, he's the Fischetti family's new *consigliere*. Nick's a guy who's always treated Joey nice and he's got the whole family's respect.

Bennie sends Sal to Minnesota, where the family's getting heavy into cheese, a job where Sal won't have a lot to do and if he does he's got Bobby and Vinnie D. to help. Tony Red Dog gets Sal's old job, and now he's *caporegime* for hijacking trucks and heisting cars. Bennie gives Tony five Gs because he likes Tony's style, and Tony gives two of this to Jill who finds a sudden need for Caribbean sun. Tony gives a grand to the actor guy Jill dug up to play the Horse, which he did real fine, considering Horse isn't the easiest guy to do.

Bennie feels kind of bad when he's got to tell Ric the bad news; hey, a guy's got his faults, he's been around a long time, he's done a job. Bennie tells Ric it's nothing personal, it's business is what it is, he wants Ric to see it that way. Bennie tells Danny Fusco to use the green Caddy, the one Bennie likes best, he wants Ric to know how he feels.

The first day on his new job, Tony spots a girl named Cecile, she works in a club down the street. Cecile's got a bod that won't quit and black eyes, and Tony knows he hasn't really ever been in love before. In spite of Cecile's great shape she cashiers in the club and don't take nothing off, and Tony's got to respect her for that.

He's been the new *capo* for two, maybe three or four days, he makes sure the guys on the street know Tony Red Dog pays his debts, this is something he feels he's got to do. He's got an idea what, because something's smelling ripe in the trunk and he remembers what it is. So he takes the potato sack out and finds a box and gets some real nice paper to wrap it up, and mails the scalps he took from the Scozarris to Dominic Tranalone. Of course he checks this out with Don Fischetti first, and Bennie, who don't think a whole lot is funny, gets a real laugh out of this, and thinks the Indian guy is okay. Listen, for a red colored guy he's okay.

MICHAEL A. BLACK was born in Chicago in 1949. A particularly shy child, his father thought it was wise to teach him the rudiments of fighting and to enrol him in a judo/karate school. This overcame the problem of school bullies and began a life-long appreciation for physical fitness and martial arts.

Black enlisted in the US Army and became a Military Policeman. Upon discharge, he worked as a security guard and taught karate until joining the police department in Matteson, Illinois, where he remains today. He has written several novels, and has had short stories and non-fiction articles published.

Michael A. Black
The Savant

'You see, Mr Shade,' Carole Snow said, pushing up on her glasses. 'Vincent is an autistic savant. Are you familiar with the term?'

She watched me carefully as I nodded. The oval-shaped lenses had a faint blue tint, obscuring her eyes slightly. I placed her in her late twenties, but, with her hair pulled back in a tight bun, she looked older.

'How long's your brother been missing?'

'Since the day before yesterday,' she answered. 'I know that doesn't seem like a real long time, but he's incapable of taking care of himself.' Her hands tightened around each other. 'I hope I didn't make a mistake putting him in that place, but after our parents died last year, there was just no way that I could work and take care of him.'

'This place?' I asked, picking up the Witherspoon Institute brochure.

She nodded and continued. 'When Mom and Dad were alive Vincent stayed at home. Mom would always make sure he had his medicine. He's prone to seizures, and can get very upset if something varies from his routine.'

'Upset? You mean violent?'

'Yes, but that usually doesn't occur often. But it increases my concern that something dreadful could happen if he isn't found right away.'

'I'll certainly do my best,' I said. 'Do you have a picture?'

'Yes,' she said, handing me a photograph. I looked at it.

Two older people I assumed were her parents were both huddled close to Vincent, who seemed to be looking off into space at an odd angle. Carole stood to one side, separated from the other three.

'Nothing more recent? Or larger?'

'I'm afraid not,' she said. 'Perhaps the Institute could provide one. Now, you'll call me as soon as there's any news, won't you?' She stood and smoothed out her dress. 'I work late at the library every night but Wednesday and Saturday. And Sunday, too, of course.'

'Of course,' I said, standing to go.

The Witherspoon Institute loomed massively as I rounded the turn and drove up the sweeping driveway. It looked more like some country estate than a mental hospital, except for the high cyclone fence strung with three strands of barbed-wire. The huge, three-story brick structure was barely visible through the large, efflorescent trees that were scattered liberally over the well-maintained grounds. Inside it looked clean and modern. Each floor had rooms attached to a central hub in spoke-like patterns. The Chief Administrator, Mr Kamen, told me how badly he felt about Vincent's disappearance and promised to help me in whatever way possible.

'I could use a facial photograph, if you've got one,' I said.

'I'm sure we can arrange that,' he smiled. 'Our photo department can duplicate one for you now.' Picking up the phone, he dispatched the secretary.

'What can you tell me about his disappearance?'

Kamen's brow wrinkled. 'We have had walk-aways from time to time. Usually it's what we term the runaway EMH cases—that's Educable Mentally Handicapped. Vincent fitted into this category. Basically, he left the hospital grounds sometime Tuesday night around six. The nurse noticed him missing, but failed to report it until eight. Naturally, he's been suspended, pending an investigation.'

'I'd like to speak to him. Can you give me his address?'

Buenoventura Marcos, the nurse, lived a few miles away in an adjacent suburb. Mr Kamen told me that Dr Wilson, Vincent's principal psychiatrist, wouldn't be in till three. I drove over to see Marcos.

The apartment building, set in a row of similar structures, looked rather run down. Several young kids played on the remnants of some grass under a watchful mother's eye. I hit Marcos's button and told him who I was. When the buzzer sounded I noticed that the security door wouldn't even lock.

Marcos was one of those small, dark-skinned Filipinos. He looked to be around thirty, and shook hands deferentially as he invited me inside. The place was clean and orderly. A small-screen TV sat on top of a coffee table. The furniture was definitely secondhand.

'Mr Kamen told me that there was a time delay reporting Vincent missing,' I said.

Marcos frowned. 'Kamen's looking for a scapegoat,' he said bitterly. 'We're really short handed at the hospital, but instead of admitting it, he suspends me.'

'That may explain why Vincent was able to wander off, but why did you wait so long before reporting him missing?'

'Well, like I said, we're usually short on Tuesday nights. I'm by myself on that floor from five till eleven. Dr Wilson usually took Vincent over to the art studio every evening at six.' He blinked twice before continuing. 'I was busy with another patient, and when I saw Vincent gone I assumed Wilson had him. Later I found out that Wilson had left on some kind of personal emergency. By that time . . . ' he shrugged.

'How did you find that out?'

'One of the security guards checked the studio for me. The gate guard remembered Dr Wilson leaving in his van real fast about six-fifteen.' His dark brown eyes studied me intently. 'Mr Shade, you think you'll be able to find him soon? This suspension's gonna finish me if this thing doesn't get straightened out.'

'Where would Vincent go?' I asked. 'Any ideas?'

He sighed and rubbed his fingers around his mouth. 'Hard to say. He was pretty reclusive. About the only time I remember him going anywhere was when Dr Wilson would take him to the Art Museum.'

'Vincent liked art?'

'Oh yeah, he's very gifted.' Marcos shook his head. 'It's just so hard to imagine him wandering off like that.'

On the way back to the Institute I stopped off at the local Police Department. The detective assigned the case was named Williams. He told me candidly that about all they could do was put Vincent in the computer as a missing person and hope for the best. A check of the area had been made the night he disappeared, followed by a more comprehensive search the next day. I thanked him and left one of my cards on his desk, in case anything turned up. Then I drove back to the hospital.

As I was pulling into the driveway I noticed a gate guard in a khaki uniform. After explaining who I was he made a call from the small gate shack, then came back and told me to drive in.

'I didn't see anybody at the gate this morning,' I said.

'We don't man this post till five,' he said.

Heading for the main building I began to wonder how Vincent could have walked out of here between six and eight if there was a guard on the gate. I made a mental note to check the outer perimeter before I left. The head nurse on duty told me that Dr Wilson was out back.

I went out the front and around the side. There was a red Camry parked next to a Chevy van. In between them were a middle-aged, bearded guy in a suit and a gorgeous woman with auburn hair. She wore a green blouse with a brown skirt. The jacket matching the skirt was slung casually over her right shoulder. They were standing close, like they knew each other well. The man spotted my reflection in the van's darkly tinted window. He stiffened.

'Can I help you?' he said.

'I hope so. I'm looking for Dr Wilson.'

'I am he,' he said.

I told him who I was and what I was doing there. The woman regarded me indifferently with cool green eyes. Wilson made no effort to introduce her.

'Mackenzie, I'll catch you later,' he said. She smiled and nodded. He watched me watch her as she strolled from between the cars, got into the Toyota, and drove off.

'Nice looking lady. Your wife?' I asked, looking at his wedding ring.

'A friend,' he answered. 'Now what exactly can I do for you, Mr Shade?'

'As I said, I'm looking into Vincent Snow's disappearance. I was hoping you could give me some ideas or suggestions.'

'On what?'

'On where he might have gone.'

He shook his head. 'None that haven't been checked out already.'

'Buenoventura Marcos told me you usually took Vincent to the art studio every night at six.' He nodded. 'Were you and Vincent close?'

'Not particularly. He was my patient, I was his doctor.'

As I started to ask another question, he heaved a petulant sigh and glanced at his watch.

'Mr Shade, I'm afraid you've caught me at a very critical time,' he said. 'I do have other patients to attend to.'

'I understand, doctor. Is it possible you could show me the art studio?'

'Why do you want to see that?'

'Maybe I can get a feel of who I'm looking for.'

'All right,' he said. 'I'll have one of the security guards show it to you.'

The art studio was a small brick building about a hundred feet away from the main complex. Heavy wire mesh covered all the windows and the door was secured by a deadbolt lock. The guard who opened it was a big-bellied, hillbilly-type named Curly.

'We gotta lock it to keep the retards out,' he said.

Inside I saw several rows of tables and some easels. There were numerous paintings in various stages of completion. Other works . . . chalk drawings, clay models and sketches, were scattered about. I asked which were Vincent's.

'Beats the shit outta me,' Curly said. 'I don't have much to do with them in here. Less'n they gits outta control. Then I snakes 'em.'

'What's that?'

He lifted his arms up and pretended he was snaring an imaginary neck between his forearms. 'Why, me and Red knows just how to grab these bastards. Some of 'em can be real strong. But you cut off their air, they can't do much.'

'I see,' I said, looking at the partially finished oil on the easel closest to us. It was a startling replication of a large photograph that was sitting in front of it on another easel. On the floor to the right was a finished painting that bore the same expert quality. In its right-hand corner was a small V.S. The finished one looked familiar. Like I'd seen it somewhere before in a newspaper or magazine.

'Maybe this is one of his,' I said. 'Has his initials on it.'

'Oh, yeah,' Curly said. 'Come to think of it, I do remember that guy. He got real funny once, cause somebody touched one of his paintings. Weirder than hell, and all they do around here is coddle to him.'

'Something you'd change if you were in charge, I'll bet,' I said.

'Damn straight,' he said.

The door slammed open and another guard came in. He was a powerfully built guy with red hair and piercing blue eyes.

'Curly, what the hell you doing in here?'

'Just showing this guy around,' Curly answered.

'Well, we're a little short-handed for you to be giving guided tours,' he said. 'Now let's get this place locked up and start making your rounds.'

'Sorry, Red,' Curly said. The muscular guy disappeared out the doorway. 'We gotta go,' he said, an authoritarian tone creeping into his voice.

Curly was brusque as I tried to ask him how Vincent might have wandered off with the gate guard on duty and the roving patrols.

'Beats the shit outta me,' he said again as he locked up the door.

'Are there any holes in the fence or anything?' I asked.

'Now listen, mister city-slicker, just because we don't carry guns like regular cops, don't mean we don't know what we're doin'.'

After Curly escorted me back to my car, I drove to the main gate and parked. I spent about forty minutes inspecting the outside perimeter. The fence was intact all the way around and there were no other exits. Not impossible for a man to escape, but it would take some savvy to scale the fence. The Institute was surrounded by thick forest preserves on two sides. The other two sides were long expanses of grass that led to the highways.

The businesses around the Institute, a couple of gas stations and convenience stores, provided me with no new leads. A couple of people said that the police had already been by asking them if they'd seen Vincent. Nobody seemed very concerned one way or the other. I drove into town and went to the library to confer with Carole. She seemed somewhat depressed by my lack of progress.

'Do you have any other ideas on where he might go?' I asked.

She compressed her lips inward as she thought.

'He has made a few trips with Dr Wilson to the art museum,' she said. 'And to the gallery.'

'Where's that?'

'The Knight Shore Gallery. It's here in town. Dr Wilson had some of Vincent's paintings on exhibit there.'

'I'll check it out,' I said. 'Can you give me the address?'

The Knight Shore Gallery was an ultra-modern looking building in the middle of a strip mall. I began wondering how an art gallery could prosper so far out in the burbs, but the lettering on the window said the main branch was in the River North area of Chicago. When I pushed open the glass doors I heard an angry voice.

'I didn't drive all the way out here from Chicago, Ms Knight, to hear you apologize.' The speaker was an older, balding man. He wore thick glasses and an expensive looking suit.

'Mr Rhetton, please,' the woman said. 'I assure you the matter will be taken care of to your complete satisfaction.'

The man shifted as he spoke and I got a better look at the woman. She was the same one I'd seen talking to Wilson earlier at the Institute.

Both of them suddenly noticed my presence and stopped talking.

'Good evening,' I said.

'I'll be with you in a minute, sir,' she said. Then, back to the man, 'We regret this unfortunate mix-up as much as you do, and I'll do everything in my power to rectify it.'

'You'd better,' Rhetton said, punching his index finger onto the newpsaper that he held in his other hand. 'Or you'll be hearing from my attorney.'

'Mr Rhetton,' she said with a trace of smugness. 'I'm sure you'll agree that litigation would be undesirable for both of us.'

He turned and stormed out, glancing at me obliquely as he passed.

'I'm sorry,' she said. 'I'm Mackenzie Knight. May I help you?'

I handed her one of my cards. If she remembered me from earlier, she didn't show it.

'I'm looking into Vincent Snow's disappearance,' I said. 'His sister told me he had some paintings on exhibit here.'

'Yes, they're over here.' She swept her arm toward the left. I followed her to a lighted section by the window. The paintings were fastened on large sections of white plasterboard. They were startling reproductions of some of Norman Rockwell's works. Each had a small V.S. in the lower right corner.

'Like looking at old *Saturday Evening Post* covers,' I said.

Mackenzie Knight laughed. 'Yes, isn't it.'

'Have you seen Vincent since the day before yesterday, Ms Knight?'

'No. What makes you think that I'd seen him?'

'Actually, I'm just trying to cover all the bases. I thought maybe he'd come here to look at his paintings.'

She regarded me closely for a moment. 'Mr Shade, perhaps you don't realize just how disturbed an individual Vincent is.'

I let her continue.

'I doubt very seriously if he even realizes that his paintings are on exhibit here.' She glanced at the framed works. 'In any case, I really just put them up as a favor to Dr Wilson. I'm afraid Vincent's work has no real style or substance. As you can see, he's quite adept at copying, but I'm afraid that's as far as it goes.'

'Any ideas where he might be, Ms Knight?'

She shook her head, the green eyes regarding me placidly. 'I'm afraid not, Mr Shade. And I couldn't even begin to tell you where to look.'

With no kick-boxing matches scheduled in the near future, my heavy training was on hold. So I took my time with my five-mile run the next morning, and thought about the inconsistencies in the case. Mr Kamen, the head honcho of the place, had bent over backwards to be cooperative. Everybody else seemed indifferent to Vincent's disappearance. And how could he have just walked away from the Institute with a gate guard on duty? With Vincent's limited social skills it seemed logical that someone would have noticed him.

By the time I'd finished the run I'd pretty much decided to spend the rest of the day beating the bushes around the Institute, trying to find somebody who might have noticed him. Getting a K-9 unit from the county police to check the forest preserves again, was another possibility.

When I opened the door I heard my beeper doing the intermittent beep of an unanswered page. It was the phone number of my answering service. They told me that Carole Snow had called about twenty minutes ago sounding real upset. I hung up and dialed her home number.

'Mr Shade,' she said, her voice racked by sobs. 'Vincent's dead.'

She told me that the police had notified her this morning and needed her to claim the body.

'Just stay at home till I get there,' I said.

The police detective I'd met earlier, Ken Williams, met us at the local hospital. They had Vincent in their morgue. I thought Carole would collapse when she saw the body. It wasn't pretty. Lots of facial scrapes and discoloration. They hadn't tried to clean him up.

Williams and I escorted her into a lounge area and got her a cup of coffee. Some guy in a gray suit, a hospital administrator named Woodcock, began pressuring Carole to call a funeral home as soon as possible.

'What's the cause of death?' I asked.

'Appears that he fell from the roof of the old Berkis Plant,' Williams said. 'It's about a mile from the Institute. Place has been closed down for years now. Some kids found him this morning. Been trying to get the county to raze that place for the longest time.'

'What're the autopsy findings?'

Woodcock broke in: 'The preliminary findings are that he died as a result of the fall. I've been in contact with the Institute, and Dr Wilson'll be by here later to sign the death certificate.'

'Without an autopsy?' I asked.

'We really don't need one at this point, Mr Shade,' Williams said.

'Our preliminary investigation seems to indicate that it was an accidental death. Vincent must have climbed up to the roof to look around and fell off.'

'Is that all right with you, Carole?' Woodcock asked. 'Dr Wilson seemed to feel it would spare you unnecessary anguish.'

'I'm not sure,' she said. 'Whatever you think is best.'

'I think it's best to have an autopsy,' I said.

'That means he'll have to go down to the county morgue,' Williams said.

'This'd be a lot simpler if . . . ' the administrator said.

'Did you say Vincent fell from the roof?' Carole asked abruptly.

Williams nodded.

'That doesn't seem right,' she said. 'He was deathly afraid of heights.' Her voice trailed off as she suddenly realized her unintentionally morbid pun. She began crying again.

Reluctantly, Williams and Woodcock agreed to contact the Kane County Coroner to make arrangements for an autopsy. It meant more paperwork and delays, instead of being able to tie everything up in a neat little package.

I took Carole out for some breakfast and tried to gently convince her that she should get on with the rest of her life. She asked me if I thought she'd made the right decision about the autopsy. I assured her that she had.

She didn't have much of an appetite. Back at her house she began making the appropriate phone calls, and I stayed close in case she needed help. But she seemed to be holding up well, imbued with that shot of adrenaline that keeps us going in times like that. She made us some coffee, and, sipping from the cup, I wandered around the living room of her old house. There was a framed, pastel chalk drawing of a man's upper torso hung above the mantel. Brilliant colors swirled surrealistically around the figure's head. In the corner was the same V.S. that I'd seen before.

'Is this one of Vincent's?' I asked.

'Yes,' Carole said. 'That was when we first realized how artistic he was. I liked it so well I had it framed. I've always called it 'The Savant'.'

Below the drawing was the photograph of Carole, her parents, and Vincent. Savant—the term came from the French verb *savoir*, meaning to know. I wondered if Vincent had ever known what an untidy wake his simple existence had caused? Or was he oblivious, locked inside his own world until it had collided with reality?

Carole asked if I could drive her to the Institute to pick up Vincent's things. When we got there they already had the room cleaned out and everything stuffed into a couple of large garbage bags.

'How about his paintings?' Carole asked.

The nurse made a call and told us that one of the security guards would meet us by the Art Studio. As the elevator doors opened to the first floor we ran into Dr Wilson.

'My condolences, Carole,' he said.

She thanked him.

'Mr Woodcock from the hospital called me and said you're requesting an autopsy.'

Carole nodded.

'Well, I must say that I feel that's a bad decision. It's best to get this over with as soon as possible. Prolonging the loss of a loved one can be a big mistake.'

'What's wrong with having an autopsy?' I asked.

Wilson turned to me, squinted, then raised his eyebrows fractionally. 'You're that detective, aren't you?'

'Right.'

'Are you the one who's put these foolish ideas into her head?'

'What's foolish about finding out what's happened?'

Wilson ignored me. 'Carole, I want you to know that the Institute realizes its culpability in your brother's death. The man responsible for allowing him to walk away has been suspended and will be dealt with sternly, I assure you. Now if you're concerned about an insurance settlement, I may be able to provide some assistance . . . '

'It's too bad you weren't this interested in Vincent when he was alive,' I said.

'Vincent made enormous progress under my care,' Wilson shot back, pointing his finger at my face. 'And don't make accusations about something you know nothing of.'

'I don't, doctor,' I said, pulling Carole away from him. 'I always wait till all the facts are in.'

At the art studio the two security guards, Curly and Red, were waiting for us. They said that all Vincent's stuff had already been packed.

'You mean there are no paintings here?' Carole asked.

'Sorry, ma'am,' Red said.

'I thought I saw a couple of his yesterday,' I said.

'You thought wrong,' Red said, looking me squarely in the eye. 'We just checked.'

'Mind if we look?' I said.

He stood aside and swept out his arm with exaggerated courtesy.

The place had obviously been cleaned up. The paintings with the V.S. initials were gone. So was the large photograph. I turned to Curly and asked him where they were.

He scratched his head and rocked back and forth in an aw-shucks posture. 'Can't remember nothing like that.'

Up until our visit I'd been leaning toward accepting Vincent's death as an accident brought on by the Institute's laxity. But Wilson's attitude bothered me. Had Vincent been given the wrong medication? Could he have OD'd? And the run-around about the paintings. Where did that fit in? These things stood out in my mind like ripples in a still pond. After we got back to Carole's I called Buenoventura Marcos.

'Was Dr Wilson close to Vincent?' I asked.

'I'd say so,' he answered. 'Dr Wilson seemed to work well with Vincent. Almost like he had control over him. Especially with the art.'

'He told Vincent what to paint?'

'Yeah. He'd get the photo lab to blow-up pictures of famous paintings so Vincent could copy them,' Buenoventura said. 'He was instrumental in getting Vincent's stuff on exhibit, too.'

'Mackenzie Knight's place?' I said. 'What's her connection to Wilson?'

He hesitated, then said, 'Oh, it probably doesn't make any difference anyway. My job's gone for sure. I think Wilson and her are lovers. He's married. She's divorced.'

'Is that how they met? When Vincent's paintings were on exhibit?'

'I'm not sure,' he said. 'Her brother works at the Institute. Security.'

'Her brother?'

'Yeah. Red Smith.'

When I set the phone down I thought back through all my meetings with Wilson, Mackenzie, and Red. Something was out of place, but I didn't know what. Then I remembered the guy arguing with Mackenzie at the Gallery. He'd been pointing at a newspaper. A *Chicago Sun Times*.

'Do you keep recent newspapers from Chicago on file at the Library?' I asked Carole.

'Of course.'

I found the article on page 47 under the heading of *Stolen Art Work Recovered.* It told how police had recovered a cache of stolen paintings that had been taken from a River North Gallery. One of the paintings by neo-realist painter Bert LeVeille was purported to be worth close to twenty thousand dollars. The paintings were believed to have been lost in a gallery fire in the River North Area last year. Knight Shore, I wondered?

The article went on to explain how the police have set up special teams to deal with the recent wave of art thefts and forgeries. Art forgeries, it said, had exploded in recent years because of the large number of novices entering the field of collecting who unknowingly buy forged or stolen paintings for some exorbitant amount and let them languish in some storage area.

I made a copy of the article and headed for the Knight Shore Gallery. It was early evening when I got there, but the front door was locked. Wilson's van sat in the parking lot. I decided to see if my lock-picking equipment would work on the rear door. After retrieving my pistol-pick from my truck, I drove around the back. Luckily most strip malls have clearly marked rear entrances for deliveries.

The door was solid metal, but the deadbolt wasn't even secured. The lock in the knob yielded in a few seconds. I slowly pulled it open and slipped inside. It was some kind of storage room with stacks of paintings, frames, and sundries clustered about. Ahead I saw the light outline of another door and heard voices on the other side of it.

'You can't be serious,' Mackenzie said. 'They'll be able to tell that?'

'All I'm saying is that if the medical examiner determines that he died of a broken neck before the fall, we should be ready with some contingency plan.' It was Wilson.

'Like what?' she said derisively. 'Take the rest of the forged paintings and run away together?'

'You know I can't do that right now,' he said.

'Well, if you think I'm sacrificing my brother just because that retard went crazy . . . ' She was snarling at him. I cracked the door open a little more. Mackenzie whirled to face me. Wilson turned too.

'Shade,' he said. 'What are you doing here?'

I stepped into the room, smiling as benignly as I could. We were in an office area, set behind the dry-wall display pillars.

'I had it figured out, doctor,' I said. 'You were using Vincent to reproduce some modern paintings. Probably to sell to *nouveau*-collectors who were interested in deals on those paintings that vanished in that River North fire last year. But something went wrong when old Red got a little too exuberant with his choke hold.'

'It was an accident, Shade,' Wilson said nervously. 'I had nothing to do with it.'

'When you left the Institute on some personal emergency in your van,' I said. 'Is that how you smuggled out the body?'

'Shade, it wasn't intentional,' he said. 'Vincent was extremely possessive about his paintings. He became violent. Red was just trying to stop him.'

'Shut up, you idiot,' Mackenzie spat. 'Don't tell him anything.'

Wilson's head swivelled to look at her, his hair flopping around.

'Darling, it's okay,' he said. 'It was my fault. I'm to blame.' He began to move toward her, hands outstretched.

'I'm not going to ruin my life over some retarded idiot,' she said, running to a nearby desk. Flinging open the drawer, she pulled out a black automatic and pointed it at me.

I ran to my left, moving between the rows of dry-wall stands, reaching into my jacket for my Beretta.

I heard the shot and the bullet smacked through one of the display stands in front of me.

'No, Mackenzie. No,' I heard Wilson say.

Another shot! The plasterboard next to my shoulder bubbled out from the impact of the high-velocity round.

She caught sight of me and fired another round, as I made a quick glance around the side of the display. I raised my own gun, and Wilson screamed for me not to shoot. He moved forward, attempting to grab her hand. They did a quick two-step, punctuated by a deadly crack. Wilson stepped away, his right hand bloody, his knees bent. But it was Mackenzie who slipped to the floor, the gun still in her hand.

The large blood stain under Mackenzie's left breast grew larger with each passing second. Wilson screamed for me to get an ambulance. After I picked up the gun I made a call. But from the bright red color of the spurting blood, and her grayish color, I knew it was already too late.

I pocketed the gun and unlocked the front door for the police and paramedics. Wilson cradled her, saying that it was all his fault and that things would be all right. He kept right on holding her, repeating the words over and over, even after the convulsions had stopped and her arms drooped listlessly to the floor.

WAYNE D. DUNDEE was born in 1948 in northern Illinois and has lived all his life along northern Illinois/southern Wisconsin state line. In 1966 he married Pamela Daum and they have one daughter, Michelle, who was born in 1968.

Dundee worked at various jobs since he was in early teens. At one time or another he has been a farmer, truck driver, construction laborer, carpet layer, door to door salesman, newspaper circulation manager, factory laborer, factory supervisor, and process engineer of a specialised steel fabricating department.

He has been an avid reader as far back as he can remember. Everything from Mark Twain to Robert E. Howard, with notable impact by Edgar Rice Burroughs and Mickey Spillane. Spillane won out in the influence category when Dundee decided to try his own hand at writing and he has been following the path Spillane started down ever since.

Wayne D. Dundee
The Slicer

'I feel pretty crappy about this,' Mike Brandish was saying. 'I hate myself for thinking the things I've been thinking, for coming here like this . . . But I can't *not* do something. Not any longer. I've been living with it for days. Weeks. It's eating me up.'

He was a big guy, thirty, give or take a year, bulky and slightly rumpled in a workmanlike way. Untrimmed reddish-brown hair poking down over a bull neck, calloused hands with unevenly chewed fingernails, the right thumb plastic-splinted and wrapped in flesh-toned tape. His jeans were faded but clean, his shoes freshly polished but old, their fake leather cracked and gouged under the stain. On his clean-shaven face he wore his troubles like a painfully pinching mask.

He was seated before me in my office on a rainy late winter afternoon. I'd poured us each a cup of coffee and had recited my standard lines reassuring him whatever he told me here would be held in strict confidence. I was ready to get on with it now and so was he, I sensed, but apparently only after a bit more nudging.

'You mentioned this has something to do with your father,' I reminded him.

He nodded, his pained expression clamping harder, more starkly etching the lines it put in his face. 'That's right,' he said. 'It does. At least I'm afraid it does.'

'You're not making yourself very clear, Mr Brandish,' I told him. 'You came here seeking the services of a private detective—me—but I can't do you much good until you tell me what your problem is.'

He hung his head and stared down at his big, blunt hands as if they had failed him somehow. After a little while he said, 'I guess you must have heard about the killings, the ones being done by the guy they're calling the Slicer?'

It was like asking me if I'd heard of the bogeyman, or the Black Plague, or the AIDS epidemic. We all have a capacity for bad news, we're all hungry for it to some degree no matter how much we might protest otherwise, at least a little bit eager to learn of dark and nasty things as long as they take place outside our own safe little patches of light. And when somebody like the Slicer comes along, the news media stands ready, willing, and able to feed our craving on a feastlike scale.

'Yeah,' I said, 'I've heard of the Slicer killings.'

Rockford's very own serial murderer. Six victims so far, all very well-endowed women, all beaten and stabbed to the point of mutilation, all with their previously formidable breasts sliced off (hence the media tag) and removed from the rest of the grisly remains. That was the only pattern. No other similarities, no leads for the cops. The women ranged in age from twenty to forty-five, ranged in occupations from a hooker (the first victim) to a church secretary, covered the spectrum as far as size and race and hair color, and had met their ends in different parts of the city.

Brandish kept looking down at his hands. 'They've done a couple of those . . . what they call "psychological profiles" on what would fit somebody who acted that way.'

'Far as I'm concerned,' I said, 'those kind of things are like police artist sketches or throwing darts at a piece of cork—sometimes they hit the mark, sometimes they don't. In this particular case, if I recall right, the nut doctors are even coming up with conflicting theories. One claims the killer has an uncontrollable obsession with large breasts, that he loves them so much he is driven to actually possess them, to take them away from their original owners, so to speak. Another feels these actions are the result of someone who *hates* big breasts and all women who have them and the killings are his way of trying to get rid of them.'

Brandish took a deep breath and let it out. 'My father has a . . . a thing for really big boobs.'

'That in itself doesn't make him too unusual,' I said, trying to keep him at ease, keep him going with it. 'Happens to be a tendency I lean toward myself.'

'My mother was a big woman,' he went on. 'Matronly, I guess, would have been the old-fashioned way to describe her. You know the type, big-boned, kinda heavy, really substantial in the chest department. She kidded about her bust, made fun of it, but it was really a point of pride with her. She was no beauty, had no movie-star figure, but she knew what she had kept the old man interested. That's the way it was around our house, even when I was a kid growing up. Lots of affection and kidding, a little fanny-slapping and grabbing on the sly. I don't mean they were sick about it or anything, but Mom and Pop really liked each other and weren't afraid to show it. It never bothered me—hell, I figured I was better off being raised in an environment like that than around some of the tight-assed parents my buddies had. Later on, after I got married, my wife let me know she thought the way my folks carried on was in bad taste, sometimes downright embarrassing. My wife, she's built pretty good, too, and when Pop tried to kid around about that she got really pissed. Said it was disgusting a guy would notice anything like that about his own daughter-in-law.'

When he paused, I said, 'No offense, but it sounds like maybe your wife was raised under some of those tight-assed circumstances you mentioned.'

He bared his teeth in a brief, rueful smile. 'You don't know the half of it . . . '

I let that one ride.

He reached for the coffee I'd poured, took a couple of long swallows. He kept the cup, holding it pressed between his broad palms. 'Anyway,' he said, 'Mom passed away a couple years back. Pop's never been the same since. She went real sudden and right up to the end they were . . . well, like they'd always been with each other. Even after all those years. Lovers, best buddies, the whole nine yards. Left a hell of a hole for Pop. He retired from the butcher shop where he'd worked for twenty-five years. Sold the house he and Mom had lived in, said it was too big for him alone and too full of memories. I made a feeble offer for him to move in with us, but he was smart enough to know it would have never worked. He took an apartment in the upstairs of a nice old house on North Main. Close to downtown, plenty of things for him to do, he said. But he doesn't get involved in all that much. Watches a lot of ballgames on TV, drinks more than he should, for sure more than he ever did before. Goes down to the river-front in nice weather and sits there for hours with a flask in his pocket, watching the water roll by. The juice is gone, you know, Mr Hannibal? It's not like he's withering up and threatening to die or anything, but at the same time the zest just isn't there—the twinkle in his eye, the lopsided grin, the jokes. I don't ever see those things any more. He's actually turned sort of sour and . . . and . . .'

'Bitter?' I suggested.

Mike Brandish winced. 'Yeah,' he said, his voice suddenly a little husky, 'he's like he's bitter.' He lifted his face and looked at me. 'You see what I'm getting at?'

I nodded. 'I think so.'

'Depending on exactly what's going on under the surface, see, my father could fit *either* of those psychological profiles. Always before he showed a pretty strong attraction to ample busts. But now that Mom's gone—now that *his* have been taken from him, so to speak, and he's turned sour and taken to drinking the way he has—maybe he hates the thought of all the big ones out there that, well, belong to somebody else.' He transferred the coffee cup to one hand and raised his free hand to rub hard at the back of his neck. 'Damn. I can't believe I'm thinking or saying that kind of shit about my own dad . . . '

'There must be something more.'

Still with the hand clamped to the back of his neck, he nodded. 'In the past few months, Pop's taken to going out at night. Something he never used to do. He says he goes down to some of the neighborhood taverns, sometimes checks out the go-go joints over on State. I phone him two, three times a week to see how he's doing—usually from work, I'm a second-shift foreman over at Pellson Foundry. More and more often he isn't home when I call. A few times I tried calling the places he says he goes to. Not that I was checking up on him, hell, he's sixty-four years old, he's entitled to a few drinks if he wants. But I worry about him, I like to hear his voice so I know everything's okay. Anyway, the thing is, some of those times he wasn't where he said he was.'

'The 'if anybody calls, I'm not here' bit is pretty standard tavern routine.'

'No, I don't think that was the case. He's got no reason not to want to talk to me—what am I going to do, scold him and tell him to get his butt home? No, he just plain wasn't where he said he was. And then there's the magazines.'

'Magazines?'

'Couple weeks back, Pop fell on the ice. Didn't break anything, but bruised hell out of his hip and shoulder, got all stiff and swollen, couldn't get around so good. He spent the weekend at my place—my wife could handle it for that long—until some of the swelling had gone down and he could at least get up out of a chair or off the bed okay by himself. I had to go over to his place to get some clothes and a toothbrush and things, and that's when I found his cache of magazines in the closet of his bedroom. I'm talking some pretty gross shit, Hannibal. Hell, I buy *Playboy* every now and then, look at a lot of the stuff the guys at work bring in. But this stuff of Pop's was pure raunch—titles like *Knocker*, *Queens*, *Jumbo Floppers*, *Stacks & Slits*, all shit like that. Strictly wack-off material, not even any text in most of them.'

'The old guy lives alone, he apparently needs to take matters in hand once in a while. That's what those kind of books are for. I can see where a fella wouldn't want to picture his father doing something like that, but it really isn't too bizarre a behavior.'

'But don't you see? More and more of it fits those damn profiles. And tracing things back in my head, at least one of the nights when I couldn't reach him was a night a murder took place.'

The kid was obviously going through a lot of torment over this. But at the same time it seemed to me he was reaching awful far to pull together some of the things he was letting bother him. I told him as much.

'There's one more thing,' he said. 'Something else I keep going back to in my head.'

'And that is?'

'When Pop fell that time, it was while he was taking garbage out. When I went the next day to get his things, he asked me to be sure to clean up the mess he left in the alley where he fell. As I was doing that, I noticed some clothes and gloves stuffed in one of the torn bags. They were smeared with what I figured at the time was red paint. Something real odd about that, though, when I stopped to think about it later—Pop's allergic as hell to any kind of fresh paint, has been for as long as I can remember.'

Then it was my turn to go back to something in my head, something my would-be client had said a few minutes earlier, something about his father *retiring from the butcher shop where he'd worked for twenty-five years*. Suddenly it seemed like maybe the kid wasn't reaching so far at all.

His eyes were pleading things. 'Do I have to tell you what those stains must have been if they weren't red paint? Do you see why I have to do something? I'm not ready to go to the cops, but I've got to know one way or the other. That's what I need you to find out—if all of this is just craziness in my head or if . . . if . . .'

He couldn't finish it, but we both understood damn full well what the 'or if' was.

As I saw it, the job would be pretty straightforward, possibly even simple. It wasn't like I was setting out to nab the Slicer and solve the string of murders that had kept the authorities baffled for going on thirteen weeks. No illusions so grand. All I figured to do was keep tabs on Old Man Brandish until one of two things happened: either another Slicer murder took place while he was at some neutral location innocently sipping suds or maybe getting cozy with a new girlfriend he was too embarrassed to tell the family about yet; or I spotted him getting ready to take a meat cleaver to some unfortunate gal with an industrial strength set of lungs. In the latter event, of course, things would turn *un*-simple.

But somehow I doubted it was going to come to that.

Mike Brandish's anxiety was very real and he'd managed to convince me there were enough quirks in his father's behavior to warrant my looking into them without feeling irresponsible about taking his money. I made it clear I'd have to turn the old man over if I turned up anything incriminating. But things don't come to me that easy—clients just don't march in off the street and present me with a lead to the hottest case going. Hell, there were probably dozens of people around town who, in the wake of these murders, were starting to look a little askance at their husbands, or boyfriends or co-workers, recalling odd things that hadn't seemed all that important before but now had them wondering if just maybe . . . And some of them likely had more to wonder about than my new client. Yet they couldn't *all* have a bead on the Slicer. So I more or less expected I'd end up tailing the old bird for a couple of nights until I discovered whatever he was doing on the sly was something relatively harmless—like the aforementioned girlfriend—and that would be the end of it.

After obtaining from Mike Brandish a retainer check and a photo of his father, I'd seen him to the door then closed the office and walked down the street for a late lunch of a hot dog and a bowl of chili. I took my time over the food. As I ate, I re-copied the hurriedly scribbled notes I'd taken while Brandish talked.

By the time I left the diner, the afternoon rain was turning to sleet that rattled like a death cough on the crust of old snow lining the streets and sidewalks. I didn't go back to the office. I knocked the ice off the windshield of my heap, climbed behind the wheel and drove to the auto window of my bank. From there I rolled uptown, crossed the river on State, then turned on North Main. I wanted to do some daylight scouting of Oliver Brandish's place of residence as well as some of the likely routes he'd be taking if and when he went out.

The house was a tall old Victorian job on a block crowded with other once-grand structures. Almost all of them had been divided into apartment dwellings.

I cruised past Brandish's place twice on the street out front, then passed once through the alley behind. Mike had told me his father lived upstairs and his comings and goings were done primarily through the front foyer. But I saw now that there was an outside stairway on the back that he *could* use. I'd have to keep that in mind when staking out the place.

Also at the back of the house, on the alley, was a rectangular shed that, judging by the old-fashioned roll-back door and the tire tracks, had been turned into a garage. Beside it, on a concrete slab, stood a row of garbage cans. Effectively blocked from the house's view by the shed/garage, I dropped my heap into park and got out for a little closer investigative work. It was here that Mike had seen the stained clothing and gloves. Really wasn't much chance I'd spot any remnants of those, but in this kind of weather you never knew—since he'd said the bag was torn, it was conceivable something could have blown out and gotten frozen into an odd corner. If I caught a break and came up with anything, I had some lab connections who could tell me PDQ exactly what the stains were.

I didn't catch a break. I got caught instead.

I'd no sooner climbed out of my car and started toward the row of garbage cans than the garage door shot back with a squawk of unoiled rollers. The woman who stood in the open doorway didn't look nearly as startled to see me as I was her.

'What's going on?' she said. 'What are you doing here?'

She was in her middle fifties, tall and sturdy-looking, with iron gray hair and sharp eyes beneath strikingly dark brows. Her facial features were plain, neither attractive nor unattractive to any remarkable degree. She wore laced, high-top shoes, jeans, and a hooded sweatshirt jacket. Through the mud and salt-splatter, the car squatting in the garage behind her bore the markings of a taxi cab; I remembered my client mentioning that the woman who lived downstairs from his father was a divorcee who drove a cab.

In response to her question, I did some fancy mental footwork. 'I'm a friend of Mike Brandish,' I said. 'His father'—pointing—'lives upstairs there.'

'That much I know. Still doesn't tell me what I asked.'

I padded the lie. 'I was here with Mike a week or two ago—when he came to pick up some things for his dad after Mr Brandish had that bad fall and was laid up for a while. I guess you must have heard about that, right?'

She nodded. I had the feeling there wasn't much that went on around that she didn't know about. Her eyes told me to get on with it.

'Well, I lost an ornament off my keyring some time recently—just a cheap doo-dad with my name on it, but a sentimental thing, you know—and it occured to me it might have happened the day I was here, helping Mike straighten up the trash and stuff. I happened to be on this end of town this afternoon, so I thought I'd stop and take a look, maybe get lucky.'

She eyed me shrewdly. 'A friend of Mike's, huh?'

'That's right. I used to work at Pellson's with him.'

Mention by name of the kid's place of employment seemed to put the lie over the rest of the way. I could see her face relax. But just a little.

'How much chance you figure you got of finding your doo-dad in all this muck after more than a week?'

'Like I said, maybe I'll get lucky.'

She grunted. 'Well, have your look then. But make it snappy. Your car's blocking my way and I got an evening's shift to get out and drive.'

So I went through the motions of looking for the non-existent lost keyring fob. Kicked at the ridges of snow around the base of the concrete, leaned down a couple of times to examine what I uncovered, paced back and forth peering intently. All the while the sleet nipped at me and the woman sat in her car inside the garage, occasionally gunning the engine, watching me with a half-suspicious scowl. Blue exhaust smoke boiled around her. When I figured I'd put on enough of a show, I turned back to my heap, pausing to favor my audience with a brief smile and an 'I give up' gesture of my arms.

She scowled and gunned her engine at me some more.

I pitied any poor fool of a fare who might try and stiff her on the tip.

Dusk found me back at the old Victorian, parked diagonally across the street out front in a car I'd borrowed from my buddy Bomber Brannigan. My vantage point afforded me a view of both means of entering or exiting the house and the borrowed vehicle afforded me protective camouflage against Oliver Brandish's neighbor, who had already seen too much of me and my own car.

The night was as dark as a pimp's heart. Intermittent bursts of sleet poured down, crackling through already ice-coated branches, pinging off the car's body. The wind blew cold and relentless.

His son had told me that Oliver Brandish seldom drove anywhere these days, especially when road conditions were bad. He preferred to walk, even in cold temperatures. It seemed unlikely he would be going out at all on a night like this, but it was my job to be sure.

As long as my tailbone and my supply of coffee held up, I'd hang in. I ran the car's engine every once in a while to keep the windshield clear and to assist the coffee in keeping me warm.

At the three hour mark—with no sign of activity on the subject's part except an infrequent shadow flicking past one of his lighted windows—it was my about-to-burst bladder that threatened to undermine the mission. I carry an empty anti-freeze jug (no embarrassing questions that way) in my own heap for such contingencies, but hadn't thought to transfer it to my temporary set of wheels. I had to make do with a quick duck over behind a frozen hedge where I left some melted snow and a tell-tale wisp of steam that, given the hour and the conditions, luckily no one was around to notice.

At midnight I watered the hedge again.

The subject's lights were still on, although it had been some time since I'd seen any shadowy movement. I wondered what happened to the notion that old people retired early and got up with the chickens. Looked like Oliver Brandish might have it backwards.

At half past the hour, his neighbor got home. I watched her park her cab in the garage, then trudge across the back yard and go inside. The bottom half of the house became as well-lighted as the upper. A thought wandered in that maybe the old guy had been waiting up for her, that maybe the two elderly, unattached people were finding solace in each other. But then I had to consider the woman's distinct lack of femininity and my subject's alleged fascination with the most feminine attributes of all. Weird hours and a gallon or so of caffeine can conjure some pretty screwy ideas. At any rate, if any cohabiting went on inside I saw no signs of it.

Around one, Brandish's lights went out and he finally turned in.

Forty-five minutes later, the rest of the house went dark.

I gave it another hour and a half, then went home and went to bed myself.

I didn't get up until almost noon. The first thing I did was check the morning paper for anything new on the Slicer killings. There was nothing except some rhetoric on the editorial page warning against the armed vigilance groups that had started to spring up in many neighborhoods and calling for the police to get on the stick and arrest the killer before these righteous citizens, in their fear and grief, spilled innocent blood trying to protect themselves and their loved ones.

After I'd showered and shaved and gotten on the other side of some coffee and a bowl of cornflakes, I called Mike Brandish at home. His end of it was done in low mutterings, leaving me to think he proably hadn't gotten around to telling his wife he'd sunk some of their hard-earned cash into hiring me. I reported on my uneventful night, told him I'd be back on watch again tonight. I mentioned my run-in with the neighbor lady—her name was Alice Gorton, I found out in the process—and made him aware of the line I'd fed her so he could cover for me if it ever came up. I assured him I'd keep him posted as things went along, then rang off.

I went to my office and spent a couple of hours doing phone work on another case, a drawn-out interstate job I was peripherally involved with. From there I drove to the library and put in some time at the microfilm viewers, re-familiarizing myself with various newspaper accounts of the Slicer killings.

After squeezing in a hearty late lunch and replenishing my stakeout supplies, me and my borrowed car were back in place on North Main as the final visible sliver of the sun was dropping out of the sky. The day had been clear and bright and considerably warmer. The streets and sidewalks were wet from melted snow.

I leaned back in the car seat and impatiently exhaled cigarette smoke. I hate stakeouts. I especially hate them when I'm only half-convinced they're liable to yield anything.

At quarter of six, Oliver Brandish came out the front door of the house and started walking in the direction of downtown. He was a big old guy, blockily built, like his son. He wore a light, short-waisted coat and an old-fashioned touring cap. He walked with his hands shoved in the coat pockets. He stepped them off pretty handily, showing no ill effects from his recent fall.

I gave him a full block lead. His broad back was easy to keep in view. I'd roll slowly into the block behind him and pull to the curb, then roll ahead again when he threatened to stretch it out too far. When he approached State Street, angling toward the downtown mall, I parked and got out and went after him on foot. There'd be enough pedestrian traffic around the mall this early in the evening for me to remain inconspicuous.

He ended up ducking into an unassuming little tavern off Court, one of the few remaining such places in this part of town that hadn't been crowded out by the failed mall or the failing Metro Center. I walked past the entrance he'd used, then cut through the closest alley and, from there, watched the joint's back door for a while. I had no reason to suspect he was on to me, but there's nothing more embarrassing than having a subject double-door you, especially an amateur. When I was satisfied that wasn't his game, I went inside where I could keep a closer eye on him and where it was warm.

Brandish spent almost two hours in the place, playing shuffleboard with a couple of pals, laughing, talking, carrying on in the relaxed, good-natured way people do in a bar like that. It was obvious he was a regular. I sat in a dim corner and sipped beer and munched cashews and watched. Soft rock music played on the jukebox and the TV over the bar was tuned to an all-sports station. The floor waitress—who, I got the impression, was the wife of the bartender—happened to be a middle-aged woman of reasonable attractiveness and ample proportions: big smile, big behind, big pillowy breasts happily displayed by a fuzzy low-cut sweater. Oliver Brandish's eyes swung often to those fuzzy mounds as the woman moved about the room . . . but so did the eyes of every other male in the place.

Just past eight, Brandish pulled his coat back on, said goodbye to his pals, and shoved out the door. I was thirty seconds behind him.

It was full dark now. The air was crisp, but still nowhere near as cold as the previous night.

We crossed the river, heading, as I'd anticipated, toward the string of go-go bars on East State. My buddy Bomber Brannigan's place, The Bomb Shelter, was among them.

Brandish went into the first one we came to. Not surprisingly, it turned out one of the dancers there was an extremely well-endowed young woman. We stayed for two of her sets. Between them, Brandish bought her a drink and she sat at the bar with him while she drank it. She laughed and tossed her long hair and shoulders a lot, causing her proudly cantilevered breasts to sway mesmerizingly. Whatever she said, Brandish smiled idiotically and nodded his head.

I felt a hard knot tightening in my stomach.

After the big-busted girl's second set, Brandish got up and left. I figured he was going to cruise the remaining go-go joints on the strip. It occured to me he would eventually make his way to The Bomb Shelter. I thought protectively of Aletha, the most voluptuous of the current crop of dancers working there—and of Liz, Bomber's Gal Friday and my special friend, herself not exactly scrawny in the body department. My face burned hotly, even in the raw night air. I had to caution myself against letting the case turn personal, to say nothing of mentally trying and convicting an individual without a shred of hard evidence. Hell, just a couple days ago I'd been the one who felt maybe Mike Brandish was reaching too far in his concern over the man.

Any further pondering along those lines was cut short by an unexpected move on the part of the subject. Instead of continuing up State as I'd anticipated, he veered off before reaching the next go-go bar and started down one of the side streets. Past the darkened windows of a row of closed businesses he went. Hanging back, watching from a careful distance, I saw then what I realized his destination must be. A modestly lighted sign jutted out over a doorway near the far end of the block: LUCY'S LACE LAND. One of those lingerie modelling shops, a recent addition to this part of town.

Oliver Brandish went in under the sign.

Since there was no way to follow him inside inconspicuously, I crossed the street and slid into a convenient patch of blackness between two buildings part-way down the block. From there I had a good view of Lucy's. Heavy drapes were drawn behind the front window and on the glass had been painted curvaceous female silhouettes. In theory what went on inside a place like that was that an individual paid a fee to view a display of the latest in fashionable ladies' lingerie as demonstrated in a private booth by a model of the individual's choice selected from the staff on duty; after the show, the individual might then be moved to purchase some of the clothing modeled to take home to his wife or loved one. In truth what went on, more often than not, were acts of prostitution performed in the privacy of the booths, additional money paid in accordance with the individual's desires and the model's willingness. When claims of such acts were brought to public light, of course, the owners of the shops would protest that they ran a legitimate business and had no control over transactions conducted in secret by the models. It was a popular scam, the old massage parlor bit dressed up in see-through lace instead of terrycloth.

In my patch of darkness I risked a cigarette, figuring Oliver Brandish had no inkling of my presence in the first place and was otherwise occupied in the second place. I now had a pretty good idea of where he'd been on the nights he wasn't where he was supposed to be. In my mind he reverted back to what I originally suspected he was; a lonely old man with some shameful—but relatively harmless—secrets.

Forty minutes and two additional cigarettes later, the old guy re-emerged and began plodding back toward State. I followed him home. He made no other stops. Maybe it was my imagination, but it seemed to me his wide shoulders slumped a little lower under his coat than they had before.

Back inside my borrowed car in stakeout position, I wondered what I should tell Mike Brandish. It had bothered him that his father kept raunchy magazines in his room; how was he going to react to this? Was it my job to tell him the absolute truth, or merely to ascertain his father's innocence regarding the Slicer killings without going into every detail? I decided it was the latter. Which meant I'd have to ride it out a little longer, until the real Slicer was either apprehended or struck again when I could verify Oliver Brandish's presence elsewhere—never mind exactly where. Besides, from a strictly cynical standpoint, the fact the old bird had gotten his ashes hauled at the lingerie joint was no guarantee he couldn't still be the killer.

Around midnight, the lights in the upper half of the Victorian winked out.

Half an hour later, right on schedule, Alice Gorton arrived home in her mud-spattered taxi. Her lights went on and then back off in less than an hour.

At three-thirty, it was my turn to go home and to bed.

I was up before ten, feeling restless and edgy. I checked the morning paper. Nothing new on the Slicer killings. It had been eight days since the last victim.

With no pressing business for the day until it was time to go on stakeout, I decided to fill in as many blanks as I could rather than coast along and wait for things to run their own course. The name of the game in detective work—public or private—is contacts. Call them snitches, informers, whatever you want, with the right voices willing to whisper in your ear the job gets done a hell of a lot quicker and easier. Rockford is a small city and it's been my home base for a lot of years. I've built up an enviable network of snitches and for matters that fall outside their areas of expertise I've developed a reputation for being willing and able to lean hard in order to find out what I want to know. None of this was worth spit for unearthing a psycho like the Slicer, unfortunately, but it was just the ticket for blank-filling.

It took me a half-dozen calls to come up with a list of the girls employed at Lucy's Lace Land and then get that list narrowed down to the most spectacularly built of those who'd been on duty the previous night. Her name was Roberta Relva and her address was a trailer park out by the airport.

I drove out to Sky Court without calling ahead and was lucky enough to catch Roberta Relva at home. On the unlucky side, I also caught her boyfriend at home with her.

'What about?' he sneered after answering the door and listening to my request to speak to his lady.

'Personal business,' I told him.

'Personal business my ass. You're one of them sick bastards from the lingerie place, ain't you?' He was broad-shouldered and blue-jawed and handsome in a torn T-shirt, brooding, moody kind of way. His mood today didn't seem to be a pleasant one. But neither was mine, particularly.

'You're right,' I said, keeping my voice level, 'I'm here about Roberta's work at the lingerie place. But I'm not *from* there, not in the way you mean.' I decided to let the 'sick bastard' crack ride.

But he wouldn't have it. 'Don't you wish,' he said with a fresh sneer. 'You got the look all over you, bub. The look of a loser who had to pay for his kicks.'

I smiled at him. 'And how do you get your kicks . . . sloppy seconds on what others have to pay for?'

He shoved the plastic-wrapped storm door open the rest of the way and came barreling out at me. Eyes wild, teeth bared, saliva spraying along with an enraged roar. I slipped the first clublike fist he stabbed at me, ducked in close grabbing a wad of shirtfront, pivoted, dragged him across my hip and sent him sailing over the flimsy metal rail of the landing. He crashed to the ground and rolled struggling through the gray slush there. I vaulted the rail and when he spun to face me on his hands and knees, I kicked him in the throat. Still on his knees, he went rigid with pain and alarm, making ragged sucking noises and clasping under his chin with both hands. It wasn't necessary to hit him any more, but his upturned face made a damned tempting target. I kept seeing that sneer on it.

I was still contemplating whether or not to skin a knuckle on the guy when a voice said from the doorway of the trailer, 'That's enough. Okay?'

I turned to look at Roberta Relva, and there was plenty to look at. She was young, maybe twenty-five, with a foam of shiny black hair pouring down around a face highlighted by almond eyes and a wide, sensual mouth. Her skin was the color and texture of heavily creamed coffee. She wore a floor-length red robe, but it was unbelted and hung provocatively open. Beneath it she had on a filmy black thing cut low to reveal lots more coffee-cream skin wrapped around breathtaking curves. In the open doorway, her hair stirred in the chill air and her bursting cleavage took on a fine pattern of gooseflesh.

'Your doorman needs to work on his manners,' I said.

'I know. He can be a shit. But he's handy to have around this time of year to keep my water pipes unfrozen and the driveway shoveled. So don't hurt him please.'

I turned back to the guy still trying to suck air. 'That's sort of up to you, *bub*. You got any more problem with me talking to your lady?'

His eyes hated me but he managed to shake his no.

'Turo,' the woman said to him. 'Go over to Rosemary's. Have her fix you some tea for your throat. I'll call when I am finished.'

The guy got slowly to his feet, still breathing raggedly, still rubbing his throat. He walked away, eyes averted, head hung low.

When he was gone, I said, 'I think his pride is hurt worse than anything else.'

Roberta Relva shrugged. 'When the time is right, I will repair his ego and make him feel like a man again.'

I looked at her. Yeah, she could do a hell of a lot for—or to—a man's ego.

Her eyes met my stare. 'You came here to talk to me about something?'

'That's right.'

'Come inside then. Where it's warmer.'

The trailer was a nice one. Lots of dark wood and brass, plush carpeting, overstuffed furniture. The air was heavy with a sweet scent. After closing the door behind us, Roberta Relva strode to a pack of cigarettes on a polished table, withdrew one and lighted it. Exhaling smoke, she said, 'Do I know you?'

'I never had the pleasure.'

She shrugged again. 'I used to do a lot of drugs. Sometimes I run into men I used to . . . know. But I don't remember them.'

'You have no reason to remember me.'

'You're a cop, right?'

'Not the kind you mean.'

'Show me something.'

I flipped open my wallet to find my P.I. ticket and held it out for her.

'Private heat,' she said. 'So I don't have to talk to you at all.'

'Nope, not if you don't want to. I can go chat some more with Turo if you'd rather.'

'Is that supposed to intimidate me?' She laughed and snapped her fingers. 'I could replace Turo like that.'

'Yeah, I suppose you could.'

'You're not as tough as you think you are, either.'

'Nobody hardly ever is.'

She let some smoke leak from her nostrils, then took a deep breath, swelling her magnificent breasts, shoving them out at me. 'Maybe you think *you* would like to replace Turo.'

I drank in a good long look. I smiled. 'Sorry, babe, I don't do water pipes.'

She smiled right back. 'Bullshit. You'd *lick* my pipes clear—and be happy to do it—if that's what I really wanted.'

I shook my head. 'Why go to all that trouble when all I'd have to do to get what you're offering is stop by Lucy's and pay a few extra bucks for a modeling session?'

Her smile went away. When she exhaled smoke this time, she blew it at me like a cannon blast. 'Not a *few* extra bucks, buddy—*plenty* of extra goddam bucks!'

It was my turn to shrug.

'What the hell do you want anyway?'

'Just a few questions.'

'Ask them then. No guarantee I'm going to answer.'

I showed her my photograph of Oliver Brandish. 'Do you know this man?'

'Maybe.'

'Come on, dammit. He was in Lucy's last night. You were on duty. He has a thing for really stacked chicks and you fit the bill, baby, in case you never noticed.'

'All right, yeah, I know him.'

'Did you do a session for him last night?'

'Yeah.'

'Has he been there before?'

'Sure. They all come back.'

'What does he like?'

'He likes to play checkers and whistle John Phillip Sousa marches—holy fuck, what do you *think* he likes?'

'Tell me.'

'Look, he's a nice old guy. I don't want to make trouble for him.'

'Nobody does. His family is worried about him, worried about what he does when he goes out alone at night. That's all.'

'You're going to tell them about me?'

'Probably not. I need to know things for myself, then I'll decide what to tell them to best ease their worries.'

She lit another cigarette. 'He's not rich, like a lot of the old guys we get. You can tell that. Sometimes he can only afford the modeling session and he . . . you know, plays with himself while I'm doing a show for him. If he's got extra or if I'm in a generous mood, I'll let him feel me up. I've given him head a few times. His favourite thing is for me to smear myself with oil and let him titty fuck me. But that's awful messy, I won't do that unless he can afford the full price. When he comes, he says "Margaret" a lot of the time—that's his dead wife. It's really sad when he does that.'

I didn't say anything for a minute or so. Yeah, it was sad all right. It was a sad bitch of a world. Sad that old guys like Oliver Brandish ended up alone seeking so desperately to fulfill their emptiness, and sadder still that sorry bastards like me took money to find out about it.

'Are you all right?' Roberta Relva said.

I turned to leave. 'No, I'm not.' I said over my shoulder. 'Most of the time I'm lucky if I'm half right.'

It was another clear night, at least so far. A raw, damp wind had blown up out of the southwest, threatening to drag a storm along with it. The first wisps of gray-black clouds were starting to skid across the glittering sky.

I sat in my borrowed car at the North Main stakeout, sipping bourbon-laced coffee from the thermos. I felt generally lousy, like a half-healed wound. A storm would suit me. Maybe it would wash away some of the crud I had to dip myself in to make a living.

Everything was normal with the old Victorian. Lights on upstairs, dark downstairs. The Gorton woman was out driving her shift, Oliver Brandish had stayed in so far tonight. It was past eight, I doubted he'd be venturing out anymore now.

The wind shook the car. I fired up another cigarette and pulled the harsh smoke deep. Shit, I hated this. God help me, but in a dark corner of my mind I was hoping the Slicer would strike again—strike while Oliver Brandish was right where he was, so I could report to his kid without telling any direct lies and be done with the whole stinking thing.

I smoked and thought my black thoughts. And watched. And waited.

Well before midnight, almost a full hour ahead of her pattern, Alice Gorton arrived home. Into the garage went the cab and across the back yard she came. Was there a little more purpose in her stride, a little more bounce, or was it just my imagination? Maybe the night had capped with an especially generous tipper and she'd been able to knock off early.

The lights in her half of the house came on, but not as many as usual. After only a minute or two they went out again, the basement lights flaring in their stead, a row of dull yellow squares skirting the base of the structure like broken teeth in a smile.

This variation in routine snagged my curiosity, but not unduly so. The focus of my attention remained a couple of stories higher. Less than ten minutes later, though, when Oliver Brandish's lights went out too, it became another matter. It was pushing midnight, not that far off schedule from his previous turn-in times (one the first night, a little earlier last night). Nevertheless, too many breaks in a pattern have to make you wonder. And the lights were still burning in the basement. What was she doing down there at this hour? The screwy notion I'd had before, about the two of them getting together with each other, played across my mind again. Maybe they slipped down to the basement for their assignations. But that didn't make any sense. They were grown people, for crying out loud, the only residents in the whole building—what would prevent them from meeting in one or the other's apartment?

The lights in the basement continued to burn.

The rest of the house stayed dark.

The clouds skidding across the sky were growing fatter, darker, sending eerie shadow-shapes swimming down the street and over the bare lawns. Picking one of the shadows, I piled out of my car and moved with it. I circled part-way around the block, went up the alley until I reached the garage/shed where Alice Gorton parked her taxi. Most of the other houses around were dark. Here and there you could see a nightlight or the bluish eye of a TV showing through curtains.

I catfooted over the slushy path Alice Gorton had worn between the garage and the house. Under the outside stairway that led to the upper apartment, I crouched and edged close to one of the basement windows. It was an old-fashioned job, sunk low in a corrugated well, awkward as hell to peer into.

Balancing on a knee and an elbow, I leaned down to see what I could see. Visibility was poor through the grime-caked glass. I seemed to be looking into an old coal bin, a box of rough wooden walls with a narrow opening affording very little view of anything else. Faintly, I could hear music playing—a soft, lilting, romantic instrumental.

I moved to a different window on the side of the house. The visibility wasn't much better, even after I rubbed the dirty glass with my sleeve. I could make out a huge furnace, rows of support beams, a stack of storage crates against one wall. The music was barely discernable from over here. Feeling exposed as hell on the edge of the open lawn, I didn't waste much time at that vantage point.

I returned to the open stairway, went past it, made my way around to another window on the back side of the house. I could hear the music plainly as I knelt beside the spill of yellowish light. Carefully I wiped the dirty glass, then leaned to look inside.

And wished to hell I never had.

Alice Gorton was down there, moving to the music, dancing with herself, swirling and dipping across the dusty cement floor on bare feet. Her toenails were painted bright red and her face was made up garishly, heavy lipstick and eyeshadow, false eyelashes that fluttered like butterflies that had landed on either side of her nose. She wore a long, flowing negligee wrap of white gossamer, her arms spread wide so that it billowed behind her as she danced. Beneath it she was nude.

Except for the thing around her chest.

At first I thought it was some sort of ill-fitting bra, ludicrous in contrast to her bushy nakedness below. But then, as she turned and turned, allowing me repeated looks at it, I noted the puckered nipples, the darkened, crusted flesh, the oddly-angled clasps and the elastic bands tied to hold the pieces together. And over on the top of what had once been a tool bench I saw the stained gloves and the knife and the plastic freezer bags. And through the red-flecked, smeared plastic, the unmistakable shapes, the carefully paired mounds . . .

Realization overcame me and my guts threatened to boil up out of my mouth and nose. I recoiled from the window as if scalded—and lurched directly into one of the two men who had come up behind me. I think the collision of our bodies surprised him almost as much as it did me. As I twisted and jerked from his grasp, I saw that he was tall and spindly, wearing a brown hunter's vest over a red checkered shirt. Past his shoulder, the second man, similarly dressed, carried a rifle. On their arms, both wore bright orange bands marking them as members of one of the neighborhood vigilance groups I'd read about in the papers.

'Hold it right there,' the one with the rifle said. 'Not another move.'

'You don't understand,' I tried to tell him.

'We understand alright, you window-peeping bastard.'

I held up my hands in protest. 'No. In the house there, in the basement . . . '

The movement of my hands alarmed the spindly one. He swung a fist from his vest pocket and aimed something at me. My body went ice cold and I thought I was dead—shot by a well-intentioned amateur. I almost wished he would have shot me. The mace he sprayed in my face felt like molten lava poured into my eyes and lungs. I flopped on the ground in an imitation of a headless chicken's thrashing. I tried to shout, to talk . . . managed only a few cuss words between the sobs and the gasping groans. Something in what I managed to get out must have pissed off the one with the rifle, though. Or maybe he just wanted to get in a few licks of his own. For whatever reason, he stepped up . . . mercifully, from my standpoint . . . and punched me unconscious with the butt of his .410.

EPILOGUE

Plenty more happened after I went down for the count. The rest of the shit hit the fan, so to speak, and grisly shit it turned out to be.

The disturbance outside the window—as the two men who'd 'apprehended' me put me in handcuffs and summoned other members of their vigilance team and eventually sent for the cops—couldn't help but gain the attention of Alice Gorton. The final slim thread of sanity she had left—the instinctive thing that had caused her to conceal her crimes—snapped at the interruption and brought her up out of the basement. In all her naked, painted glory she came, wearing her ghastly flesh bra to cover her shame and wielding her knife with surprising savagery.

She slashed the guy with the rifle before he had any idea what was going on. The spindly one ended up macing her, too. But her madness threatened to carry her even through that. She cut him as well before he managed to finally subdue her.

When the cops started arriving, the scene was chaotic. Nobody had any comprehension of what they'd stumbled onto yet.

It was only after I regained consciousness at the hands of the paramedics and screamed for somebody to look in the basement that the pieces began falling into place for the rest of them.

It took days and weeks of psychiatric probing for it all to come together, to form the final twisted picture of what had gone wrong with Alice Gorton, what had turned her into the Slicer. Eighteen months earlier she'd had a double mastectomy. Prior to that she had been a big, heavy-breasted woman, her endowments (so ironic, considering the Brandish situation that had brought me onto the scene) the pride and joy of her husband of twenty-five years. After the surgery, he could no longer bear to touch her. The physical side of their relationship crashed and burned in a series of tearful, painful, unfulfilled bedroom confrontations. He left her seven months after the operation. She took a job as a night-shift cab driver to make ends meet. She tried dating other men, but always her 'deformity' (her word) got in the way. She became sour and abrasive to the world.

Then came the night the black hooker and her 'date' flagged Alice Gorton's cab. In the back seat during the brief ride to the hot sheet motel, the drunken john had taken out the hooker's ample breasts and kissed them and played with them, accompanied by much pleasurable moaning and murmuring from both parties. All of this audible to Alice Gorton, and visible in the rearview mirror. Her reaction had been embarrassment and humiliation and then, slowly, a gripping, all-consuming rage. When the hooker came out of the motel some time later, Alice Gorton's cab was conveniently cruising by. The black girl might still have been all right if she'd kept her mouth shut. But no, she had to flaunt her roll of bills and giggle and brag about her fun at the expense of the 'big-spending titty man'.

Alice had pulled over on a poorly-lighted side street, taken the knife she kept for protection from under her seat, turned and stabbed the black whore. Stabbed her repeatedly, slashing and hacking, unleashing a fury that had been building pressure inside her for long, agonizing months. As the madness gripped her to its fullest, she had removed the woman's breasts and then kept them after dumping the body. The whole exercise, in addition to abating her rage, had generated a breathtaking, near-sexual release. That night, in her bed, possessively clutching the severed breasts over her own scarred chest, Alice Gorton had masturbated to a series of shattering climaxes. After that, the stalking of new prey, the seed for new pleasures, so accessible through the cab service and so trusting due to her own femaleness, had begun in earnest . . .

When all was said and done, I managed to keep my name out of most of it, at least for the public record. I let the neighborhood vigilance boys take the credit for ferreting out the dreaded Slicer. While a certain amount of publicity can be good for business, too much can become notoriety and that can work against you in my racket. The cops were pissed when I wouldn't name my client or state my specific reasons for being on the scene, but they were too relieved at having the Slicer in custody to push it. I didn't want Oliver Brandish to find out I'd had his house under surveillance and maybe start asking why. I saw Mike Brandish once more, to settle up my fee, and he seemed pretty down on himself for the suspicions he'd had about his father. I tried to tell him it had all been a sign of caring on his part, but I don't think he bought it. I hoped some day the kid found a way to turn his caring into a more positive demonstration of affection the old man could know about and appreciate.

Before she could be proclaimed competent to stand trial, the cancer that had already gnawed away part of Alice Gorton spread to her liver and kidneys. She died painfully in the mental ward of the county hospital less than six months after her last victim.

Sad. That was the word Roberta Relva had used. That's what the whole damn mess was. Sad and tragic. Except for potential victims who'd been spared, there were no winners in any of it. Only losers.

And then there was me. Somewhere in between.

ROSE DAWN BRADFORD grew up in Washington, DC, and now lives in Southern California. She's published fiction with a variety of small press magazines. Rose Dawn's most recent sale was a short horror story to the bi-weekly magazine *Pulphouse*. She is working with Dark Horse Comics at the present on a graphic adaptation of two of Andrew Vachss' short stories. She also writes non-fiction for a local CA newspaper.

Rose Dawn Bradford

Principles

'Ideals are sometimes more important than individuals. Anyone with any sense would have to agree.'

Marjorie Bates smiled at the man from Channel Six, pulling aside her chalk-striped suit jacket to show the folks at home her T-shirt—blue on white background, with the words *Censorship is un-American!* in bold red letters across the front.

Her mind on auto pilot, Marjorie went off into the standard spiel: the First Amendment protected the free expression of ideas, even those the majority of society might consider repugnant, blah blah blah, all Americans must pull together to defend the rights granted under the Constitution, blah blah blah, Nazi Germany, blah blah blah, right-wing book burners, blah blah blah.

The man from Channel Six (who looked like a Vidal Sassoon poster boy) smiled, nodded encouragement, and tried to look wise. Marjorie smiled, nodded back, and turned away from the camera, pausing for a final still shot, arms around two of the gold-encrusted hip-hoppers she'd successfully defended against charges of obscenity.

Ideals were *usually* more important than individuals.

'I'm proud of you, Mom.' Cherie held up the latest newspaper article: *Marjorie Bates, crusading civil liberties attorney strikes again.*

'I clipped it out this morning.' Cherie smiled, waiting for approval. Marjorie returned the smile, absently stroking a strand of apricot-colored hair away from her daughter's brow.

'Thanks, hon. I'm glad you're glad.'

'I mean, I really, really *like* the Rich Mothafuckas, and I don't know how anybody could say they're obscene. Music isn't obscene *ever*, is it, Mom?'

Marjorie bit back the complaint—it *was* the group's name after all—and sighed.

'The kids in my class think it was really dope. Except a few of the nerds, and who cares what they think. Only . . . '

Cherie paused, trouble and adoration warring on her face.

Marjorie waited.

'Well, Tasha says it's way fresh what you did for the Mothafuckas, but . . . ' She stopped again, then continued all in a rush, 'But she says you're helping some white supremo group now, and they want to kill all the African Americans, and she can't believe anybody would help them after all the stuff they've done.'

Marjorie placed an arm around her daughter's shoulder.

'Look, baby. What Tasha says is true, to an extent. The firm is defending a member of the Aryan Army. He wasn't charged with killing anyone, or beating anyone up, or anything like that. If that was it, I'd stay out of it.'

She rotated her head, easing the tension in her neck. 'This kid was arrested after organizing a public meeting to explain his group's philosophy. That's all. Sweetie, you know I find everything the Aryan Army stands for disgusting. But please try to understand. If one group has freedom to express its ideas, then *all* groups need to have the same freedom. Get it?'

Cherie nodded. She knew what the words meant, but Marjorie was sure, had no real grasp of the beliefs behind them. As was well and good. Cherie was ten, and a pretty neat kid.

Sometimes it was even hard to justify the shit she did to herself. Blind trust. Blind trust in the good intentions of a bunch of slave owners who wrote a bunch of cool-sounding rhetoric over two hundred years ago.

Marjorie sighed. 'Okay, kiddo. Let's get dinner started.'

'There is a difference between art and pornography.'

'Yes, there is,' Marjorie agreed. But who could say what the hell it was?

She'd found herself actively disliking those she was called to speak for in the past; the dead-eyed street boys, every other word out of their mouths 'fuck', 'bitch' or some seemingly innumerable combination thereof; the raging skinhead warriors; the sad little perverts making phoney snuff flicks in their garages. But never had she felt such disgust as the man now sitting across from her in her plush office evoked.

And, much as she hated to admit it, even some fear. Marjorie prided herself on her composure—at least when the cameras were running or the jury was sitting.

Another attorney had once called her 'Brass Balls Bates,' and she'd immediately corrected him: 'Brass *ovaries*, buster.'

Sighing, Marjorie opened the case file again. This wasn't a case she wanted; this was not a man she wanted to be in the same room with, much less defend.

She looked again at Frank Lawson. Franklin Lawson, III, a new money guy from an old money town. Rancho Santa Fe, California, a gated community whose residents considered their La Jolla neighbors barely one step above white trash. He wasn't doing what he did for the bucks, that was for sure. He'd earned his the old-fashioned way; waited for Daddy to croak, then inherited the bundle. Nope, Franklin III was in it for fun.

Art, she reminded herself. His photo-essays were all the rage in LA, New York, and even the hipper, more yupscale sections of San Diego, the biggest little town in the USofA. The alternative newspapers called him an artist. The ACLU called him an artist. The young angsters in their black clothes with their black hair, their little cups of black expresso and little balloons of black heroin shipped over the border from Mexico, called him an artist. Maybe he even bought it himself.

All Marjorie knew was that the senior partner wanted this case. It was a high-profile case, Marjorie was a high-profile attorney, and she despised that prick sitting across from her. Frank III, the latest 'artist' to be busted on a pornography rap.

But not just any kind of pornography. Kiddie porn, the DA called it. There were even rumors he planned to RICO old Frank, but Marjorie knew that was just talk for the headlines. Well, at least she could dump her Hitler Youth rabble-rouser off on one of the other lawyers. It'd take a lot of time, a lot of energy, to figure out how to get a podunk San Diego jury to let Frank III walk.

She looked through the portfolio, the material that had brought the law down on Frank's head. Though the photos were going to be a problem, the words that went with them were what disturbed Marjorie the most. Ironic. Every stinking, putrid word the man—if you wanted to call him that—had written could easily be proven protected under the mighty First Amendment. But the words . . . Christ, the words.

This wasn't some ghetto boy rapping about jamming flashlights up some 'ho's snatch; or a skinny, pizza-faced kid with swastikas tattooed on his arms, talking about the 'superiority' of the White Race, when he himself was a walking advertisement against it.

This was an intelligent, monied man spewing filth that shocked Marjorie in spite of herself. Whether he meant what he said or was simply out for publicity, which seemed the more logical explanation, she didn't know or care.

Either way, the bile rose in her throat when she read the words penned by Franklin Lawson, III. First some bullshit justificatory language about the proven superiority of 'Man', then . . .

Lesser men may be put off by the laws of the system. Only the truly courageous few are able to take what they want, no matter what the consequences.

I do not admire pedophiles, in general. They whine, they claim to have been 'abused' themselves, they try to gain sympathy in order to remain free, at the expense of true valor.

I am also dismayed by the sadomasochistic crowd, with its emphasise on consensuality. What is consensuality but an admission of weakness; that one is not strong enough to have one's way without fear of reprisal?

No, those I admire are Men like myself. Those brave enough to say FUCK the laws of the system. We will follow the law of nature: the weak are consumed by the strong. I admire Men like Thomas Bradbury, serving five consecutive life sentences at Tracy as these words are written, who found five little girls he thought pretty, and decided to take without apology. Five little girls, each fucked in every little orifice of her little body before Bradbury took a knife and carved his mark upon them; slowly, lovingly.

The police and the Courts in this so-called land of the free and home of the brave call him a murderer. Thomas Bradbury, I call you brother. No excuses for you! You took what you wanted, and are paying the consequences at this very moment, and the world of wimps and whiners has been denied the privilege of containing you, that your light might provide a beacon which all Men may someday hope to follow.

She shuddered, glanced up, saw that Frank had caught it, the gleam of amusement in his eyes. *Asshole.* Yeah, he was just writing this trash to get attention. A real crusader. But, much as the words disgusted Marjorie, they were fairly unimportant in the overall scheme of things.

Frank III wasn't copping to any rape, sodomy, mutilation or murder of children; just stating his admiration for those who did.

But the pictures that accompanied the text . . .

She thought she could make a go of it. An entire page filled with photographs in rows of four. A nude child; an adult male ejaculating. Over and over and over again, repeated in sickening detail.

But the photos were obviously separate. No penetration, no overt sexuality at all in the poses of the children, other than the fact that their pre-pubescent nipples and genitalia were exposed. Most of them wore bright smiles. Here, a little blonde girl licking a lollipop, coquettishly nude. Then the cock, looking so huge in contrast with her tininess, spurting semen. There, a small Mexican boy, his eyes so large and dark that looking into them was like gazing out at the night from a windowless room. Then the adult penis, a man's hairy paw wrapped around the shaft, come dribbling over the bulbous head. Again and again, the pattern reasserted itself.

She forced herself to look at the man without flinching, found his mouth drawn into a small smile as he watched her.

Having avoided looking directly at him, Marjorie now found herself studying Lawson. He was dark-haired, jet-eyed, pale as an albino. A full beard framed lips lush to the point of corpulence, his nose a sharp jib between yards and yards of stone cut cheekbone. Muscles rippled beneath the silk suit jacket. It was cut to fit him perfectly, stretching across his chest, nipping in at his impossibly flat stomach. He was all peaks and planes; an altar boy at a church of debauchery. Marjorie wasn't sure whether, meeting him under different circumstances, she'd find him shockingly attractive or simply shocking.

She cleared her throat, embarrassed, but Frank III didn't seem discomposed by her stare. 'The pictures,' she said. 'I don't see any real problem with what you wrote—covered by the First Amendment.'

'God bless the First Amendment,' he sneered.

'Mr Lawson.' She couldn't resist. 'If you disdain the rules of the cops and the Courts so much, why ask me to defend you? Why not just take what you want, then accept the consequences?'

'Good girl,' he said, the words sounding like profanity from his lips. 'You actually read the words, didn't you? The truth is, I could give a good fuck about what your government does to me. But isn't it better that I be free, free to distribute my art without hindrance? That I be given a forum to speak up for my beliefs? That, sweet crusading bitch, is why I've come to you.'

His tone was so silky, she almost missed the word. 'So you think I'm a bitch? You want a bitch as your advocate?'

He laughed. 'I think a *bitch* makes the best advocate, don't you? Won't back down, right? And you surely didn't seem to mind the word when you were speaking out for the Pretentious Motherfuckers, or whatever they call themselves.' He laughed again. 'Look, let's get on with it. The words aren't a big problem? Neither are the pictures.'

'Well, a jury might . . . '

'Fuck a jury. I have signed consent forms from the parents of every child in every photograph that was seized. And none of them even saw the men in the other photos. The men never saw them. Parade the kids, in all their innocence, before the cameras, let them tell you what fun it was to help me with my little art project.'

Marjorie chewed the end of her Cross pen, eyes locked with the creature across the desk. 'You have signed consent forms? The parents are willing to testify that they gave permission for you to photograph their children nude?'

'Of course they will, my dear little bitch . . . or lady, if you prefer. Of course they will. And I strongly suggest you put the children on the stand. They'll tell you nothing untoward happened. They'll tell you they had . . . a ball.' Again, the sickening chuckle.

Repressing her revulsion, Marjorie stood. 'All right, Mr Lawson. I think we just might be able to pull this one off.'

Leading him to the elevator, she thought about what he'd said. A bitch to defend him. What it really boiled down to was, a *woman* to defend him . . . a *mother* to defend him. Like having an African American defend that Aryan punk.

As Lawson entered the elevator, Marjorie smiled. What the hell? Striding down the hall, she knocked on Steve Goldberg's office door, poked her head in. 'Steve? Got a case for you. I'm gonna have to spend some time working with Frank Lawson—'

'The baby raper?' Goldberg's bushy eyebrows drew down. 'What a world, huh?'

Marjorie smiled impishly. 'Yeah, what a world. Guess who your new client's going to be? Arthur von Stilwagen.'

'The *Nazi*?'

'We're true believers,' she reminded him. Then, laughing, closed the door gently.

Marjorie was on the phone with the ADA. 'Did you know my client obtained permission from each child's parents before photographing them? Did you know that not only the parents, but the children themselves, are fully prepared to testify that neither Mr Lawson nor anyone else behaved inappropriately with them? You *did* notice, didn't you, that the photographs of the kids and the photographs of the men were obviously taken at different times, in different settings?'

Of course the ADA didn't know anything. Lawson, the publicity-leech, had never bothered to disclose his little facts to the cops or anyone on the DA's staff.

Marjorie knew the DA. She knew he loved press, but only as long as it was positive. She knew she had this sucker nailed as far as the facts went. She also knew juries were apt to ignore facts and go with emotions. So it was a gamble, trying to get Frank III off the hook. On the other hand, the entire DA's office knew as well as she that every major obscenity case they'd tried to make lately had been a dismal, headline-grabbing failure.

Waiting for the DA to call back personally, she flipped through Frank III's file one more time. The happy-faced nymphet babies in stark contrast to the hideous, protected words that encaptioned their pictures. She felt she could get the charges dropped even before the Prelim. She was pretty certain she could win the bastard at trial, if it came to that. She still wasn't convinced she wanted to.

Victory! When she'd called to give Lawson the good news, he'd been unctuous, oily, grateful. Now he could produce and distribute his 'art.'

'But I don't really like this town,' he'd sighed. 'I think I might head for someplace where people like me are better understood. Europe, perhaps. But I really want to thank you, my dear. I wasn't looking forward to having to get up there on that stand, you know. So draining.'

He chuckled. 'In fact, to express my deep appreciation, I'm taking the trouble to give you a small appropriate gift. Something that will indicate the respect I feel for your prowess.'

Now that she'd gotten him off, she wasn't a bitch anymore, but a dear, and one with prowess at that. Chalk up another one for Brass Ovaries Bates.

She stepped off the elevator, returning to the office after her late court appearance, ready to put Frank III's file away. Out of sight, out of mind. But when all was said and done, Marjorie knew she'd done the right thing. Principles were principles, *no matter what.*

'Put a package on your desk,' the receptionist called as Marjorie turned toward the door. 'That guy—that artist—dropped it off for you, said it was real important.'

'Okay,' Marjorie said, smiling. What would a self-aggrandizing fraud like Lawson pick to indicate the respect he felt for her? *I just want to produce my Art. I want a public forum.* Asshole just wanted to get some free publicity, sell pictures of happy, unharmed children, and stay the fuck out of the pen. Oh well . . . ideals were more important, and all that.

She dropped her briefcase on the floor, straightened the frames that encased Cherie's smiling face, and peered at her desk. 'Personal and Confidential' was stamped in red all over the surface of the thick manila envelope, her name written in blood-bold letters across the front.

Picking up the letter opener, Marjorie pulled the single sheet of bond out. 'A token of my appreciation,' typewritten across the center of the page. That was all.

She frowned, then pulled at the rest of the package, separated from the note by a thin cardboard backing.

Catching a glimpse of childish legs, a hairless body, Marjorie's stomach lurched, in spite of knowing she'd been right to defend the . . . prick. A token of his appreciation? More sick photos of little Lolitas, obligingly sucking lollipops for the camera.

As she pulled the first 9' x 12' photograph free, she averted her eyes from the hairless pussy, the barely-budding breasts, wanting to toss the whole packet of filth immediately.

As the first of a horribly thick bundle of pictures cleared the envelope completely, Marjorie glanced down . . . into the wide, terrified, horror-stricken eyes of the little girl. A little girl about the same age as . . .

She doubled over, clutching her stomach, fighting to keep from vomiting all over the surface of her shiny oak desk.

Not a little girl the same age as . . . not a little girl who looked like . . .

Cherie's eyes. Cherie's nude little body. Cherie's terror, Cherie's humiliation, Cherie's anguish.

Trick photography. That had to be it. Some kind of psychopathic joke. A token of his gratitude—to indicate the respect he felt, the esteem he held her in.

With a cry like a gut-shot dog, Marjorie tore her eyes away, punching buttons on her telephone with savage, Parkinsonian fingers.

One . . . two . . . five . . . ten . . . with each empty, hollow ring, Cherie's wide, glazed eyes peered up at her mother. Petrified. Trapped.

Accusing.

JAMES COLBERT's first novel, *Profit and Sheen*, was praised by Charles Willeford in the *Washington Post Book World* as 'a stunning first novel, and if you plan to read only one mystery this season, this is the one to buy.' Colbert's second novel, *No Special Hurry* (the first chapter of which is presented here), was also well received, as was his third, *Skinny Man*, which was published by Atheneum in 1991. Colbert has been a marine, an air-traffic controller, a cabinetmaker, a bartender, a Latin tutor, and a police officer. He lives with his wife, Veronica, in New Orleans and is working on a fourth novel.

James Colbert
No Special Hurry

For almost an hour I had watched as he worked on the crude, star-shaped design, etching it carefully with a sewing needle into the soft skin between his thumb and first finger. Now he sat on the corner of the metal-frame bunk, hunched over, intent in that rapt way only a seventeen-year-old can be intent, a bottle of ink clasped tightly between his knees, the marked hand draped over the edge of the rusting iron sink.

He dipped the needle into the ink and lifted it out, a shiny black drop quivering on its tip, and I asked, 'You know a tattoo will never come off?'

He smeared the ink into the design, then looked at me irritably, lips pursed, one eyebrow arched scornfully in a way that reminded me of myself at his age, when I had practiced bad-ass looks in the mirror, T-shirt sleeves rolled up, muscles flexing.

I added, 'It's going to hurt.'

He shook his head indulgently, then dipped back into the ink, smiling slightly as he did so.

'Everyone who sees it will know you've been in jail.'

His smile broadened, rounding his dull features, and without looking at me again, he set his shoulders in a preoccupied way and tossed his curly red-brown hair over one narrow shoulder.

His name was Randy. I had found him two nights before, wandering up and down the cellblock, newly admitted and not exactly certain why the tough guys, the ones with their solid bodies and their long, dull stares, were whistling at him and laughing as they invited him into their cells. So I had taken him in, reluctantly giving myself the role of his protector, and after a time I had explained to him that *white meat* was a term not always reserved for the breast of a chicken. And he had looked at me then just as he had looked at me a moment before, indulgently, half-amused, as if *I* were the one who needed help, and said, 'Give me a break, Tony,' to which I had simply raised and dropped one shoulder in a resigned shrug meant to convey certain knowledge.

Now he added, 'You remind me of my mother.'

'Wait until it gets infected,' I warned.

'It's not going to get infected,' he replied sourly. 'I watched the guy yesterday, start to finish. He showed me what to do.'

'What guy?'

'The tattoo-guy. You know him.' Randy gestured behind his back, pointing with the needle.

I looked away, not bothering to observe that his description fit half the men locked in with us, then asked over my shoulder, 'How much did he charge you?'

Randy did not reply right away but again dipped the needle into the ink and brought it out. As he held it close to his face and studied it, he answered absently. 'He charged five dollars for the needle, three for the ink. Eight dollars.'

My head jerked around involuntarily. By prison standards—for men who were paid ten cents an hour, *when* the prison could find them paid work—eight dollars was a considerable amount of money.

'At what interest?'

Randy smeared the ink, dipped into the bottle, smeared more ink.

'He didn't say anything about any interest.'

'He will,' I said.

'I won't pay it,' Randy replied with a teenager's smug, that-settles-that finality.

He will, I thought, and for a moment it was hard to look at his young face, *and you will.*

He was jabbing the needle now, going into his design too deeply, and blood was mixing with the ink, causing it to smear and to run along the weblike little creases in his skin.

I looked away and for a few minutes watched the cons moving idly back and forth, killing time on the strip, the ten-foot-wide floor that ran the length of the cellblock, from the door to the showers; cells on one side, steel wall on the other. A guard passed on the overhead walkway, whistling and tapping his stick on the steel rail. I looked up, following his progress without interest, imagining through the long, narrow windows behind him New Orleans's downtown, not a mile away: the secretaries in bright dresses on their way to work, the men in suits, the newsstand where I used to buy the morning paper. I pictured the newsman's hand, tough and callused, stained with newsprint; the cup of coffee I customarily drank standing up, glancing only briefly at the headlines before I turned to the commodities reports, the neat, orderly columns of numbers that prepared me for the day's work ahead.

For nine years I had managed one of my father's offices, advising wealthy Central American clients how they might maneuver around whatever currency restrictions prevailed at the time. Invariably these clients wanted to get their money out of their home country and into this one; it was my job to recommend that they convert their money into goods—timber, coffee, stamps, bananas, tin, anything that had intrinsic value—and then to arrange for those goods to be moved up here and sold. Since my fee was based upon the number of US dollars my clients deposited after the sale of the goods, it seemed to be in my own best interest to stay abreast of the market trends. My interests seemed to coincide with those of my clients—although later I learned that most of my clients were representing my *father's* best interest, and the fees I had worked in good faith to earn were nothing more than money to keep me distracted.

I turned back to Randy and asked, 'How big a man is the tattoo-guy?'

'You know him,' Randy repeated. He dabbed at his hand with a folded tissue. 'He wears a bandanna all the time.'

It would be him, I thought, picturing the glassy-eyed biker who wore a bandanna because he chewed tobacco with his mouth open and occasionally liked to wipe at the brown spittle that drooled down his chin. A massive gut encircled him; his fat arms stuck out from his sides, a veritable showcase of tattoos.

'Pleasant fellow,' I observed drily.

'Not really,' Randy said.

The skin betwen his thumb and first finger was now smeared with ink and oozing blood and looked as if he had caught it in a closing steel door.

I turned away again, in time to see the tattooed biker approach our cell in that oddly tentative way prisoners go from one cell to the next. I knew he would not enter without permission from us both and simply glanced past him.

He called out, 'Hey, Randy, how's it going?'

Randy looked over his shoulder, saw with relief who it was, and replied, 'Come on in. I think I have a problem.'

I know you have a problem, I thought, but the most immediate part of it was the mess he was making of his hand; so I pushed myself upright and stood outside the cell door, allowing, if he turned sideways, room for the biker to enter.

As he started to pass he smiled dimly, showing in the gap where his front teeth should have been a dark brown wad of tobacco.

I moved just slightly, but enough to block his way, and said, 'Eight dollars is too steep, pal.'

It took him a moment to comprehend that, and I could see it coming, the way he was working up to his hard-ass look, squinty-eyed and malevolent.

'What's it to you?' he asked.

'My money,' I replied.

That sank in slowly.

'You two married?' he asked, jerking his head to the left, indicating Randy.

I said evenly, 'As good as in church.'

He nodded solemnly.

'Two dollars for the needle, a dollar for the ink. Three dollars.'

I nodded agreement.

'I'll pay you this afternoon,' I said.

He did not seem to hear me but leaned in close, close enough that his breath was warm on my face and the cold, flaccid skin of his gut pressed against my arm.

'And I get first use of him when you two get divorced.'

I glanced at Randy before I nodded again, a barely perceptible movement of my head, the same nod I had first learned to use when trading currency for my clients.

They sat side by side on the lower bunk, Randy twisted around so that he could clasp the biker's fat knee with the hand he had marked.

'You dumb shit,' the biker said in a mild, almost friendly rebuke, 'you let the ink run.'

Randy did not reply but looked at me instead and smiled conspiratorially, as if we shared some private joke.

I shook my head and turned around, turning my back on both of them, leaning against the wrist-thick metal bars at the front of the cell. After a moment I noticed an unfamiliar man looking down at me from the guard's walkway above. Even standing still he seemed to be in motion, waving his arms, jerking his head, so I looked back at him curiously until he turned to say something to the person standing next to him, a woman, I was almost certain. Then she stepped back to look at me too, and I *was* certain. Her hair was dark brown, and it was fluffed fashionably, styled to appear un-styled. Her dark eyes were calm and level, holding my gaze so easily it was a moment before I noticed her gray suit, coat open enough to reveal the swell of her breasts, ripe in a way that reminded me I had served only one year of my three-year sentence.

Behind me, Randy said, alarmed, 'Hey, what are you doing?'

I turned quickly, in time to see him pull back his hand and slap the biker's arm ineffectively.

The biker laughed. A dark brown ball of tobacco rolled out of his mouth. He tried to catch it but missed; it fell onto his fat thigh and crumbled into a wet, fibrous wad.

Randy looked at me and said, 'He put my hand between his legs'—he hesitated, embarrassed, but incensed enough to get past it—'on his thing.'

Still chuckling, the biker unconcernedly picked up the wad of tobacco and put it back in his mouth.

'The boy won't keep his hand still.' His smile was suddenly mean and challenging. 'I was giving him something to hold on to.'

I took my hands out of my pockets and stared at him hard, putting a lot into it. He gave me his squinty-eyed look, chewed twice, looked away; angrily he grabbed Randy's hand and placed it firmly back on his knee.

I moved into the cell and stood in close to the bunks, my hands ready at my sides, waiting for the biker to look at me again. When he did I leaned in under the top bunk as if I were going to whisper to him, then grabbed his long, greasy hair. I yanked it back, slamming his head against the steel wall. He came up fast for a fat man, and as his weight shifted, I sprang back, yanking him forward and up, smashing his face against the welded metal frame of the upper bunk. Before he could fall back I yanked him forward again, throwing him sideways through the open cell door, where he hit the steel deck, coughing, choking on his tobacco, but rising quickly to his knees. I shot Randy a vicious look and stepped out of the cell, onto the strip.

The biker swung around as he got to his feet, crouched low, arms wide, an ugly red welt across his forehead. And he charged just like that, fast, trying to get his fat arms around me. I jabbed for the welt on his forehead, missed, caught his nose, kicked at his feet as he went past.

He turned quickly.

I heard Randy shout, 'Hey, you started it.'

The biker charged again.

I moved left, bumped Randy as he came out of the cell, pushed him out of the way.

One fat hand caught my shirt, and I hammered the arm hard, four quick shots to the elbow as he dragged me toward him and then threw me against the wall.

In close now, my feet off the ground dangling uselessly, ribs crushed, unable to breathe, I twisted his sodden bandanna with one hand, holding his head away, and I pounded that snarling, gap-toothed face. Around the edges of my vision I saw black. A guard's whistle sounded over and over in short, frantic, heart-pounding blasts.

I awoke on the floor, in time to see the dog burst into the cellblock, a big German shepherd straining against its leash so hard its front feet hardly touched the ground as it lunged, ears flat, lip curled back over those teeth, the snapping, frenzied sound of it reverberating off the steel floors and steel wall. Behind it came the guards in blue helmets, overhead lights flashing on their clear plastic visors as they screamed unnecessarily, 'Move it. Move it. Move it.' I rolled myself into a tight ball, face against the ringing steel.

I felt my ankles shackled, my arms pulled behind my back and cuffed. I was lifted to my feet, then, guided by a strong, firm hand, prodded by a hardwood stick, I was marched behind Randy and the biker to the lock-down cells, tiny, dark, one-man cells, where we were confined without any hope of privileges—exercise or showers—close enough together that I had to listen to the biker's obscene threats and Randy's adolescent whining. My whole body ached as I lay down on the narrow bunk; after a while I napped, the sound of angry voices intruding into a fitful sleep.

When I heard keys jingle and the hollow, metallic thump of the lock, in the first confused moments of waking I thought it was my wife coming in, out and back early on a Sunday morning: a run for pastries and the *Times-Picayune*. Just for a moment I could feel her next to me, legs and hips warm down my side, arms moving, turning pages noisily, skipping right through to the gossip columns before she began to read; slipping me a bite of her eclair, knowing I was waiting for it and would chew languorously, eyes closed, feeling as much as tasting the flaky, delicate crust and the smooth, rich whipped cream inside. Then I felt a tug on my foot and remembered: she would have to be back from the dead, too.

Without opening my eyes, I said angrily, 'What?'

A nasal voice came back sourly, loud and harsh: 'Man, what's your problem?'

I sat up enough to see at the foot of the bunk the same man I had seen watching me from the guards' walkway, in motion again, waving his long arms loose-jointedly as he said, 'Hey, chill out. This is Skinny.' He thumped a finger against his own chest, referring to himself as if to another person. His shrewd, almost feral eyes flickered around the cell, then stopped suddenly, locked on me. 'Show some respect. You are going to work for Skinny.'

'Is that right?' I said, starting to grin because I could picture him standing in my father's office, dressed as he was in dirty jeans and a sleeveless green fatigue jacket, unshaven, his hair matted with its own dark grease. I pictured him at work, boots tracking mud on the powder-blue carpet as he moved from desk to desk, reviewing exchange rates and approving transactions.

'That's right,' Skinny said, stating it as a fact. 'You are going to work undercover. That's different from being an informant. Get that straight. Informants tell on their friends. Undercovers don't have any friends.'

Skinny reached into his pocket, took out a can of beer, popped the top.

'Hey, Curbelo,' he said brightly, 'it'll get you out of jail.' He held the beer out to me, then shrugged indifferently. 'Or you can stay here until you're leaning back for the strip-searches—that's up to you.'

Curbelo, I thought. *How does he know that?*

I was christened Antonio Curbelo, but just after my seventh birthday, after we had moved here from Honduras, my father changed our surname to Curbel—'just lopping off the extra vowel' he said—and shortly thereafter he had changed Antonio to Anthony, too, a change I had protested until I was the first Hispanic to attend one of New Orleans's more exclusive private schools. I confessed to one friend my real name, and after that I learned to fight.

'My name is Curbel,' I said, and took the beer, trying to appear casual about it. 'Tony Curbel.'

Skinny raised and dropped both shoulders at once in a way that caused his elbows to flap loosely at his sides.

'That's okay with Skinny,' Skinny said agreeably. 'He could give a shit. He's an equal opportunity employer.'

Ignoring him, I took a short swallow of the beer, eyes closed, savoring the nearly forgotten taste of it; then a long swallow, gulping it down greedily. When I opened my eyes I saw that Skinny was watching me. He smiled without humor, a hard glint in his eyes.

'It's easy to forget about the good things, right? Skinny knows. He did his time in here.'

'Yeah?' I said doubtfully, holding the can of beer, not offering it back.

'Yeah. Skinny did three years.' He put one grimy canvas boot on the end of the bunk. 'In those days, cons didn't have civil rights. When they brought in the dogs they let the furry motherfuckers nibble at your pants.' He lifted the leg of his jeans to show a round, deep scar on the back and side of his calf. 'Those dogs are something, aren't they?' he added admiringly, looking at the scar himself before he pulled down the leg of his jeans. 'But Skinny got off easy—you'll get off even easier, thanks to Skinny.'

I took another swallow of the beer and ran my tongue over the inside of my lips.

'Why?' I asked, not really interested in any deal he could offer but letting him talk while I drank his beer.

He smiled knowingly.

'Because Skinny thinks you know what a shit your father is,' he said. 'Skinny thinks you know he's the one who put you in jail—'

'You know that for a fact?' I snapped.

Skinny eyed me coolly, looking me up and down.

'Skinny knows about your uncle, too,' he said. 'Skinny knows about the slaves he keeps out on Airline Highway.'

He shook his head slowly.

'You got one peach of a family, Curbel.'

I squeezed the beer can until the light aluminium flexed and popped.

Ni puedes imaginartelo, I thought. *You can't even imagine . . .*

GARY LOVISI is the force behind Gryphon Publications, a small press which publishes all manner of books on Pulps, Sherlock Holmes, reference, mystery and SF as well as the magazines *Paperback Parade* (about collectible paperbacks), and *Hardboiled* (new fiction and non-fiction). He also writes his own hardboiled fiction and is presently completing a series of stories chronicling the rough life of his detective character, Vic Powers. Lovisi lives in Brooklyn, NY, with a very patient, understanding woman named Terry, and some very impatient, non-understanding cats.

Gary Lovisi

VORTEX

They hated painting, but they painted. They had to. They had to do it. They made sure they painted well. But they ran out of paint. They must have put too much on the walls and now they'd run out of paint.

That would make mommy and daddy very mad. That was not good. They could not leave the room. They could not get more paint. But the older brother had an idea. So they made the cuts, mixing their blood together with what remained of the paint, binding themselves together in blood.

And mommy and daddy didn't get mad at them that night.

When police detective Bill Crow and his partner Clyde Burkshaw entered the old tenement in Brooklyn they had no idea what they would find. They were on the hunt for a killer and they'd finally found him, but so had the press and what looked like half the curiosity seekers in New York. The block had been closed off by uniformed cops, but there were still people everywhere. Nosing around. Full of rage. Crying at the horror that rumor said lurked within the apartment. Hundreds of people, dazed at this latest urban horror. The media everywhere sticking their cameras in everyone's faces.

There was a sickly sweet smell of blood heavy in the air, thick as gravy, hanging in the stagnant summer breeze like a vise around everyone's neck. Growing tighter. Just about to pop the top of everyone's head off. Tension and anger were growing. It was hot and it was getting hotter.

Right in the center of it all were Crow and Burkshaw, trying to figure out what the hell had happened. Why it had happened? How such a thing could occur?

They'd have to go back now, piece it together bit by bit, try to get some meaning or reason. They knew it was impossible, but it was their job.

The Voodoo Stranglers owned this section of the city. Roaming the streets in packs, talking the talk, walking the walk, taking what they wanted to take, doing what they wanted to do. Hurting anyone they felt like hurting. It was a great life.

They usually went out hunting Friday night. Scare the people. Get off on the fear. Rob and steal to buy drugs and booze. Do the stuff they got and get crazy. Then go out on a spree for a few days more. Sexing.

They weren't widely known. They weren't a big gang. No one spoke of them much. But the other gangs knew who they were and sidestepped for them, the other gangs called this a serious gang, intense dudes—and off-the-fucking-wall crazy!

The rage burned deep, like the seething coals of a blast furnace. Hot and red. Firelike. Consuming—the darkness—the light—the life that flowed and ebbed in the city like a rusty dripping faucet in the sink of a sleazy burntout tenement. A faucet that was never fixed.

The Fixer would change all that. He was on the prowl. Working. After the hated transgressors, entering the vortex of life and purifying it.

Police detective Bill Crow looked at the photos again. There wasn't much to tell from the mess depicted. You could bearly determine the sex of the remains without a scorecard. He read that scorecard now. Read the preliminary report and the Coroner's determination.

Victim: Alonzo Ruiz, member of the Voodoo Stranglers, the gang rumored responsible for the kidnapping of the Thompsons—that nice young white yuppie couple captured on Riverside Drive after their car had broken down in the lonely hours of predawn. They'd been abducted and forced into an old van. Then driven to an abandoned tenement in Harlem. Then . . . well, you get the idea. The girl was eventually butchered, but not before they had their fun with her—and the husband was forced to watch it all. He was later found nude and chained in the basement of the abandoned building almost starved to death. Deranged. Later institutionalized. The officer on the scene said the husband had been trying to rearrange his wife's body parts as though she were a big jigsaw puzzle. Trying to put her back together again, but so far gone he couldn't even get that right.

And now Alonzo Ruiz, member of the feared Voodoo Stranglers, was dead the same way. Sliced and diced.

Clyde Burkshaw wiped the sweat that glistened from his old black face. He knew that coincidences don't happen like this in real life without reason. But sometimes reason has very little to do with certain situations.

Crow sat back sucking on a Marlboro and waited for his partner to drop the other shoe.

Clyde had a table full of photos and rap sheets spread out before him. It was a grim assortment of human tragedy.

'Lot of dead people listed here, Bill. A lot of the usual, some unusual. Some strange coincidences. I figure our boy is responsible for killing some of these guys that deserve killing. Guys the law can't get, guys that got off from soft-bellied judges on technicalities. First-class garbage that they set back on the streets. It looks to me our boy is going after them.'

'Yeah, at least members of the Voodoo Stranglers. He's a fixer, no doubt, but he's still a psycho. Look at what he does to the one's he's caught. He's just a serial killer—who hunts down other killers—but he's still bad news.'

'Sure, Bill, still and all I kinda like him. You know, I thought I'd seen it all by now.'

'Me too, Clyde, but he's gotta fall, man.'

'I know. He's gotta fall.'

The Voodoo Strangler was tied and hanging above a huge vat. The vat was one of those old industrial metal containers and it was full of foaming, boiling water—the burning embers underneath causing the water to churn and bubble as if in furious rage.

The Voodoo Strangler's mouth was taped, his hands and feet tied with heavy chain. His face and body bleeding heavily from numerous razor cuts. His blood dripping down into the bubbling water, mixing with it, giving it a pretty pink hue.

'I have to go now. I'm sorry we can't play more but you have a lot of friends I have to meet yet.'

The Strangler squirmed, tried to talk, yell, cry, tried to do anything—anything at all but watch as the crazy one slowly lowered him down into the churning water below.

Clyde fished around the hole in his molar with a toothpick. Worked it around a little bit and then looked to his partner with a face full of disgust.

'Well, he sure cooked that son-of-a-bitch. Not a bad end for Juan Garcia, really. A kid that likes to rape children won't get any sympathy from me, Bill.'

'But it's getting out of hand, Clyde,' Bill Crow said. He studied the scene again, went over Garcia's record, it made for some heavy reading. 'We got a problem here. We gotta watch these Voodoo Stranglers and they don't want us watching. Someone's evidently after them—or at least the ones we think were involved in the Thompson mess. I'd like to know why.'

'Yeah, Bill, but I've run checks on the Thompson family and relatives and they're clean. It looks to me our fixer is not involved with the Thompson's at all. He seems to be a free agent, an outside agency. I figure he's a psycho who heard about the case on TV or something, was so incensed by what he'd heard, he decided to fix it right himself when we couldn't make an arrest. Anyway, it's our best bet so far.'

'Lovely, and you might just be right. Which means we've got a very deranged and dangerous guy running around the city offing gang members. We gotta get him before the lousy papers turn him into a damn saint.'

The club house of the Voodoo Stranglers was in a run-down abandoned tenement on the outskirts of Harlem. A barrier between Harlem and the Barrio—a no-man's land that even the cops tried to stay away from if they could.

There were only four Voodoo Stranglers left from the original group of a dozen or so. Of course Ruiz and Garcia had met the Fixer already. The others had been killed in various rumbles and drug disputes. Two were upstate in prison for murder and drug charges. The attrition rate in a gang like the Stranglers was always very high and going up day by day now.

The Fixer made it worse. Being a Voodoo Strangler just wasn't as much fun as it used to be.

'Police protection for the likes of this trash is a damn insult to every victim of crime in this city,' Crow grunted. He and his partner, Clyde, sat their shift across the street from the Stranglers clubhouse. Watching. Waiting. Doing nothing and drinking a lot of beer. Just like the night before.

The Stranglers refused to have a cop stationed inside their clubhouse or anywhere near it. Most people thought it odd, but the gang claimed discrimination and police harrassment, and actually had the spineless politicians downtown supporting them—after all, they said, weren't *they* the victims? Two of their members had been murdered by a killer that was supposedly gunning for the rest of the gang. Their leader, a big tough named Roche, actually accused police death squads of being behind it all. The media ate it up.

'That logic sticks up my ass like a month-old turd. Here we are protecting these slimeballs, and not only are they not cooperating—they're blaming us for the whole mess.' Clyde hocked up a phlegm and spit a juicy bit of it out the window.

'And they're crying about being victims,' Crow added, 'that's what bugs me—and they may be right! It looks like they are victims, at least with the Ruiz and Garcia killings. What a world! And they accuse us. It stinks.'

'Well I hope this Fixer fixes their asses, but good, messes them four up like they never been messed before. They deserve it, if not for this crime, then for all the others. I'm sure they've got enough under the belt to each hang if we had any kind of justice in this city.'

'Meanwhile we just wait it out, Clyde. And if this Fixer is here when we are, we'll let him do the dirty deed—then put him out of commission—afterwards. The world won't be in any worse shape minus four Voodoo Stranglers. In fact, we'll be doing everyone in this city a big favor.'

The Stranglers had the clubhouse set up like a fortress. They brought in guys from an out-of-town gang to stand guard. They trucked in weapons—heavy-duty stuff they didn't usually keep close to hand. They had plenty of firepower and plenty of muscle—but when the bomb went off in the early morning hours the entire building was obliterated. Only a small crater was left.

'Son-of-a-bitch must have had a damn suitcase full of plastique,' Crow growled once he and Clyde were able to get out of what remained of their car. The whole area looked like a scene from

Hiroshima, rubble and fires everywhere, broken glass and shards sent in a 360 degree maelstrom. It was a miracle they'd lived through it. The blast alone took out every window on the block, knocked down the abandoned buildings on either side of the clubhouse. Later on there were gas leaks, fires, watermain breaks, and downed power lines. It was a scene from Armageddon. There wasn't anything left of the block or the Voodoo Stranglers.

'I thought it was all over.'

'So did I.'

'It's been a week. The gang guys are dead, but something is wrong.'

'I guess we were both wrong on this one. Do you see how he did it? See what he did? That guy, the one called Roche. His body was never found. That didn't mean much at the time but now I've heard hints of talk, hints he's still alive and hiding out somewhere in Brooklyn.'

Crow nodded, 'The last of the Voodoo Stranglers. Roche. Alive. It has to be, just has to be when you think of it. An inside job, by one of the gang's own members. Who else could pull off an explosion like that, and who better to do it than Roche himself, the leader of the gang.'

'We've been shitted. The guy who wouldn't accept police protection,' Clyde said, 'did this just to screen himself. Who's he hiding from? Now everyone thinks he's dead—the Fixer too. But I wonder?'

'We gotta track him. A dozen people died in that clubhouse—even if they were only gang members—even it they were only Voodoo Stranglers—they were still people and it looks like Roche murdered them all in cold blood. If he did it—he's gotta be made to pay.'

Crow and Burkshaw dug around on the streets in Brooklyn. They had a lot of contacts there from previous days. Set them to work. They didn't mind snitching on an outsider if the price was right. They got a tip on where Roche was staying. A girlfriend in Bed-Stuy, she'd been Roche's main woman a year ago, now she was just another crack whore. Her mother moved her in with the grandmother in Bed-Stuy hoping to get the girl away from gangs and drugs and into a better environment. Silly idea, if you know Bed-Stuy.

My eyes are on fire.

My hands twitch with anticipation.

My brain cries out, 'Kill them! Kill them all!'

I just laugh and get ready.

The knives are sharp. They glisten so pretty, even by the dim light of a dirty bulb in a grimy tenement. I have two knives. They are called Mommy and Daddy.

Mommy likes to cut up top. Necks and tits. Fun things like that. She likes lots of blood. Always *so* much blood.

Daddy likes to rip open stomachs and intestines until the guts flow onto the floor and you slip on them and fall into the mess. It likes to cut off balls. Rip your penis to shreds. Shove itself into your ass. Daddy is mean and nasty. He means business.

Mommy and Daddy are angry. They want to go after a bad boy. My brother is a bad boy. A very bad boy. Mommy and Daddy are going to fix him.

I'm going to help.

'There's something just came in.'

'What's that?' Crow said. He and Burkshaw were on their way to an address in Brooklyn's Bedford-Stuyvesant section. A run-down demolished section of a dying city that long ago should have been put out of its misery.

Clyde said, 'This kid, Roche, has a half-brother. From what I make out he wasn't an actual member of the Voodoo Stranglers but he did hang with them. Everyone figured he was put away upstate at a mental hospital for the criminally insane. He wasn't. He's been loose in the city for the last six weeks, hanging with the Stranglers. He's not on the sheets. Not listed in the records. He's Roche's half-brother with a different surname and he's been missing for a couple of weeks. He seems to have left the gang after the Thompson's were murdered.'

'Got a rep?'

'Yeah, they say he's *real* crazy. Serious. He also likes to play with knives. His brother, Miguel, El Roche he calls himself now, used him to handle problems in the gang—until he got out of hand. It seems even they couldn't control him. He's a cutter, Bill.'

'Sounds like a natural to be the cutter on the Thompson case, Clyde.'

'Just what I'm figuring.'

The neighborhood in Brooklyn was old and run down. So were the houses. So were the people. So were their dreams. If they had any left that hadn't turned into nightmares yet.

The mother was at work.

The old lady, grandma, was at a Seniors' Center, losing her money at bingo.

Miguel, El Roche, was in bed with the daughter, Clarise. They'd just finished doing the dirty deed—now they topped it off with a pipe of crack.

'This really makes it good, baby,' Clarise said, toking on the pipe, taking the warm smoke deeply into her lungs, and feeling it move up within her, blasting her mind, setting her flying. This was better than doing the dirty deed, but Miguel was a man, and men only wanted one thing from a girl. At least afterwards he always turned her on to the best stuff. It was all worth it once the pipe was lit.

'Yeah, baby, you're so hot today. I likes it when your folks be out . . . ' and he moved closer, rubbing her small hard breasts with one rough hand, while the other reached over and pulled the pipe out of her sucking mouth.

'Oh, wait, baby,' Clarise protested, but Miguel already had the pipe, toking away madly on it himself.

'Ease up, girl, we got more. Don't get greedy or I'll kick your ass.' Then he pulled her close to him, hard, down low, and held her down there—near *it*. She knew what he wanted. She didn't like doing it.

'Do it!' he said.

'I don't like that,' she said.

'You like it. Come on, baby. We'll have a little smoke afterwards.'

He is a very bad boy. He has always been a very bad boy. He makes me do bad things, like the things I did to those people we took off the highway. That bitch was so pretty and he made me rip her face off. Bad thing. I had no choice, I had to do it. I always have to do it. I always have to do what Roche says. He's the older brother. He made me bleed when we painted the room. We mixed blood together. You cannot deny that. So I do as he says—unless Mommy and Daddy tell me different.

Everyone laughed while the woman died. We all watched her. Roche laughed the hardest, the Stranglers laughed very much, and I laughed . . . but for some reason her husband did not laugh at all.

That upset me. It started thoughts in my head.

Then the husband began crying and he could not stop. I felt bad for him. Later I went out and found the parts for him, so he could put her back together again. It was no big deal. We tried to do it for a long time but we couldn't figure it out. I was there helping him, but I don't think he really knew I was there at all. After a while it got boring. Maybe some parts were missing, maybe I had cut some the wrong size. I couldn't figure it out but it was sure fun for a while. When I left him he was still trying.

And then Mommy and Daddy were mad at me for what I had done. What they'd done. What evil brother Roche and the others had made me do.

And Mommy and Daddy talked to me. From where they lived underground. Deep, from where I put them a long time ago, before I went away. They talked to me again.

They told me more people had to die.

Mommy and Daddy told me so.

It had to be done.

Now I come for the last one.

'Roche! Roche!'

When Clyde and Bill got to the scene the smell of blood was heavy in the air. Everywhere. They saw the girl, Clarise, her mother and the grandmother being taken out on stretchers. They were all tied down. Clarise was hysterical. So were her mother and grandmother. The girl was still hyped-up on drugs. They couldn't get a coherent sentence out of any of them. They looked shattered. They'd seen things. It had affected them.

Crow didn't need to get a statement just then. One of the uniform guys called him over to a room down the hall.

'It's the girl's room,' he said, holding a handkerchief over his mouth. 'It's pretty terrible in there. We found the girl, her mother and the grandmother all tied up in there. They were forced to watch it. They saw it all. It did something to them. I think he did it purposely so they could watch, almost like he did it *for* them. Like a show. Pretty sick, huh?'

'Yeah,' Crow replied quietly as he and Clyde approached the girl's room.

Crow and Burkshaw had finally found their Fixer, but they were too late. They wondered what twisted cord connected the Fixer and his killings, with Roche, the Voodoo Stranglers and the Thompson murder. They were sure they'd find out soon enough.

They went inside.

Clyde closed the door behind him. They moved deeper into the tiny room.

It was dark.

The window was covered.

Crow bumped into something big, moist.

Clyde turned on the light.

Bill Crow stood looking at an indistinguishable form about five inches from his face, suspended by bound wrists from a ceiling light fixture. The body had been stripped of all its clothing—stripped of all its skin. And if that wasn't bad enough, blood had been drained out of it, leaving a wet, pulpy hulk, a twisted rictus leering insanely at the two detectives.

Crow swallowed and took a deep breath. Calmed his nerves. 'I guess we've found Roche,' he said.

'Jesus!' Clyde said, starting to shake visibly now, 'Why? What the hell . . . where's the blood?'

Crow moved around the hanging body, careful not to touch it, moving closer to Clyde as he pointed to an empty bucket and a trail of dark and dry brown spots on the floor.

Crow and Burkshaw followed the trail. The blood trail. To another door. It opened into another room like old railroad apartments that are connected to each other. An empty room. The furniture had all been moved out. But it was not really empty.

There in the center of the room, his body propped up against the far wall watching them was another kid. He looked just like the mug shots they had of Roche. Definitely a family connection, definitely the lost half-brother. Definitely the Fixer.

He sat there, dead and cold now. Staring out with lifeless eyes. Another hollow husk.

His left arm was out, extended, hanging over a big pan. One of those pans painters use with a roller. The vein had been slit and a few viscous drops still hung from the incision threatening to drip into the pan. They never did. Nearby was a paint roller. It was full and stiff, but whether it was with dried paint or dried blood they couldn't tell. But something told them it was the latter. It still smelled sickly sweet. In fact, the entire room smelled this way—for the entire room had been painted with human blood!

Clyde lost it then. Would have lost it all if he had eaten yet. As it was he got the dry heaves and had to get out of there.

Crow stayed. Looked around. He knew he'd never understand this stuff. How could it happen? Why did it happen? The kid had painted the entire room with his brother's blood. And his own blood. He'd forced the three women to watch it all. Made sure they saw it all. And they weren't talking. There were all too gone at this point. Maybe for good.

Crow looked around in wonder. The walls were still a little wet in places. Dripping unevenly in one spot. Probably the last to be painted. And yet, it was done rather neatly. No spots missed. And it appears he'd had just enough paint—blood, Crow reminded himself—to finish the job.

The kid was dead. Suicided. Not from the bleeding though. He had two knives dug deep into his heart—and written on his chest in his own blood was—'I love Mommy and Daddy!'

Crow looked at the words.

They began to dance in front of him.

He had to leave the room too now.

JOEL A. DVOSKIN has come to his knowledge of crime honestly. While this is his first work of published fiction, he has been involved in the world of crime for most of his adult life. For the past 15 years, he has worked as a clinical and forensic psychologist and administrator in prisons and maximum security psychiatric hospitals in Massachusetts, Arizona, Virginia, and New York. He has consulted widely on issues related to mental illness and criminal justice, and believes that preventing child abuse is the only way to reduce the size of our next generation of violent criminals. Along the way to obtaining his PhD in clinical psychology, Dr Dvoskin has worked as a carpenter's helper, bartender, soda jerk, basketball coach, and live musician. He spent two years as a US Peace Corps Volunteer in Senegal, West Africa. His great passions are his wife and two children, basketball, and bluegrass music. He currently lives in Albany, New York.

Joel A. Dvoskin

B-B-B-Billy

i have a gift for seeing things that other people can't see. It's a special talent, really. i am very grateful, and i don't really mind the way they punish me for it. God wants me to understand things and to explain them, but it must be in code. It must always be in code. i can never betray God, who has made me special and entrusted me with this gift. It is odd the way they treat me. As if it were worse to be special.

i'm not stupid. You can tell that, can't you? Yet the Doctors talk to me real slow, as if i were a child, or worse, a foreigner. They speak very kindly to me, always before they hurt me somehow. The worst hurts are when they humiliate me in front of my—i cannot call them peers, because they are mostly troubled, and really not a very bright group at all—before my colleagues at the hospital.

But i digress. i am here today to explain to you who killed B-B-B-Billy. That's how he always said it. He never stuttered, except when he tried to say his own name. The poor shit. i miss him more than i will tell anyone. He was one of the only ones who understood me, and the gifts i have been given. i miss him terribly. One day he was alive, and the next he was dead. Strangled. No one had any idea who had killed him. The police came and investigated for weeks, trying to get sensible answers to stupid questions out of people who have been condemned to this hell hole precisely because they never made any sense. Go figure.

The patients were a riot. They were so amused by the fact that anyone wanted to hear what they had to say. Word quickly spread. Whoever helps them find the killer will be punished, because then the police would leave forever and life would go back to normal at the hospital. Ordinarily, i never allowed myself to drop to their stupid level of social masturbation. i am not of them. But this time i really thought they had a point. It had been so long since anyone really listened.

There was a great irony to all of this. You see, i had succeeded where the men in blue had failed. i knew who killed Billy. And i knew why.

B-B-B-Billy had arrived at the hospital the same way as many of his fellow patients. He was living at home in Sheepshead Bay with his parents, who couldn't quite get over the fact that he wasn't working. The idea of disability had never occurred to them, so they assumed their schizophrenic son just wasn't trying hard enough. Billy told me of horrible fights with his parents, often late into the night. Often, push would come to shove—literally—and Billy would come to the hospital, bruises and all. Funny, he never won the fights.

Billy's father came to visit sometimes, but you could tell he hated the humiliation and the son who had caused it. He would laugh at Billy, curse him, and tell him he was stupid. He was right, too. Billy was pretty stupid. Stupid he didn't smack the shit out of the old man, in front of God and the whole visiting room. The Father's hate smoldered nevertheless, and he visited that night, the night Billy died. So he was a suspect.

Then there was Billy's boyfriend. Stephen was a homosexual. Billy wasn't, but he spent so much time on locked all-male wards, he learned to find comfort wherever he could. i never soiled myself, with men or women, but i am special. Billy needed love. He needed to be touched, and Stephen was all too glad to oblige.

Then Billy and the Chaplain hooked up. The Chaplain—how i hate those pious fools—took away Billy's only comfort, when he told Billy that it was a sin to love a man. Billy told Stephen he was evil and to stay away from him, and Stephen took it real hard. Maybe too hard. i thought Stephen was going to kill the Chaplain, but the Chaplain's still alive, so to speak. And Billy's dead, so Stephen was a suspect, too.

There was one more suspect. Billy wanted to die sometimes. Real bad. He knew the value of his life. i always read with great interest when a mental patient is killed somewhere in these United States by some of the 'treatment' staff, or when a prisoner dies. The State never fights too hard about the cause of death, because they figure they can keep the damages low by proving that the deceased never would have earned a dime or mattered to anyone. They didn't matter to me either, for i am not one of them, but at least i never pretended to care.

So Billy knew what they thought of him. How little they valued his underdeveloped little self. He knew he would never be allowed any joy. He wanted to die, so Billy was a suspect, too.

You might think that i didn't care. That i would encourage Billy to end his miserable existence, so inferior to my own. But you would be wrong. i meant it when i said that i miss him.

It's lonely at the top. It's lonely at the top. It's lonely at the top. You all say that, but none of you have any idea what it means. Only Billy could make me feel like part of you. He needed my help. He understood my gifts. He believed with all his miserable little heart that only i could heal his damaged spirit. And now he is gone.

B-B-B-Billy had grown up in a rat-infested hole in a Brooklyn apartment house. His parents kept him. Like people buy a pet, and then decide it's a pest, but somehow they never have the energy to get rid of it. i had thought for a long time they abused Billy when he was little, but now i know better. They wouldn't have bothered. They didn't have the energy for that, either. He wasn't special enough, i suppose. So they just let him stay. Eating what they ate and going where they went, but never a part of anything or anybody.

i had to be his salvation. i know that now. Brooklyn left no scars that were beyond my powers to heal. i taught him things. i nurtured his spirit in a way his parents couldn't have imagined. i would have hated them, if i was of such human things as hate. But you have seen enough of me to know better.

The New York City Police. They were astonishingly superficial. A man had died, for God's sake. For B-B-B-Billy's sake. For my sake.

They asked so many questions. Every question leading to another dark and barren branch of the tree of knowledge. i could barely restrain myself. With all their imagined power. Their uniforms and their impotent weapons. Their grade-school notebooks. With all of these things they knew nothing. Yet they scoffed at me, as if i were one of the others.

One officer, though, was different. He was a dark Italian. Short, with eyes that were too close together to be fully trusted. His straight black hair was oily, and he had bags under his eyes, from worrying about who killed Billy. i wanted to help him. Only him. He was Billy now. i made him stutter, but only a little, only when he said his own name.

'Mr Anderson? I am Sergeant P-P-P-P-Peluso. I have a few questions to ask you, if you don't mind.' (Smile)

'i don't mind, Sergeant.'

'Did you see Billy on the night he was killed?'

'We are a small community here, Sergeant. Of course i saw him.'

'When was the last time you saw him alive?'

'i would say it was before bedtime, Sergeant. He had been talking to Stephen. About evil.' i began to laugh. 'i really am not at liberty—no pun intended—to divulge any more secrets.' He needed for me to laugh. i knew exactly what was bothering him, and what his quizzical look meant. i looked out the window at Brighton Beach, and wondered if the warm sand still felt good.

'You know, Mr Anderson, you seem a little different to me than your friends. What are you doing here, anyway?'

'They are not my friends, Sergeant, and i could ask you the same thing.'

He smiled. Touché. 'Yeah, but I'm the cop, so tell me, what gives?'

'You might say i am on a mission from God, if you were so inclined.'

Suddenly his partner appeared, and i disappeared. 'I'm getting nothing out of this turkey,' said Sergeant Peluso. 'He thinks he's God or something.' The stupid, stupid man. i do not think i am God. i know exactly who i am and why God put me here.

Now i would never tell him. Nothing. He was a disrespectful little man and he would never be told. That night Billy and Stephen had argued, long into the night. Stupid petty quarrels. The Chaplain, his bloated throbbing curiosity aroused, had poisoned Billy's mind. He had asked Billy for the sordid details of Billy's only comfort, his leering smile not of divine love, but of ugly little men and their secrets. i knew these men. i knew everything about them. They were the messengers of all that was bad and unholy on earth. They were at their worst in the clothes of the pious, and they would be punished.

Billy became distraught. His mind was so weak and vulnerable that even Stephen's manipulations could not ease his mind. You see, Stephen was hardly a person to be admired, but his sins were of weakness. He lay with Billy neither to hurt nor to love, and even simple Billy had understood and accepted the deal. Till the poison penguin man made simple Billy sad and afraid.

Billy went to Stephen and begged to be left alone. He tried to pray with this Godless stupid man. Stephen was enraged, and pushed Billy hard into the wall. Bruise. Clue? Maybe to the stupid police, but not to me. i saw Billy crying alone on the floor. Unhealed. My precious work in a heap on the terrazzo tile floor of the end of the world. i so wanted to go to him, to repair the damage wrought by stupid little men. But rules are rules, and i had to watch.

Stephen stood over Billy. His anger now was beyond any control. To be rejected was to die, or to kill. 'Billy,' he said, 'if you don't, I will have to kill you.'

'No, no, no!' i screamed inside. This was all wrong! Billy cannot die at the hands of this stupid barbarian. The Chaplain cannot be allowed to win. The Chaplain. The Devil. This was all wrong, and not at all according to Plan.

i am suddenly aware of an intruder. Sergeant P-P-P-P-Peluso seems to want to talk again. 'Mr Anderson, I have a few more questions for you, if you don't mind.'

i minded. i am a turkey, i believe you said, little man. 'Gobble, gobble, gobble, gobble.' i glared at him and then he knew. He knew that i was neither crazy nor his equal. He knew everything i wanted him to know. That his new-found stutter was my gift, and that i had given him to B-B-B-Bily, and B-B-B-Billy to him. But he had disrespected me, and must be humbled.

'Okay, man. Sorry about the turkey thing.' (Not good enough.) 'I didn't know you guys cared about stuff like that.' (Now you're making it worse.) i continued to glare at him, always teaching.

'Okay, man, seriously, I'm sorry.' (Better.) 'It was a stupid thing to say.' (Yes, and you are a stupid little man, but you are forgiven.)

'Yes, Officer?' (Demoted, now, no longer a Sergeant.)

'You said that Billy and Stephen were talking.'

'What is your question?'

'Talking, or arguing?' Now i began to doubt the wisdom of my silence. i could lead them anywhere. It was also clear to me now that they were leaving soon, one way or another. Was Billy's death to be avenged? By God or man? My mind was filled with questions, and so little time to decide.

'Arguing.' The other patients would be mad, but they were of littleness and not to be considered now.

'About what?'

'i believe you call it homosexuality, Sergeant.' (It suits me to reinstate you now.)

Off he went, in his sloppy trenchcoat uniform, chasing the goose i had lent him, and allowing me to return to my thoughts. i was still watching, remembering, Billy and Stephen in the hall, destroying all that was Planned. Billy was unable to answer. Stephen's violence left him whimpering, unsure. The Chaplain's probing, judging, had left him feeling guilty and ugly. My beautiful little Billy, unhealed and writhing now in confused terror. i am enraged! But not impotent. Never that.

Yet touching is not allowed. Neither in love nor in rage. It is not in the Plan.

Stephen's lust is now abated, by violence this time, and he seeps into the night.

Billy's father is a bad man, but in a wholesome, ignorant sort of way. He visited Billy the night he died. Visited. Visited. Like a plague was visited upon the land. Like a Board of Visitors. Bored of visitors, indeed. How could he hurt this beautiful, miserable little son? This man needs to die, the father. But who shall i chose to do the deed? He sat in the visiting room waiting for the fruit of his loins, scratching his belly like the ape he had become. 'Where is that stupid kid? He knew I was coming to visit tonight.' To no one in particular.

You might wonder what i was doing in the visiting room. i who am not of this world, with neither friends nor relatives. Yet i knew how to be where i was needed. i used the stupid church lady, who came to give comfort to the wretched. She was a wretch, and i comforted and used her to be where i was needed that night. i arrived long before Billy. Just when his father was about to explode with impatience—lust of yet another kind?—Billy showed his face. He was soiled, but his father couldn't see.

'Hi, Dad.' What cruel irony. To greet this monster with such naive hope, after all the years of rebuke. Hi, Dad, indeed. i must make his killer say it, too. The last words Billy's father will ever hear must be 'Hi, Dad.' But don't be alarmed. Billy will not kill this heathen. His father will not die this night. Not here. The Plan does not say so now. Soon, i will make it happen. Soon. But not here, and not now.

So Billy looks up with preserved innocence, and his father gutwounds him for a thousandth time. 'You idiot. I told you I'd be here at 4. Where the hell were you?' Tears. More tears. Must i watch bad men hurt my Billy forever?

'Yes, Lieutenant.' (It was Sergeant Peluso. i am allowed no fun, officially, but this was coming close.)

'I'm only a Sergeant, Mr Anderson.' (Pity. i could change that, if i choose.) 'Can you explain why Billy might have been in your room last night?'

'No, Sergeant. Why do you ask?'

'Chaplain Osbourne says that he saw Billy enter your room at 9 p.m. It's the last time anyone claims to have seen him.'

'Curiouser and curiouser, Sergeant. I last spoke to Billy in the visiting room. (Not the last time i *heard* him, though, but you didn't ask that.) He was with his father.'

'What time was that?'

'Around 7.'

'Why would Billy go to your room?' Now came the dilemma. You see, i was in my room from 8 p.m. on. What do i tell this untective?

'i don't believe that he did.' Here it comes.

'How do you know? Were you there?'

The dice are tossed. 'From 8 o'clock on, sir.' i knew what i was doing. The Plan was finally clearing up. i am now a suspect.

'Mr Anderson, I'm going to have to ask you to come with me. You have the right to . . . '

'i have seen you on TV, Sergeant, but your warnings are not necessary. i have decided to help you find your killer. The other patients will be most upset, but Billy will be avenged. You see, i know who killed Billy. In a way, i am responsible, but it has nothing to do with your laws.

'i am not sorry that Billy has been killed, though i miss him terribly. He had been soiled by evil men of power. Beyond my powers to heal him. By now you have figured out that Billy and Stephen had lain together. Many times. This had been forgiven. Life here provides no—how shall i describe it—*accepted* outlets for physical contact. i do not need such things, but the other men are not so strong. Stephen was what you would call an aggressive person, who would have taken Billy. But Billy was gentle and lonely, and needed to be touched. Stephen touched his body, and i touched his soul. All was well.'

'So who killed him?'

'In good time, Sergeant, in good time. But it wasn't Stephen. He was too selfish to kill Billy. Stephen was a mean child who only broke the toys of others, you see. Anyway, all was well, and Billy was being healed. But when he met his father that night, he was injured again. All of the healing, to body and soul, was again undone at the hands of this beast who sired Billy.'

'So the old man stuck around and killed the kid?'

i so wanted to sell this point of view, but i am not allowed to lie. 'What do you think, Sergeant?'

'I think you're jacking me off, Mr Anderson. Billy's father has an airtight alibi between 8 and 11, half an hour from here. Since Billy was seen at 9, and dead by 10, Billy's father couldn't possibly have killed his son. But maybe you did. So, you have the right to remain silent . . . '

'You are becoming a bore, Sergeant. i am well aware of my right to remain silent.' (i had once refused to speak for more than a year.) 'Now do you want to know who killed my friend?'

The policeman waited now. Respect?

'Very well. Billy's father would have killed him, and deserves to be punished for Billy's death, but you are right. Technically, he did not kill Billy. Billy was distraught. He left the visiting room at quarter till eight, moments before his father left the hospital. So much for your airtight alibi. Billy ran down the hall in tears. Why he cared about the approval of this beast is beyond me, but he did. Had he run into me, or even stupid Stephen, he might well be alive today. But he didn't. He ran into the Chaplain. Man of godlessness. Evil man.

'The Chaplain saw Billy's tears and his opportunity. He pulled Billy into the interview room, thinking no one saw them. I leaned against the wall outside the door. Listening. Billy told the Chaplain of his pain, his fears, his need for love and touch and approval. He was so confused. He had no idea of the difference between his father's missing love, Stephen's loveless sex, or the purity of my own feelings for him. The Chaplain could barely conceal his joy. His lust. His evil.

'The Chaplain made Billy tell him, in vivid detail, of his activities with Stephen. Every touch a confession. Every confession bringing hypocritical condemnation from the godless one. Like a freak censor clucking avariciously over a dirty book, he scoured Billy's soul for sins to condemn. Worst of all, Billy began to believe him. Believe that he was evil for being himself. For needing.

'Yet who put these needs in Billy's soul? Was he not acting out the Plan when he lay with Stephen?'

'Skip the philosophy, Mr Anderson.' My Sergeant was getting interested. 'If you didn't kill him, then who did?'

i continued. 'As Billy cried louder and harder, the Chaplain began to comfort him. Soothing words at first. Then Billy's cries became muffled, and i knew. The Chaplain was Stephen, and Stephen was the Chaplain. Good was bad and black was white. And Billy would die that night. What i didn't know yet was at whose hand. i won't lie to you, Sergeant. It might have been me . . . but it wasn't.

'Suddenly Billy screamed. Not loud, but it terrified me. Suddenly this damning pervert was seen for what he was. Now Billy understood. The Chaplain and God had never met. "You're a freak," yelled Billy. "Worse than Stephen and me put together." Billy threatened—promised—to expose the living Satan. I rushed off to my room. As i said, i was there by 8. i smelled death, but did not know whose. i was rooting for Billy to kill the pig, but it wouldn't have helped. Billy's spirit had already died. Killed by his worthless superiors.

'Billy couldn't have come to my room at 9 o'clock. Your tests will tell you that he was already dead by then. His death will be in the interview room, along with the stench of the man who killed him. i suggest you speak to the Chaplain again.'

'Sometimes I amaze myself,' he replied. 'I actually think I believe you.' He hesitated.

'Don't worry. i'm not going anywhere.'

He started to run off to make his arrest, but again he hesitated. 'You know, Mr Anderson, I owe you an apology.'

'Indeed. You will be a Lieutenant, now.'

'Hey, you might be right. How about that . . . Lieutenant Peluso. I like the sound of it.' The stutter was gone.

Stephen escaped from the hospital two weeks later. For a person so treacherous, you'd think it would have only taken a suggestion, but it took hours of preparation to give him the courage to go. Programming people used to be so easy. As i watched him leave, i sat back with a satisfaction i rarely get to enjoy anymore. i closed my eyes and watched him; watched him as he walked most of the night. He avoided any suspicious activity, as he was taught. By morning he was far away from the Hospital, back in Sheepshead Bay, Billy's source and Stephen's final destination.

i watched him as he left the subway at the Neptune Avenue station. He blinked away the angry sunshine. Much work to do. Finally, i watched him walk up the drive to the house of Billy's father. He would speak but once—'Hi, Dad.' It would be the last words Billy's father would ever hear.